Dark Entities

R. Scott Campbell

Copyright © 2013 by R. Scott Campbell
First Edition —July 2013

ISBN
978-1-4602-1011-6 (Hardcover)
978-1-4602-1009-3 (Paperback)
978-1-4602-1010-9 (eBook)

All rights reserved.

No part of this publication may be reproduced in any form, or by any means, electronic or mechanical, including photocopying, recording, or any information browsing, storage, or retrieval system, without permission in writing from the publisher.

Produced by:

FriesenPress
Suite 300 – 852 Fort Street
Victoria, BC, Canada V8W 1H8

www.friesenpress.com

Distributed to the trade by The Ingram Book Company

CHAPTER 1

Lightning flickered along the skyline, igniting the night into an explosion of dazzling brightness. Moments later, thunder grumbled and growled in the distance, finally fading away to silence.

As an ear-splitting thunderclap boomed above the aging van, Jackson woke up with a choked cry and jerked upright in his seat. His hands clenched the armrests and he looked around fitfully. "Jeez," he said. "What was that?"

"Huh?" said his mom, half-turning from the steering wheel. "Oh, just more thunder. It's been going on like that for a couple of hours now."

"Really?"

"Yeah, but that was the loudest one yet."

He sat up and rubbed a hand over his face. "I must have drifted off. I was just in the middle of some really weird dream." He tried to remember what it was, but only caught a fleeting image of something like a shadow entering his bedroom. Crazy.

"It must have been," she said. "You were yelling about something creeping out of your closet."

"Really?"

She nodded and turned her attention back to the road. "Oh yeah. I'm surprised you didn't wake your sister."

Jackson eased back on his seat and yawned. He felt disoriented and fuzzy headed— completely out of it. He turned and checked the back seat. His younger sister didn't seem too bothered. She was fast asleep, snoring lightly. Talk about lucky. "I don't think you have to worry about Suzy. If that thunder didn't wake her up, nothing will."

His mom nodded in agreement. "Well, she's probably just exhausted with all the driving we've done." She glanced at the odometer. "We travelled a long way today."

"Yeah?" Jackson said. "No wonder I feel so crappy."

He turned and stared out the side window, gazing past beads of water gliding down the glass. He wished that they never had to leave St. Rogers and all his friends, but after his dad died and they lost the house, the only alternative was to move to Boswell when they found out they'd inherited a distant aunt's house.

It had been a crazy few months, though.

In the dim glow of the headlights he could see they were passing two large cornfields, the corn struggling to keep upright as a strong wind buffeted the fields.

It looked pretty nasty out there.

He caught a glimpse of his reflection in the window. He looked awful. His short blond hair was greasy and spiked up like a punk rocker. His face looked drawn and haggard. He scowled at his reflection

Yeah, the Sid Vicious look.

"Having fun?" his mom said, grinning.

"Just looking out the window. Trying to see if I can see a road sign saying where we are."

"Sure," she said, trying hard not to smile.

Irene Ralph flipped a loose strand of hair behind her ear. "I think we should be approaching the outskirts of Boswell. At least... that's what I think." She thought for a moment, her face scrunching up. "Problem is this storm has really slowed us down, so I'm not sure where we are."

Jackson nodded, looking up as the rain really started to pound down on the van roof. It sounded like marbles were pinging on the metal.

"We'll just have to take our time," she said, increasing the wiper speed.

Jackson watched the windshield wipers flap across the windshield, barely able to carve away the rain sluicing down. "It's almost impossible to see the road."

"I know," she said, leaning forward over the steering wheel and wiping away fog from the windshield.

Jackson felt the van slow. "That's a good idea. We can just take our time and get there when we get there."

"Exactly."

"Say, how big is this town supposed to be?" Jackson asked.

She ran a hand across her face. "Oh, maybe ten thousand. More if you count the cows and sheep."

He had to laugh. "How about things to do in town?"

She navigated around a bend in the road. "I read on the Internet they've got a pretty good sized recreation centre."

"Oh," he said, waggling his hands in the air. "I don't think I can handle it. Next you'll be saying they've even got a mall."

She nodded. "Yes, as a matter of fact they do."

Jackson leaned back and folded his arms across his chest. "Yeah, I can just see it now. Three or four stores lined up along the main drag. Yep. A shopper's dream come true."

His mom took her hands off the steering wheel for a second and waggled them in the air. "Oh, I don't think I can handle it! All that shopping. I can't wait." She glanced at Jackson and laughed.

"Yeah, yeah. Glad to see you're enjoying yourself," he said, shaking his head. He turned his head and stared out into the black abyss beyond his window. Jeez, don't they even have streetlights out here?

There was a clattering of gears, metal grinding on metal as his mom pumped the clutch pedal.

She shook her head in disgust. "The transmission's almost had it. I just hope we make it into town."

"Hey, I thought you said we were almost there?"

She shrugged. "I don't know anymore. I just hope we are."

Jackson saw that the cornfields still ran alongside the road. They had to be huge. Jeez, they must really like corn out here. He shook his head. They must eat it with everything.

He could see that the wind was really picking up. Corn plants whipped about crazily in some kind of weird, frenzied dance. Leaves and pieces of plants were torn off and sent sailing into the night.

He started when a huge, black shape thudded onto the windshield, slid off and disappeared. "What was that?"

"I don't know," his mom said, taking a deep breath. She held a hand over her heart. "It scared the crap out of me."

Jackson leaned forward, seeing vague shapes moving along the cornfield, flitting over the tops of the plants. He squinted into the blackness, trying to make out details. "What in the world are those?"

"What?"

He shook his head. "I'm not sure. It's crazy… but it looked like a couple of dark shapes moving along with the van. Almost pacing it."

She looked him. "Are you serious?"

He nodded. "Oh yeah. I don't think I was dreaming that."

She ducked her head and gazed out his window. "I don't see anything. Just a lot of corn."

He turned back to the window, staring out for a moment. "I'm sure I saw something out there." He used his sleeve to wipe a clearing in the fogged window. "Weird. There's nothing now."

"Maybe… maybe you just *thought* you saw something," his mom said. "You know, you were still half asleep."

He turned and looked at her and said more sharply than he intended, "No. There was something out there. I'm sure of it."

She shrugged and focused on the road. "Okay. Just keep an eye out and let me know if you see it again. It might be something as simple as branches flying around out there."

"Okay." He kept looking out the side window. S*he thinks I'm seeing things.*

He could see that the wind was definitely picking up. Large leaves were being ripped away and sent somersaulting through the air. On a couple of occasions, he saw entire plants ripped out by their roots and sucked into the black void of the night. Maybe that's what he saw—a bunch of corn plants flying about.

"Anything?" his mom said.

He shook his head. "No. Just the wind tearing up the field big time."

He listened to the wind whistling and howling through the car's air ducts. It sounded kind of creepy—like something was trying to crawl in, but got stuck partway. He finally leaned forward and closed his vent, just in case.

"Careful," Jackson warned, as he felt strong gusts of wind buffet the van and push it to the side.

"I'm on it," his mom said.

As they came around a curve in the road, the headlights raked over tendrils of mist slithering across the highway. A jagged stitch of lightning stabbed down, illuminating the mist with almost an otherworldly, pearlescent glow.

More lightning sizzled down, and in the afterglow Jackson thought he saw dark shapes scrabbling through the mist.

Not again, he thought, leaning forward and gripping the edge of the dashboard.

"What in the world are those?" he said.

His mom leaned forward, stared into the distance and shook her head. "I don't know what it is. It looks pretty strange." She took her foot off the accelerator and let the van slow down of its own accord.

Jackson watched vague shapes drifting across the road. They faded in and out of sight in the thickening mist. Could it be more corn plants torn from the fields and drifting across the road?

As they drew closer he could see dozens of them moving across the road. "They look like giant spiders!"

"What?"

"Look at them. They're spiders crawling across the road!" Jackson said. He watched the dark shapes claw their way across the road.

His mom stepped on the gas pedal and the van started to slide.

"Hey…hey!" Jackson said, grabbing hold of his armrest.

"It's okay," she said, taking her foot off the gas. She slowly and carefully guided the van back into their lane. "Hey, I can see them now."

Jackson squinted into the heavy mist. "You've got to be kidding!"

"Yeah?"

He shook his head. "They're branches. Nothing but branches probably torn off in the storm."

"Certainly looks like it," she said.

He ran a hand through his hair. "I thought they looked like giant spiders."

She shook her head. "I think you've been reading too many horror stories. You're starting to imagine things."

He shrugged. "Yeah, maybe."

She nodded to the novel splayed across the centre console. "I mean, look at the cover on that thing. It's enough to give *me* nightmares. What if Suzy sees that?"

Jackson nodded in agreement. "Yeah, you're right."

Slowly they wound their way around the mass of churning branches, weaving back and forth, finally accelerating once again.

His mom glanced in the rear view mirror. "Well, I'm glad that's behind us. Those giant spiders had me worried."

Jackson folded his arms. "Yeah, yeah."

His mom chuckled. "Spiders."

"Give me a break," he said with a smile.

They drove for another twenty minutes, still following a road that had more curves than a racetrack. Rain was lashing down once again, pounding on the van roof.

"What's that?" his mom said.

"What?"

"Not sure," his mom replied.

"Looks like there's something on the road again," Jackson said. He leaned forward, trying to see through the pouring rain.

Another burst of lightning illuminated the road before them with pulsating light.

"I'm not sure what it is," Jackson said.

The headlights illuminated a figure thrashing about in the middle of the road.

He leaned forward, staring at it for a long moment. "What the? What is *that*?"

"Probably just a giant spider," his mom said, snickering.

Jackson shook his head. "I don't think so. It looks like some kind of animal."

"Are you sure?"

Jackson looked at her. "Can you hit the high beams?"

She thought for a second. "Yeah, good idea."

She reached past the steering wheel and switched on the high beams.

Jackson watched them rake across the highway, illuminating what looked like some kind of struggle near the centreline.

There was frenzied motion out there. Something—whatever it was—was wrestling with what looked like a glowing ball.

What the heck?

He watched as the figure fell to the concrete and started rolling about, looking like it was trying to pull the sphere off its back.

"What are they?" Jackson said.

"I have no idea," she said, leaning forward and squinting into the driving rain.

As his mom applied the brakes, the van slid again. This time it felt like they were on ice. The van started to spin sideways.

"Mom!"

"I'm trying," she said as she twisted the steering wheel, trying to counteract the spin of the vehicle.

Jackson saw a glowing shape rise from the pavement and hover for a moment over a vague shape moving on the pavement.

"Hang on!" his mom said. "We're going to hit!"

CHAPTER 2

Jackson jammed his feet against the floorboard and grabbed hold of the armrests.

In the kaleidoscopic flickering of the headlights, the *thing* on the roadway tried to get out of the way, but was hit mid-stride. It flipped up and smashed into the windshield, buckling it in. A bloody and distorted face hung on the windshield for a brief moment before it was gone, disappearing into the darkness.

The luminous globe he'd seen earlier was no longer in sight.

As the van suddenly veered off the road, he could hear Suzy's undulating scream echoing through the van. They crashed into the cornfield and bounced down a slope, flattening everything in sight. Finally, they rammed through a wooden fence and came to a stuttering stop beside the remains of a battered scarecrow.

The van engine shuddered, coughed twice, and then died. Jackson let out a breath, hearing only the soft, melodic ticking of the engine.

"Is everyone all right?" his mother rasped.

Jackson nodded. "Yeah, I think so." He rubbed the side of his face, opened and closed his mouth, and winced with a stab of pain. "But the side of my face sure is sore."

"Let me see." She reached up and turned on the dome light and craned her neck to look. In the dim glow of the overhead light, she checked the side of his face. "Oh, you're going to have a nice bruise by tomorrow."

"Oh, great. It'll probably look like I've been in some kind of brawl."

His mom checked the backseat. "How about you, Suzy? Are you okay?"

"Yeah," she said with a sniffle. She wiped her forearm across her nose. "I think so."

"Good girl," her mom said, patting her on the leg.

"How are we going to get back up to the highway?" Jackson said. "It looks like we've travelled a long ways downhill."

"I'm not sure how far we've come, but we'll have to check what the damage is to the van," she said. She started to open her door.

"Don't you go, Mom," Suzy said. "I'm scared."

"Yeah," Jackson agreed. "It's probably best if I check it out. Remember, I took an automotive course, not you."

"Okay. Just be careful."

Jackson nodded and turned to his door. Outside, the corn slapped and rustled against the side of the van with the howling wind. He unfastened his seat belt and turned to his mom.

"Any idea what we hit back there?"

She shook her head. "Must have been some kind of animal. Maybe a bear."

"A bear?" Jackson said. *No way we hit a bear. The hide of that thing was smooth. And those eyes.*

"What about that luminous sphere?"

"Probably just ball lightning," she said. "It's pretty rare, but it does happen in some lightning storms."

Suzy leaned forward. "What's a luminous sphere?"

Her mom waved her off. "Just when lightning comes to the ground like a big, glowing ball."

"Oh," Suzy said, sitting back in her seat.

Irene ran a hand across her face and saw blood smeared across her palm.

"Mom," Suzy said, pointing to her mother's hand. "You're bleeding! There's blood on your hand!"

"I know," Irene said, running a hand over her face and checking it again. "I must have hit the steering wheel harder than I thought." She glanced at the steering wheel. "Look at this. I've put a crack in the steering wheel."

Suzy chuckled.

Jackson leaned over and saw a small crack running along the outside of the steering wheel. He shook his head in disbelief. "Jeez, Mom, you must have a head made of stone."

"Yeah, I guess so." She tilted the rear view mirror and examined her eyebrow. "It's nothing major, just a small cut."

Suzy tapped her mom on the shoulder. "Are you sure you're alright?"

"I am," her mom said. She grabbed a tissue and held it over her eyebrow. "It's just a bit of a scratch where the steering wheel bit me."

Suzy laughed and wiped at her eyes. "Mom, you're funny."

"Yeah, a real comedian," Jackson said, turning about. He tried to open his door but found it was jammed tight. "Hey, this thing's jammed."

"Well, my door's okay. Maybe I should check the van."

"No way," Jackson said. He twisted around and, bracing his feet on the door, started to push. "I'll do it."

It took a couple of attempts, but finally he was able to push the door open most of the way. With a grunt and one final kick, it opened far enough to let him squeeze through.

"All right," his mom said.

"I'll see how bad things are," Jackson said. He hung his head through the opening, pushing aside a mass of corn leaves. "Well, at least I can't smell any gas leaking out."

"That's good because we can't afford to lose any. The tank is almost on empty as it is."

Jackson pushed the door the rest of the way open with a noisy creak. "All right, let's see what the damage is."

"Wait a minute, maybe we should all go outside," his mom said.

"I'm not going out there," Suzy said, pulling the quilt tightly around her. "That thing we hit could be out there waiting."

Jackson felt his stomach lurch. He hadn't thought of that. He turned around and faced the cornfield. It was so dark. He couldn't see a thing.

"Well, I guess," their mom said.

Jackson stepped out into the night as a blast of cold air howled in. It sent candy wrappers and loose papers fluttering about the van.

"Can't you close the door, Jackson," Suzy said. "It's freezing in here. Besides, I don't want anything to get in."

"Yeah, yeah," Jackson said, squeezing through the narrow opening. He turned towards Suzy. "Get in? Like what?"

Suzy leaned forward and whispered, "Like the Bogeyman."

He stood outside, mud and rainwater seeping into his runners. Just great. The Bogeyman. As he began to close the door, his mom leaned over and waved to him.

"Yeah?" he said.

"I just remembered. There're a couple of flashlights under your seat, take them with you."

"Perfect," Jackson said. "I need all the help I can get." He ducked back into the car, and started to dig through the layers of junk under the seat. His hand slipped past mouldy fruit, empty fast-food containers, soda cans, and a lot of old candy wrappers.

"Anything?"

"Nothing yet, but—hang on—I found them."

He straightened, thumbed both flashlights on and was rewarded with two blasts of powerful light. He turned and gave thumbs up. "Great, they both work!"

"*Now* can you close the door?" Suzy said.

"Yeah, yeah," Jackson said. "I'm out of here." He backed away, pushing his way through a mass of corn. He closed the door until it was almost shut, but left it open just a crack. No telling when he might have to get back in quickly. He just hoped it wouldn't come to that.

The dank smell of wet dirt assaulted his senses, and with the wind howling and gusting though the field, he couldn't hear anything of the conversation from inside the van. Even if they shouted out a warning to him, he doubted if he would hear it.

He started pushing his way through the thick strands of corn pressed up against the van. It was like going through a jungle. It was nice to have a pair of flashlights that worked, though. Their beams sliced through the darkness like two lasers and showed everything.

The van actually looked a lot better than he expected. Sure, it was dented and pitted, but otherwise didn't look too bad. When he finally pushed his way to the rear of the van, he stepped out onto a mass of flattened corn plants, and directed his light beams up the corridor they'd created. It looked like a roadway of flattened plants and churned up mud.

He flashed his lights up to the top of the hill. Man, it would certainly be a job to get back up there.

As he stepped to the other side of the van, he heard his mom's voice.

"How does it look?"

He flashed a light down the driver's side of the van. His mom had her window open and she was peering back at him.

"It doesn't look too bad," he said. "Just a lot of dents and stuff."

She chuckled. "That's pretty much how we started the trip."

"Well, there're a few more." He motioned back up the hill. "It's going to be tough getting back up to the highway."

"Yeah, I know."

"Mom! Can you *please* close the window! It's freezing back here," Suzy whined.

"All right, all right. Just give me a minute." She motioned to Jackson. "Can you head up to the highway?"

"Sure." He hesitated. "Ah…what for?"

"Well, if you leave one of your flashlights on the ground and angle it to shine this way, I can use it as a guide to get back up the hill."

"You got it," he said.

As Jackson turned and started to climb the narrow passageway, his lights showed an alleyway of shifting shadows and windblown corn moving in a frenzied dance. Leaves were being stripped away and fluttered through the air like giant bats. He let out a sigh. What was it Suzy was afraid of? Oh yeah, the Bogeyman. Just great.

Jackson started up the hill, his flashlights licking over the wall of corn on either side of the passageway. No way was he going to walk too close to that stuff. He'd seen the movie *Signs* enough times to know anything could be lurking just beyond the front layer of corn. What a time for him to think of that movie of all things.

He hurried up the middle of the clearing, breathing a sigh of relief when he finally stepped onto the highway. With reluctance, he placed one of the flashlights on the ground and angled it so the light shone down the dark corridor.

As he turned back to gaze along the lonely stretch of highway, the only sounds were the hissing and rattling of the corn and the distant hoot of an owl.

CHAPTER 3

Jackson slowly walked to the centre of the highway, looking one way and then the other.

It was eerily quiet.

After a moment, he could hear the sound of leaves scraping and whispering as the wind blew them along the wet pavement. It seemed utterly desolate. Now he knew how the character in the movie *I Am Legend* must have felt when he realized he was the last person left alive.

Somewhere, not too far from here, was where they had hit that thing. He turned in that direction and flashed his light beam over the pavement.

In the distance, the engine struggled as his mom tried to start the van. He hoped she could get it going. There was no way he wanted to stay out here any longer than necessary.

As he turned and swung his flashlight beam across the highway, he could see the shimmer of tiny particles of glass twinkling like stardust.

That's it, he thought, *the point of impact.*

He started in that direction, panning his flashlight from one side of the road to the other. Jackson knew it was kind of crazy, but another part of him had to know what it was they'd hit. Maybe a bear crossing the road, like his mother said, or… something else completely. The part of him that thought it was 'something else completely,' was bothered, and the idea of Suzy's Bogeyman sent a chill reverberating through his body. Swallowing to moisten his dry mouth, he started off in the direction of the glass.

Heavy clouds hung low in the sky and occasionally he could feel droplets of rain spitting down. After about five meters, he could see larger chunks of glass scattered across the road, as well as something else. It looked like oil, or maybe coolant, that had leaked after the crash. He'd have to check the underside of the van when and if it got back up to the road.

When he got closer, he shined his light over the closest pool. *No way*, he thought when he realized what it was.

Blood.

Further along, he could see more pools dotting the road. He took another couple of steps. His light showed where the blood trailed across the pavement. It angled off to the side of the road and disappeared at the road's shoulder.

This was crazy. Whatever they'd hit had managed to drag itself to the side of the road. It could still be alive, then.

Jackson followed the bloody trail to the edge of the road, pausing at the road's shoulder. From here on there was only a large cornfield extending upwards along a rise.

This is crazy, he thought, playing his light along the wall of corn.

As he swept along the wall he found where a hole had been punched into the field. Jackson crouched down, shining his light into the black maw of the cavity, illuminating where blood had been smeared over the leaves.

There was no way he was going any closer.

Stepping back, feeling the road under his feet, he heard a loud *snap* from somewhere off to his right.

He froze.

What the heck? Jackson tilted his head, listening. The only sound was the hiss of the wind through the corn.

He stepped backward again, slowly retreating across the pavement. Maybe he was just overreacting, making something out of nothing. Cocking his head, he listened. He could hear the wind whistling along the road and stirring the corn into motion again. He started to relax. *I'm making too much out of the one noise*—a loud crash and something tearing its way through the field made him jump. Something was coming!

He shined his light over the field. Quickly panning from left to right, he saw a massive furrow cutting through the corn. Behind him, he barely heard the roar of the van as the motor finally kicked in.

He staggered back a few more steps, his legs feeling like putty. There was a roar of the vehicle behind him, and he glanced back to see the glare of the taillights as the van backed up onto the road.

He started to backpedal as the roaring sound of the van echoed through the night. It bumped up onto the highway and screeched to a stop.

The van window squeaked open. "Okay, Jackson. Let's get going before—" His mother's voice cut away.

"Oh my word! Run Jackson! Run!"

Jackson heard a massive crash that jolted him into action. He turned and sprinted for the van. He rounded the rear of the van and jumped into the open passenger-side door. "Go!" he said, slamming the door and turning to watch the field.

A massive shape burst out of the field, pausing for a moment, and then started towards the van.

"Oh my!" their mom said, and stepped on the gas pedal.

The van accelerated slowly, growling and stuttering, picking up speed as the thing closed in on them.

Suzy screamed as she watched it lurch closer to the van, and Jackson watched in horror.

Suddenly, the van surged forward with power, accelerating rapidly. Jackson watched through the rear window as the thing faded from sight and melted into the darkness.

CHAPTER 4

Jackson slowly climbed out of the van, his muscles sore and aching from sleeping in a cramped space. He stretched his arms over his head and groaned aloud. It felt like he'd spent the night in a sardine can. After the events of last night, though, he was just happy they'd had enough gas to reach town.

For a few moments there, they had all thought the van was going to die when it stuttered and slowed. Luckily it was only air in the gas line—at least that's what his mom thought, and it made sense to him.

Now, images of what they hit kept dancing through his head. It had been a fitful drive, constantly checking behind them every time the van sputtered and threatened to stop.

After they found a place in town to stop at, they managed to sleep a couple of hours at best. Even with the doors locked and windows closed, Jackson kept waking up and checking outside. All he could see were the lights from the factories around them.

"Man," he groaned, massaging his shoulder. Every muscle seemed to be in pain, especially his jaw. He gingerly touched it and winced. "Crap!" He hoped it wasn't broken. He gingerly moved his jaw from one side to the other. It seemed all right, but it was sure sore.

He turned and let the early morning sun fall on his face as he glanced at his watch. It was only eight and it was already getting warm. After all the rain they'd been driving through, it felt pretty nice to see the sun again.

He thought about last night, turning to examine the van. It was a mess. The sides of it looked more banged up and pitted than they had last night. The windshield was a write off, with smears of dried blood caked onto to where the glass had been shattered.

He strolled away from the van, stepping over rapidly drying mud puddles and skirting his way around dog droppings. They had parked in the middle of some kind of industrial area, from the looks of it. A narrow, potholed dirt road wound past where they had parked, and in the near distance he could see the backs of what looked like trucking firms.

Jackson turned to eye one of the local businesses and heard the throaty roar of a truck starting up. Exhaust billowed skywards as it moved alongside a large warehouse before turning and accelerating out of sight.

He strolled along a deserted boulevard that was lined with heaped mounds of garbage. A garbage truck rushed past in a hurry, papers fluttering out of the open rear door like birds taking flight. The driver changed gears, and a cloud of black smoke spewed out as the truck disappeared out of sight.

Jackson shook his head in disbelief. What a busy place.

He turned around, shaded his eyes with a hand, and gazed up at a lengthy building sprawled along the summit of a small hill. A winding staircase zigzagged back and forth across the face of the hill, leading up to what looked like some kind of patio deck adjoining one of the businesses.

The stairs hadn't been painted in years. Long streamers of paint fluttered from the handrails like tiny flags.

Past the hillside, off in the distance, he caught sight of dozens of small farms or ranches dotting the ridgeline, their windows shimmering gold in the morning sun.

Nice.

Jackson flexed his shoulders as he continued along the curb.

There was garbage everywhere. It was piled up against the side of the curb like debris washed up to the high tide mark at the beach. Old candy wrappers and pages of newspaper scooted along the road like tumbleweed.

Pausing and planting his fists on his hips, he thought: *This is it? This is what we moved to Boswell for?*

He glanced at his watch. It was time to wake everyone up. Their appointment was in twenty minutes.

Circling back, he saw a newspaper dispenser on the other side of the road and jogged across to check it out.

Huge bold letters said: **Third Murder in a Week. Police Continue to Investigate.**

He tried to read the first paragraph, but the dirt-streaked glass made it impossible to read more than a few words. Further down, he saw another large headline:

The Creeper Strikes Again.

Three murders in one week? And the 'Creeper'? What the heck was that all about? He shook his head. It sounded like some kind of giant caterpillar. So much for a quiet life in a small town.

The creaking of a car door drew his attention, and he turned to see his mom easing her way out of the van. She was rubbing the back of her neck.

She squinted at him, holding up a hand to block the sun. "I can barely see you."

Jackson chuckled. "Yeah, but it's a lot better than all the rain we've had."

She walked towards him rubbing her eyes. "Yeah, that's certainly true." She came up beside him and turned to survey the area.

"Nice area, isn't it?" Jackson said with a grin.

His mom turned and frowned at him. "You need glasses."

Jackson let out a dramatic sigh. "Well, here we are in scenic Boswell. I'll have to remember to send the guys a postcard."

"Don't push it," his mom said, looking over the industrial area they'd camped next to. "At least we were able to make it to town in one piece."

Jackson motioned to the newspaper dispenser. "You'd better check out today's headlines."

"What?" She stepped closer to the paper dispenser and leaned over to read it. She squinted against the glare of the sun's reflection. "You've got to be kidding, a serial killer? *Here?*" She straightened, shaking her head. "I don't believe it."

"Does it really say that?" Jackson asked. "A *serial* killer?"

His mom nodded. "Well... that's how many you need to be considered a serial killer—three murders."

She pointed to the newspaper dispenser. "And how did they ever get the name Creeper?"

Jackson shrugged. "Who knows? Maybe he leaves certain clues after the murders, or it's something the papers came up with."

She turned to face him. "How do you know all this stuff?"

"By watching *Criminal Minds*, of course," Jackson said.

His mom straightened, dug through her pants pocket, and counted the change. "Good, I've got enough." Plugging the coins into the newspaper dispenser she swung open the door and pulled a paper out. She glanced at the front page. "Huh, the police aren't giving away any details, but they're increasing patrols on the west side of town."

"Which way did we come in?" Jackson asked.

His mom looked at him for a long moment and then said, "From the west."

Jackson shook his head. "Mom, I've got a bad feeling about this. What if that thing we hit was the Creeper?"

"I don't know," his mom said, staring at the front page. "But we'd better get to the local police and tell them what happened."

"Good idea," Jackson said. He looked at the van. "I hope Suzy's going to be all right after what we went through last night."

"I'm okay," Suzy's muffled voice said. "Come on over here and see what I've found."

Jackson turned to look at his mom. "I hope it's nothing bad." Something like streaks of blood along the side of the van, he thought. That would even freak him out.

His mom shaded her eyes and glanced up to the realty office. "Well, it doesn't look like its open yet."

Jackson squinted up to the realty building. "Everyone's sleeping in, probably."

"Come on, guys." Suzy said impatiently. "I found all kinds of stuff stuck to the front of the van."

Jackson's mom must have thought the same thing he did. She yelled: "Suzy, don't you go touching anything!"

Suzy's head popped up. "Mom, it's only a bunch of bugs."

Jackson looked at his mom. "Maybe we'd better go look."

As they drew closer, Suzy stood up and pointed. "Look, there must be hundreds of them stuck here."

"Wait a minute, I thought you were asleep?" Jackson said.

Suzy shook her head. "Nope, it's too hot for that. Besides, I heard something moving around up here."

"You shouldn't be wandering around here by yourself," Jackson said.

Suzy ignored him. "Here, check this out." She held up something moving about in her hand.

Jackson squinted at the squirming form in her hand. "Cool! It's a dragonfly."

"Not just that. It's a *giant* dragonfly," Suzy said dramatically. "We don't have anything this big back home."

"I suppose not," Jackson said. He frowned at it. "What are you going to do with it? The wing's busted."

Suzy frowned, eyes crossing as she examined the dragonfly carefully. "I think I'm going to keep it and try to nurse it back to health."

"Are you sure?" her mom asked.

Suzy nodded animatedly. "Oh yeah." She pulled a magnifying glass out of her pocket and peered at it. "It's a real beauty, as well."

"It looks pretty banged up," Jackson said. "What are you going to do if he dies?"

Suzy shrugged. "Then I'll add it to the rest of my bug collection so he won't be lonely."

Jackson shook his head, thinking of the hundreds of dead bugs Suzy had found and stored in a variety of cardboard boxes and pill bottles. He looked over at his mom. "How did she ever get into collecting bugs?"

"Your father, of course," she said.

"Well hey there, folks" a voice called from above them. "You wouldn't be the Ralph family would you?"

Jackson turned and squinted against the sun. He saw a large man waving at them from behind a guardrail.

"Yes, that's us," Jackson's mom called back.

"I'll be right down," the man said. "My name's Harry."

Jackson watched as the balding man started down the stairs. The stairs wobbled back and forth dangerously, looking like they would collapse at any moment.

"You sure it's safe to walk on that thing?" his mom asked, a hand shielding her eyes from the sun. "It looks ready to collapse."

"Not a problem," the man called back. "It's been like this for years."

He finally made it to ground level and walked towards them, wheezing and wiping a handkerchief over his face. He exhaled loudly. "It's going to be a real scorcher today. I can feel it already. It'll sure make up for all that rain we've been getting."

"No doubt," Irene said.

The man took in a deep breath, wiped his face again, and waddled over extending his hand. "Ma'am, my name's Harry Long." He turned and shook hands with Jackson and Suzy, as well.

Harry hitched up his pants and stared across the empty lot. "Don't tell me that's your van."

"I'm afraid so," Irene said. "We had something of an accident on the outskirts of town."

"I'll say," Harry said. "That thing is a wreck. What did you do? Hit an elephant?"

"Worse," Suzy said in a quiet voice.

Harry looked at her. "What could be worse than hitting an elephant?"

Suzy looked up at him and said, "We hit the bogeyman."

Harry laughed, and then slapped his thigh with a hand. "Oh, that's a good one. You hit the bogeyman."

"It's true," Suzy said with indignation. She planted her fists on her hips. "I'm not making that up!"

Her mother let out a sigh. "It's true. We hit something out on the highway last night." She shook her head. "We aren't sure what it was."

"Is that so?" Harry said, turning to face them. He wiped the sweat from his face again. "Well, we'd better get over to the Sheriff's office and let him know what happened."

"Yeah, I guess so," Jackson said.

"Lead the way, Harry," Irene said.

CHAPTER 5

"Well, that's it," Harry said, motioning to a corner building that had a sprawling veranda wrapped around the front.

"Are you serious?" Jackson said. "It looks like something out of a movie set."

Harry chuckled. "I'll have you know it's one of the oldest buildings in Boswell. It's even been designated as a historic monument." He paused for a moment. "They had a film crew here using it for an upcoming movie."

"Really?" Jackson said.

"Yep," Harry said. "It made the town famous."

"Huh. That's something."

"That's where Tim Russell works out of. He's been a lawman here for over twenty years. Before that, his father was sheriff, and before him, his grandfather was sheriff. So you might say it runs in the family."

"I guess so," Jackson said.

"Yep," Harry said, "He's probably dealt with almost everything you can think of."

"Even the bogeyman?" Suzy asked.

"Ah... well, I'm not sure about that," Harry said, glancing up at Irene. "I guess you'll have to ask him yourself."

Suzy nodded. "I guess I will."

"Come on, I'll introduce you," Harry said. He opened the heavy plank door and pushed it open.

Jackson looked around and then peered inside. "It looks pretty quiet in there. Sure anyone's working?"

Harry nodded. "Yep, but that's the way we like it—nice and quiet. Besides, I'm sure most of his staff is out checking up about the latest...ah... death."

"You mean murder?" Jackson said.

Harry nodded, his face drawn. "That's right."

"Hey Tim! You in here?" Harry asked.

"Back here," a muffled voice called out.

They walked in together, Jackson's head swivelling about as he took in all the details. To his right, a big board of Wanted posters. To his left, four desks, each cordoned from the others by wooden railings.

"What's all the commotion, Harry?" Sheriff Tim asked, coming out to the front.

"Tim, these nice folks have just moved into town, and seems like they had some trouble driving in last night."

"Really," Tim said, sipping at a coffee. "What happened, folks?"

"Well – " Jackson's mom started to explain.

"We hit the bogeyman!" Suzy blurted out.

Jackson saw the sheriff choke on his coffee

"You hit what?" Sheriff Tim asked.

"We hit the bogeyman," Suzy repeated.

Tim stood for a long minute—his mouth open and a look of disbelief on his face. He turned to Harry and said, "Harry, if this is another one of your goofy jokes—"

"No, no," Harry said, waving his hands. "They told me the same thing."

"I think we should all discuss this in my office," Sheriff Tim said, waving them in.

As they entered Tim's office, he motioned to a set of chairs in front of his desk. "Take a seat and tell me what happened."

"Like I said," Suzy huffed. "We hit the bogeyman on the road last night."

Tim laughed and shook his head. "That's a good one."

"I wasn't kidding," Suzy said in a huff. She folded her arms and scowled at him.

"Oops," Tim said. "Mom, why don't you tell me what happened."

As Irene recounted what had happened at the edge of town, Jackson surveyed Tim's office. There were a number of framed certificates for shooting, and a number of photos of Tim with various locals—probably the dogcatcher and a storeowner.

One thing that caught Jackson's eye was a large map thumbtacked to the wall behind the sheriff's desk. It was filled with an assortment of coloured pins. A second map beside it showed only a handful of pins, but only red ones.

Jackson stared, trying to make sense of them. Sheriff Tim seemed to read his thoughts. He cleared his throat and motioned to the map with the multi-coloured pins. He smiled at Jackson and said, "I bet you're wondering what all the pins are for?"

Jackson scratched his head for a moment, his family and Harry turning to look at him. "I'd guess that they all represent a crime that's been committed around Boswell."

"Dead on," Tim said, nodding his head. "You may have a future in law enforcement." He motioned to the more colourful map. "These are all crimes that have happened over the last five years. They're everything from shoplifting to assault."

"What about the map next to it? The one with only red pins?"

"Red pins signify murders," Tim said. He rolled his chair back and to the side so he could look at the red-pinned map, as well. "All these have happened over the last six months."

"The last six months?" Jackson said. "But there isn't even a red pin on the map for five years."

"That's right," Tim said. "For some unknown reason, we've now got someone killing people."

"The bogeyman," Suzy said in a whisper.

Tim rolled his chair around to look at them. "Now why is it she keeps talking about the bogeyman?"

Jackson sat back, stretched out his legs as his mom related what had happened on the drive into town the night before. Tim wrote everything Irene said on a notepad. When she finished, Tim sat back in his chair, staring up at the maps and pins.

"You're sure of this?" Tim asked.

"You should see our van," Jackson said, motioning with a thumb over his shoulder. "It's banged up pretty good, and there's a lot of dried blood on it."

Harry nodded. "Yeah, it looks as though they hit a moose. I'm surprised they even made it to town. It's pretty banged up."

Tim wrote something else down. "All right, I'll send a crew to check it. DNA analysis may give us a few answers."

Someone came behind them and knocked on the doorjamb.

"Yeah, Walt?" Tim said.

As they turned around to look at the deputy, Walt glanced over the collection of people in the office. "Ah... we need to talk to you, Tim."

"Is there a problem?" Tim asked.

Walt nodded. "Ah... same thing we've been working on for a while now."

Tim sighed and pushed himself out of his chair. "Well, folks, looks like duty calls. I'm going to have to get back to you later. Are you going to be staying in town?"

Jackson saw his mom shrug. "We're not sure where we'll be," she said. "We've just inherited my great aunt's house."

"Who's that?" Tim asked.

"It's the Baxter place," Harry said. "I can take them out there if it'll help."

"That'd help," Tim said. He turned to the rest of them. "Look, I'll have someone come out to talk to you a bit later. From the looks of it, we're going to be a bit busy."

CHAPTER 6

"All right, everybody buckled in?" Harry asked.

"I think so," Irene Ralph said, turning around and checking the back seat. "I sure appreciate you helping us out this way."

"No problem," Harry said.

"I'm just glad we're not going back the way we came."

"Can't say as I blame you," Harry said. He snapped his seatbelt on and checked the rear-view mirror. "There have been a lot of weird things happening around here."

"Really? What do you mean?" Jackson said, snapping his seatbelt on.

As Harry started the car, he said, "You know that map with just red pins on it?"

"Yeah," Jackson said.

"Well, like Tim said, that's where there've been murders. Not only that, a lot of stuff had been stolen from the businesses where the murders were committed. There's been wire, HDMI cable, electronic stuff, and computer stuff taken. No one's been able to figure out why, but Tim will put it all together. He's smart."

"That's good," Irene said.

"I'll give you the guided tour as we leave town," Harry said. "Your new home is just a short distance away from the Tor."

"The *Tor*?" Jackson asked. "What the heck's that?"

Harry ran a hand over his bald head. "It's probably the most unusual and most striking feature in this area. Basically, it looks like a miniature volcano set in a bowl of mist."

"What?" Jackson said. "That doesn't make any sense."

Harry flicked on his blinker and pulled out onto the road. "It will once you see it."

Jackson shrugged his shoulders. "Okay."

As they accelerated, Harry turned and said, "Rumour has it the Vikings may have been out there. Some kind of an ancient colony, I've read."

"Are you serious?" Jackson said, leaning forward from the backseat. "That's got to be hundreds of years old."

"That's right," Harry said. "Maybe even older. Some local kid, about the same age as you, found a stash of Viking coins by the river. I think he was using one of those metal detectors."

"Good idea," Jackson said, nodding in admiration. "They must have been worth a lot of money."

"It's hard to say. He donated all the coins to the local museum," Harry said. "The historian at the museum dated them back to the 12th or 13th century."

Jackson eased back in his seat. "That's cool. That's practically ten centuries old." He remembered doing an essay on the Vikings in school. He hadn't realized they'd travelled so far inland. When he looked at the location of Boswell on the map, it was virtually in the middle of nowhere.

He looked at Harry. "Why would the Vikings come here? I mean... it's in the middle of nowhere."

Harry glanced at Jackson in the rear-view mirror. "It's very simple. It was gold."

"Gold? Are you serious?" Irene said. "In Boswell?"

Harry nodded. "Oh yeah. They've been pulling gold out of these hills for a long time now. Although a prospector or two will still come into town with big nuggets, I think most of the main deposits have been played out."

"Jeez," Jackson said, shaking his head in disbelief, "that's amazing." He sat back in his seat, folded his arms, and stared out the window. He was suddenly becoming interested in the area. Gold. Who would have thought it? Who knows, maybe there's still more to be found. And to think the Vikings were here as well.

Harry glanced back towards Suzy. "How about you little lady—you're pretty quiet back there?"

"I was just thinking about my new pet," Suzy said.

"Oh, I see."

"I'm hoping that he will be feeling better soon."

Harry grinned. "Is he feeling sickly?"

"Yes, he is. Let me show you."

Harry chuckled. "Sure, why not?"

Suzy leaned forward, squeezing herself between the two front seats.

Harry turned his head as he sensed movement from the corner of his eye.

Suzy held up the still-struggling dragonfly and brought it towards Harry's face. "Watch out Mr. Harry, or you'll get stung."

Harry's head snapped back as if he'd been slapped. "Jeez kid, get that thing away from me!"

Suzy laughed and moved the dragonfly in a series of loops and swoops. "Look out Mr. Harry, my dragonfly is going to sew your lips shut!"

The car swerved across the road, tires squealing.

"Suzy, stop it!" Jackson said.

"Suzy, you stop that right now!" her mom said.

"Okay, I was just kidding," Suzy said, easing herself back into her seat. She folded her arms and looked at her dragonfly. "He's afraid of you, Mr. Dragonfly, and I don't know why."

Harry clutched a hand to his chest. "Jeez, that kid almost gave me a heart attack." He gulped air noisily.

"Are you all right?" Irene asked.

Harry nodded and muttered under his breath: "Crazy kid."

Jackson cleared his throat. "She doesn't mean any harm, Harry. She just likes to collect bugs."

"Really?" Harry said drolly. "I guess when you get back to your van she can add *Mr. Dragonfly* to her scorpion and spider collection."

Suzy laughed. "Mr. Harry, you're a real funny guy."

"Yeah, I'm a real bundle of laughs," Harry said. He turned to Irene. "You know what? When your daughter grows up she could probably get a job as a snake handler at the zoo."

Irene had to smile. "You're probably right."

Jackson gazed out the side window, noticing that they had now moved out of town into farm or ranch country.

Harry brightened. "Hey you guys, if you look out the back window, you can see a cloud of dust behind us. Kind of looks like a rocket taking off." He chuckled.

"It looks like some kind of storm," Suzy said, looking out the rear window.

Harry let the SUV slow down. "This thing goes like a rocket when I want it to." He leaned forward and flicked a button on the console. "Watch this." The sunroof glided open silently.

"That's cool," Suzy said, leaning forward and gazing up through the opening. "I wish we had that in our van."

Jackson saw a crossroad coming up as Harry turned on his signal light. They turned right at the intersection and quickly accelerated.

"Hang on to your hats!" Harry said. "We're going to go to warp speed." He punched the accelerator and the SUV took off.

"Whoa!" Jackson said.

Harry said, "Mr. Scott, give me... warp nine." Then, in a bad Scottish accent, "Captain, the engines canna take it!"

Harry chuckled away, obviously pleased with himself. He turned his head. "I bought the entire *Star Trek* series on DVD."

Jackson just looked at Harry and shook his head sadly.

Harry glanced in the rear-view mirror and asked, "What?... What's wrong, kid?"

Jackson said, "That had to be one of the worst Scottish accents I've ever heard."

"Hey, it's still a work in progress," Harry said. He motioned to a large tree to the right. "Anyway, from that tree to your house it's exactly three kilometers."

Jackson sat up and checked the surroundings. "Jeez, it looks pretty desolate out here."

Harry nodded in agreement. "Yeah, a bit, but it's certainly nice and quiet. You'll get used to it. I had a friend live up here when I was a kid, and there're lots of things to explore."

"Is there a school around here?" Suzy asked, her face pressed up against the window.

"School? Oh, yeah, but it's closer to town," Harry said. "There's a bus that comes out here to pick up the kids."

"What do people do way out here?" Suzy asked. "I don't even see a store."

"Mainly ranching," Harry said, "but a lot of people travel to town for work."

"What about our place?" Jackson asked. "What's it like?"

Harry thought for a moment. "It's big and it's on a five acre parcel of land. The house… well, it needs a bit of work."

"Five acres," Jackson said. "Nice."

"Is it a nice house?" Irene Ralph asked.

Harry thought about it for a moment, and finally nodded his head. "Oh yeah. I think it's what they call a Cape Cod home. It has four bedrooms and even a library."

"A library? Are you serious?" Jackson asked.

Harry nodded. "Yep, dead serious."

"Four bedrooms!" Jackson said. "How cool is that? Now I can finally get my own room."

"Hang on," Harry said, turning onto a gravel road. "It's not much further now."

CHAPTER 7

"Hey," Harry said, "I just thought of something. Most kids are interested in science—especially *you*, dragonfly girl—and there just happens to be an amazing science store in town."

"Really?" Jackson said. "Are you kidding us?"

Harry shook his head. "No way. I take my niece and nephew there every time they come to town. It carries all kinds of neat stuff," Harry said.

Neat? Jackson thought. "What kind of *neat* stuff?"

Harry thought for a moment. "Butterfly nets, all kinds of rocks and minerals. Fossils, telescopes—you name it, they've got it."

"Sounds pretty... neat," Jackson said with a smile.

"And they've got stuff for collecting bugs?" Suzy asked, leaning forward in her seat."

"Oh yeah, lots of stuff," Harry said. "And if they haven't got it, they order it in for you. Even the science teachers hang around there."

"So they've got rocks and minerals, you were saying?" Jackson said.

"Yeah, all kinds of stuff for rock hounding. Rock hammers, chisels, backpacks, lots of books on rocks."

"Cool," Jackson said. "Hey Mom, maybe we can check it out when we go to town sometime?"

"Well, let's see how things go," Irene said. "We also don't have a way back into town."

"That shouldn't be a problem," Harry said. "I think your aunt had an old car around the house somewhere."

"That would help," Jackson said. "We could get into town to see a store."

"And if you get to the Nature Store, you might run into one of the science teachers there," Harry said.

"Really?" Irene said.

"Oh yeah," Harry said. "They go there a fair bit. I've run into Mr. Rutledge a couple of times when I've been there." He pulled out and accelerated past a tractor pulling a load of hay. "Odd guy though."

"What do you mean?" Irene asked.

"Well, Mr. Rutledge gets most of his science stuff from the Nature Store, but a lot of people wonder where he gets the other stuff—you know, the stuff that isn't carried by any science store."

"What do you mean?" Irene asked again, looking at him intently.

Jackson nudged Suzy with an elbow and leaned forward. Now this was becoming interesting. He had a feeling Harry was up to something.

"Well, people have been wondering where he gets the skeletons he uses in class for demonstrations."

"Skeletons? He uses skeletons in class?" Irene said, gawking at Harry in disbelief.

Harry waved a hand dismissively. "Ah, it's probably just a rumour. You know how kids make up things."

"Yeah. Maybe," she said.

Harry paused for a moment and then slapped the steering wheel with his hand. "Wait a minute, I just remembered something. A while back I heard a bunch of teens talking about the human skeleton he has hanging in class. I think he keeps it in some kind of narrow closet and pulls it out when he uses it."

"What? Isn't that against the law or something?"

"You would think so, wouldn't you?" Harry said, shaking his head slowly. "If that's the case, if it *is* true, where did he get it from?"

"The Nature Store?" Irene asked.

Harry turned to look at her with a, *you've got to be kidding* look. "I don't think so."

"Then where?"

Jackson shook his head, grinning away. He knew his mom was gullible, but this was something else. He thought he'd play along. "Yeah, you wonder where he got it from."

They drove onto a hard-packed dirt road, the loose dirt spitting up against the undercarriage.

He waved a hand in the air. "Now don't get me wrong. He seems to be a nice guy, but you never know. Especially with some local tombs being broken into."

"What?" Irene said. "What did you say?"

Jackson leaned forward, fighting back a smile. "Wow, I can't wait to start science class."

"Don't even think about it!" his mom said. "I'm going to get you switched to the arts program."

"Ah, Mom…"

Harry roared with laughter and shook his head. "Sorry, but I haven't pulled a good joke like that in years." He wiped tears from his eyes.

Jackson's mom folded her arms and stared through the windshield, shaking her head slowly. "You mean you were only joking? You jerk!"

They wound their way around towering monoliths of stone, slowly leaving the grasslands behind. It began to look like they were on a different planet.

"This is bizarre," Jackson said, pressing his face up against his window.

Harry turned his head. "In a minute, you'll see the Tor."

"Yeah?"

"And then you'll think you're on a different planet."

"Cool," Jackson said.

CHAPTER 8

As they slid through a tight corner, the SUV accelerated up a steep hill, trees blurring past it on either side.

"Mostly fruit trees," Harry said, "Apple and pear, I think."

Jackson could see the crest of the hill approaching fast and grabbed hold of the armrests. A moment later they were airborne, humming through the air for a few seconds and then bouncing down on the road.

What a contrast to the bottom area, Jackson thought. It was a lush green with fields on both sides of the road.

"Oh my goodness," Irene said. "It's beautiful!" She turned towards Harry. "I think you can slow down now."

"Oh yeah, sorry," Harry said, taking his foot off the accelerator and letting the car slow down.

"Whoa," Jackson said, resting a hand on his stomach. "I think I left my stomach back there somewhere."

"That's the reason I love coming up here," Harry said. "I can drive my car like a sports car. When my wife is with me, I have to stick to the speed limit."

"I see," Irene said. "Well, you can always race your car on the way home."

"Good point," Harry said, nodding.

He slowed and gestured to the right. "All right ladies and gentlemen, coming up on your right is the world famous—or perhaps I should say, *infamous*—hill called the Tor." He paused dramatically. "A photograph of it even made it to the cover of National Geographic."

"Why infamous?" Irene turned to ask.

Harry thought for a moment. "Well, I say that because of the amount of people who have lost their lives trying to get to it. At last count, I think over fifty people have died out there."

"Oh my," Irene said, covering her mouth with a hand.

Harry nodded grimly. "I lost a relative out there a few years back."

"Oh, I'm sorry," Irene said.

"What happened? A plane crash?" Jackson asked.

"Got caught in quicksand when he was hiking," Harry said. He looked in the rear-view mirror at Jackson. "A few years back, a Japanese film crew went down when their helicopter got caught in a crosswind." He hesitated. "At least that's what the official story is."

"Hey, what's with all the fog?" Jackson asked, looking down into a barren landscape. "It's the middle of summer."

Harry nodded knowingly. "We have fog twelve months of the year down there. I think it's something to do with thermal—"

"—Hey, what's that?" Jackson asked, motioning to the right.

In the centre of a blanket of the swirling fog, Jackson could see a conical hill standing straight up from the fog like a lonely sentinel. "Now it *does* look like we are on another planet."

"That's the Tor," Harry said.

"Incredible," Jackson said, shaking his head in disbelief.

"Yep, that's the usual reaction when people see it for the first time." He turned to Irene. "That's the view that has filled local calendars and tourist stuff for years."

Irene nodded. "I can see why. It's spectacular."

Harry let the car slow down. "A lot of people have likened it to some place in England. Ah, Glastonbury Tor, I think they called it. The *Tor* means some kind of a hill. I read they even have an old building on it."

"Really?" Jackson said.

"Yeah, something like eight or nine centuries old," Harry said.

As they drove around the edge of a natural bowl in the landscape, Jackson could make out streams and ponds with pillars of steam writhing into the sky.

"See those pillars of steam climbing into the sky?" Harry asked.

"Yeah," Jackson said. "What are they?"

"They're volcanic vents. Holes that run through the Earth's crust."

The area looked dead, Jackson thought as he looked down at the bleak landscape. It was as if someone had detonated a nuclear device that had carved out a huge bowl from the rock. The only thing remaining was a rock spire in the very centre.

"Not a lot of plant life," Jackson said. "I can't even see a hint of green."

"Nothing lives down there," Harry said. "Absolutely nothing. That's why folks refer to it as the wastelands."

"Did they ever test a nuclear weapon out there?" Jackson asked.

Harry cocked his head. "What? Nuclear weapons? I don't think so. What makes you ask?"

Jackson shrugged. "I don't know. It just looks so… lifeless and bleak."

"Yeah, it does, doesn't it?" Harry said.

"It also looks pretty weird with that fog down there."

"You should see it in the fall," Harry said. "It's even thicker and pushes its way right up into town."

"Sounds spooky," Suzy said.

Harry turned in his seat. "Anyone ever see that movie *The Fog?*"

"Yeah," Jackson said. "A couple of times."

"Well, it kind of looks like that, but really thick," Harry said. "You get the fog rolling into town so thick you can barely see next door. And worst of all is that nauseating smell of sulphur."

"Sulphur?" Irene said. "Where—"

"Most of the fog comes from all the volcanic vents, and with that you usually get a lot of sulphur fumes," Harry said.

"Really?"

"Yeah. It also makes it hard to breathe," Harry said. "Weird thing is that sometimes you could swear there were *things* moving around in there."

Irene shivered. "It sounds kind of creepy."

"Yeah, it is," Harry said, pulling into the driveway.

"What kind of things?" Jackson said.

"No one knows," Harry said. "And no one wants to know."

"Oh."

Harry quickly changed the subject. "Well, here we are. Your new home."

CHAPTER 9

Jackson looked out at a massive house set back from the driveway. He'd never seen a house that size. "Jeez, that thing's huge!"

Suzy gawked at the sight. "You mean that's *ours*?"

"You bet," Harry said, stopping in front. "It's almost three thousand square feet and it's on five acres."

"Nice," Irene said.

"Now, if you find it's too large, and you'd like to move closer to town, give me a call."

Irene nodded. "I'll keep that in mind. Thanks."

Jackson shook his head in disbelief as he gazed at the front façade. It looked like a mansion compared to the small, dingy apartment they'd left. He let out a contented sigh. "Wow, no more sleeping on the sofa."

"No," his mom said, "I don't think so." She rubbed the nape of her neck.

Jackson took in the details of the house. The yellow paint was faded by the elements and flaking off in areas, while shutters bracketed each window. Some of them were so tilted that they looked like they were ready to fall off.

If anything, a fresh coat of paint would make the place look new. He just wished his dad could have survived to see it, Jackson thought.

"Why are all the windows covered up with boards?" Suzy asked as she scrambled out of the car.

"It's just to make sure nobody gets in and makes a big mess," Harry said.

"Oh, you mean like party animals?"

Harry chuckled. "Exactly, kid."

Harry paused on the grass-covered sidewalk and stretched his back. He then pointed to the second-story windows. "The four bedrooms are on the second floor, so you'll get a spectacular view from any window."

"Cool," Jackson said. "I can't believe there's a library, as well."

"Well, apparently your aunt was quite the reader. Of course, that's probably why she enjoyed working as a librarian at our public library."

"Gosh, you mean there's even a public library in Boswell?" Jackson said, smirking.

Harry looked at Jackson. "Funny guy. Yes we've even got a library."

Irene said. "I didn't realize Agnes worked at the library."

"Yeah, well she was also the library cop," Harry said. "Heaven help you if you ever had overdue books. She would literally come to your house looking for you."

"Did she spend a lot of time looking for *you*?" Suzy asked.

Jackson laughed. "Huh. Aunt Agnes: the library enforcer."

Harry waved an arm. "Come on, let's take a closer look."

They carried on, walking along a curved sidewalk that meandered through waist-high grass that was burnt brown by the sun. A few meters away, a set of aging wooden stairs led to a sprawling veranda that wrapped around the front of the house.

As Jackson paused to gaze up at the house, his mom stopped beside him.

"It looks like it's going to take a lot of work to get the place back in shape," she said.

"Just some time and money," Jackson said. He motioned with a hand. "You know, if we fix up the place it'll look spectacular."

"There are lots of tools in the garage," Harry said, passing them and continuing up the veranda stairs.

"Any neighbours nearby?" Jackson asked, looking around from the vantage point of the veranda.

Harry motioned behind them. "Oh yeah, there's a small subdivision of houses back behind your property. I think there're about fifteen houses on small acreages. I think there're kids about the same age as you."

Jackson nodded. Cool. At least they wouldn't be totally isolated.

Harry looked around, shading his eyes with a hand. "It's going to need a lot of work, but I'm sure you guys will do fine."

"It'll just take a bit of money," Irene Ralph said.

"Probably not a lot," Harry said. "The first thing I'd do is to check the garage for paint, tools, and supplies. I just think your aunt let it go after a while. It was probably too much work for the old gal to keep it up."

"Just cutting the grass will make a difference," Jackson said. "I'll check out the garage later on."

"You'd better look for a scythe first," Harry said. "The grass it so high you could get lost in it."

"Cool," Suzy said, watching a butterfly fly past the veranda.

"Well, shall we take a look inside?" Harry asked. "It's been a while since it's been opened up, so it's bound to smell musty."

"Let's do it," Jackson said. "I want to see if I can snag a bedroom for myself." He turned to his mom. "Can I have first pick?"

"We'll see," his mom said. "We'll see." She turned and nodded to Harry. "Well, let's open it up and see what we've got."

CHAPTER 10

Harry slid a key into the padlock and opened it up, dropping the massive, rusting chain to one side of the door. The weathered oak door obviously hadn't been opened in a while, so Harry had to force it open with a shoulder.

It opened in small, squeaking stages.

"Need a hand, Harry?" Jackson asked.

Puffing hard, Harry shook his head and grunted. "No, I've got it now." The door finally opened all the way, creaking loudly. "Nothing that a bit of oil won't cure."

As they stepped into the house, clouds of dust plumed into the air.

Irene sneezed. "How long has it been sealed up?"

Harry rubbed a hand over the back of his neck. "Probably close to a year and a half."

"That long? We only found out about the inheritance a few months back."

Harry shrugged. "From what I heard, it took a while to trace where you were."

"Well, we were forced to move a few times," Jackson said. "So it's no wonder." He remembered that after his dad died, they had to keep moving to places they could afford.

As everyone tramped into the entrance foyer, more dust clouded into the air.

Jackson waved a hand through the air. "This is going to take more time to clean up than the outside."

Harry stepped forward, squinting through the clouds of dust and into the deep gloom. "Well, at least it looks like everything's in one piece. We covered all the furniture with sheets to protect them."

"It's a good thing, too," Irene said as she stepped away from the entrance. She paused beside an umbrella stand full of umbrellas and surveyed the living room. "It's absolutely *huge*. This room alone is larger than our entire apartment was."

"I know," Jackson said.

Harry shook his head slowly. "Your apartment was smaller than this? You've got to be kidding me."

"Afraid not."

Jackson noted that other than sheets covering all the furniture, everything looked in pretty good shape. He crossed to an adjoining wall and tried the light switch. "Hey!" he said in surprise. "It works!"

"We had the hydro and gas people turn everything back on when we heard you were coming," Harry said. He motioned to the windows. "Once you pry off the wood from the windows, you'll have lots of natural light."

"Great," Irene said. "Then we won't feel like we're living in a cave."

Past the foyer, Jackson could see a curving staircase leading up to the second floor. "Hey, I'm going to check out the upstairs."

"Sure, go ahead," Irene said.

As Jackson started up the stairs, Suzy said, "I want a bedroom close to Mom's."

"And I would love one with an ensuite," Irene said.

Harry called up after him. "Turn right at the top of the stairs and check out the room at the end of the hall."

"Great," Jackson said, pounding up the rest of the stairs. "I'll see how everything looks."

Harry glanced at his watch. "You know what? I've got to get going. I forgot I've got an afternoon appointment."

"Well, thanks for all the help, Harry. You've been a lifesaver," Irene said.

Harry flushed. "Hey, no problem. If you need anything, just give me a call." He passed her one of his cards. "And I took the liberty of getting your phone hooked up."

"Thanks again," Irene said, glancing at the card.

"Remember, if you ever want to sell this baby give me a call." He waved. "Hey, I'll see you, kids."

"Thanks Mr. Harry," Suzy said. "I'll collect some bugs for you, to keep you company."

Harry let out a groan. "Oh, I can hardly wait."

Jackson hurried down the hall, checked the door on his right, and ducked his head to find the library. Shelves covered the walls from floor to ceiling, and there were so many books stuffed on them that the shelves bulged downward.

I'll check it out later, he thought. *First, my bedroom.*

Jackson closed the door and opened the door on the opposite side of the hallway.

A room veiled in darkness awaited him.

Reaching back, he threw on the light switch and gawked at the massive room in front of him.

Panels of plywood had been nailed over all the windows, not only protecting the glass from breakage, but creating a dark, cave-like atmosphere.

The sprawling room looked part bedroom and part workshop. It was huge.

A bed was pushed against one wall, and the centre of the room was filled by a plywood sheet suspended on three sawhorses.

What it had been used for was beyond him.

An art table, maybe?

A beat up sofa with stuffing falling out was the only other furnishing in the room. It looked a bit like a gutted fish.

"Not bad, not bad," he said aloud.

"What's not bad?" his mom said, walking into the room.

Jackson started, clutching a hand to his chest. "Jeez, Mom. Let a guy know you're standing there. You almost gave me a heart attack."

"Nice. Very nice," his mom said, slipping past him and into the room.

"I was just about to see if I could get some natural light in here," Jackson said.

"Go for it," she said.

Jackson nodded and went to the bank of windows on one side. He unlatched the window and pushed it up as far as it would go. Then, pushing against the plywood secured to the outside wall, he sent it fluttering to the ground.

He looked out over the landscape and said, "Jeez! Will you look at that."

A spectacular view of the Tor and the surrounding wastelands seemed so close, he felt he could almost reach out and touch them. A swirling mist hung around the hill and gave it an eerie, primordial look.

"Pretty nice view," his mom said.

"Yeah," he nodded. "How's your room?"

"Just going to check it out now," she said, turning and leaving.

Jackson gazed out the window. The dark outline of the Tor was striking. He could see sinuous threads of mist creeping up the slope like grey tentacles.

Below him, the property stretched back until it reached an old wooden fence. It looked like parts of it had fallen away with age. The backyard must have been an orchard at one time because there were a lot of apple trees.

He was looking near some of the trees, when he saw movement.

Jackson waited for a while, and then saw it again. *What the heck?*

There was something moving down there, on *their* property

He turned and hurried down the stairs. "Mom, I'll be right back. I'm going to check out something in the backyard."

"Okay," the muffled response came back as he slammed the door behind him.

CHAPTER 11

Jackson skirted a Laurel hedge that cut across the middle of their property like a knife. He slowed as he heard the soft murmur of voices.

"Come on, Cheryl, give me a hand?"

"Forget it, Carl. You know how Mom has a fit when I come home dirty."

"Yeah, but there's no way I'm going to be able to pull anything out by myself."

"Yeah, yeah. It's your bad back. I know," Cheryl said.

"Well, it is," Carl said defensively.

"Let's worry about it if we find anything. For all we know, there may be nothing buried there other than a couple of tin cans."

"I don't know," Carl said. "My metal detector says otherwise. Whatever it is, it's big."

Jackson crept closer to the hedge and cocked his head. What the heck was going on over there? There were at least two of them, a male and a female, he could tell that much.

He found a break in the hedge and peered through. He was right, just two of them. The only names he had heard were Carl and Cheryl. The girl was just sitting there, watching and tapping a hand on her leg as she listened to some tunes. The guy was standing in a huge hole, digging in what looked like a grave.

What the heck are they doing?

Carl took a break and wiped an arm across his forehead. "It must be a lot deeper than we thought."

Cheryl took out one of the headphones. "What's that?"

"I said: it must be a lot deeper than we thought."

"Yeah, I guess so. Just keep going, you're doing great," Cheryl said, leaving one earphone in. She promptly started bobbing her head to a tune.

Carl exhaled loudly and said, "Easy for you to say, Cheryl. Maybe you should try digging for a while and see what it's like."

Cheryl shook her head. "You heard what Mom said—to not get my new clothes dirty."

"Yeah, yeah," Carl said, resuming his digging.

Jackson moved on, found a larger break in the hedge to peer through, and paused there. Yep. There were only two of them, and based on their conversation, he knew they had to be brother and sister. For a moment, he thought of what Harry had said about some of the students bringing in bones, and wondered if that's what they were up to.

He just hoped it wasn't something like a skeleton.

The girl stood up shaded her eyes from the sun. "I think we'd better get out of here pretty soon."

"Now what? You getting sunburnt or just bored?"

"No, it just looks like there're people moving around in the house."

"What?" Carl said, turning and looking towards the house. "You've got to be kidding. That place has been deserted for months."

"Not any longer, it looks like."

"All right, let's get this done and get out of here," Carl said.

"It's what I've been saying all along," his sister said.

Jackson watched as the guy went back to work. This time Carl was really putting in an effort. Jackson could see shovelfuls of dirt flying through the air every few seconds.

"Yeah, put your back into it," his sister said.

The guy paused long enough to glare at her. "Hey, maybe you'd like to take a turn."

"Afraid not," she said wagging a finger at him. "You know what Mom told me."

"Yeah, I know," he grumped. He started digging again.

"Hey, maybe that metal detector of yours is broke," she said.

"Nah. I checked it out before we left home. It works fine. I just don't think we're deep enough."

"You keep digging. I'll keep an eye on the house," she said.

Jackson wondered what to do. Phone the cops? It might take hours for them to arrive. No, he needed something else. Maybe a ruse of some kind. He thought about it for a moment while Carl continued to dig furiously. Then, thinking he had an idea that might work, Jackson took a step forward, and then another. He purposely stepped on a twig and heard a soft crunch. Perfect. He froze position and waited.

"Carl?"

"Now what?" he said, pausing to gulp air. He leaned on his shovel, breathing hard.

"I don't think we're alone," Cheryl said.

"Of course not, you already told me that you saw people at the house."

"No, I don't mean that," she said.

"Okay," he said. "What do you mean?"

"I—I heard a noise."

He stared at her for a moment. "That's it?"

She looked around nervously. "Isn't that enough?"

Jackson grinned, covering his mouth so he wouldn't laugh out loud. He kept perfectly still. He bent over and peered through a tiny break in the branches. He could see the guy frowning and looking around.

"I don't hear anything," Carl said, shrugging his shoulders.

"Well, there was something."

"Sure."

His sister's eyes grew wide as she said, "What if it's the Creeper?"

Carl shook his head. "Don't get carried away, Cheryl. The Creeper was way on the opposite side of town."

"Maybe he's moved out here," Cheryl said.

"Well, I'll keep an eye out," Carl said. "Besides, I've got this baby," he said, holding his shovel in the air.

"Okay." She kept looking around nervously. "Let's just hurry up and get out of here. This place is giving me the willies."

Jackson remembered the blurb he had read about the Creeper. It seemed like it really had the townspeople spooked. He let out a breath. He'd have to make sure he didn't overdo it.

Cheryl kept looking around while her brother worked at shovelling as fast as he could. Jackson wondered what it was they were digging for. Somehow, he had to find out. Then, he hit upon another brilliant scheme and laughed to himself. *Mwah ha ha.*

Reaching out, he grabbed an overhanging branch and shook it briskly from side to side. Cheryl's eyes grew even wider and her mouth opened to form an O. She pointed at the swaying branch. Carl, who had his back to him, dug his shovel into the ground and there was a loud *clunk*.

"Look!" Cheryl said, pointing.

Carl grinned. "I told you my metal detector worked! We've found it!"

He bent over and started digging frantically, then began to scrape away dirt. He got down on his hands and knees and started to clear the dirt away.

Peering through the opening, Jackson wondered what they had found. He stood on his tiptoes and tried to see what it was.

Carl turned to his sister. "You'd better give me a hand. This thing is a lot heavier than I thought."

"But… but—" she said, still pointing.

"Never mind the motor boat impersonations, get down here and give me a hand," Carl said.

"The branch… moving," she said.

Carl turned and checked behind him. "There's nothing there! Come down and give me a hand, will you?"

With his sister grudgingly helping him, and still glancing at the hedge from time to time, Carl and Cheryl heaved a massive metal trunk out of the hole and threw it on the ground.

"We found it, Carl! We actually found it!"

Gulping air and trying to catch his breath, Carl said, "Yeah, I know. I know."

"Let's open it," Cheryl said, rubbing her hands together.

Carl nodded, still breathing hard. Then, motioning to the trunk, he said, "There's a huge padlock on it. There's no way we're going to get that off."

"We should have brought some tools with us," Cheryl said.

Carl shook his head. "It's too late to say that now."

"We could run home and bring some tools here," Cheryl said.

Jackson shifted position, stirring some of the branches into motion.

Carl looked around for a minute. "Did you hear something?"

"Oh, don't you start," Cheryl said. She looked at him. "You're kidding, right?"

"Probably just the wind," he said. "Best thing is to carry that thing out of here back to our place."

"Yeah?"

Carl nodded. "We're too exposed out here, and it'd be better to try and open it in our garage with some tools."

"I think you're right."

They were lifting the metal chest off the ground when Jackson decided it was time to move into action.

He cleared his throat and in a gruff voice said, "Leave that chest right where you found it!"

CHAPTER 12

"Wha...What?" Cheryl stammered.

"You heard me!" He cleared his throat again. "Leave it where you found it. You're trespassing on my property!"

Cheryl's hand fluttered to her mouth. "We...we didn't know!"

"Leave. Now!" Jackson said in his scariest voice.

"Carl?" Cheryl turned and said in a whisper.

"Sorry, we didn't know anyone lived here."

"Well now you do!" Jackson growled. He bit his lip to keep from laughing. He felt like the great and powerful Oz. "Now leave!"

Carl nodded. "Okay, okay." He leaned over and grabbed one end of the chest.

"Leave the trunk where it is," Jackson said.

"Wait a minute. We found it," Carl said.

"Carl," Cheryl said in a pleading voice.

Carl gave her a dismissive wave, and shook his head.

"My property. Sorry," Jackson said. "So pick up your tools and beat it." For a brief moment, he thought of singing Michael Jackson's *Beat It,* but then thought he better not.

"Wait a minute—" Carl began.

"Leave!" Jackson said, cutting him off. He covered his mouth, grinning like a fool. Somehow, he lost his balance and started to fall.

Arms wind-milling the air, he tumbled into the hedge and burst through to the opposite side.

When he lifted his head, Jackson saw two angry faces glaring at him.

"Look," Carl snarled. "He's a teen, like us!"

Cheryl's head swivelled about like a praying mantis focusing on its prey. Her lips pulled back in a snarl. "*You're* the one who's been taunting us? You're the guy pretending to be the Creeper? You jerk!"

Jackson got to his feet, held his hands up defensively. "Now wait a minute."

The girl charged at him, bent low and put her shoulder into his midsection, driving him heavily to the ground.

Air exploded from Jackson's lungs and he lay there trying to catch a breath. Finally he managed to throw Cheryl to one side. He heard her scream, "Don't just stand there, Carl, help me."

Carl raced over, grabbed hold of Jackson's leg, and started to pull him across the ground. "You'd better let go of my sister!"

Somehow, Jackson managed to get his belt buckle tangled up in Cheryl's sweater. Every time her brother yanked on his leg he dragged his sister along the ground. "Come on, let go of her!" Carl shouted.

Jackson tried to kick himself free from Carl's grip. They were thrashing around so much that Jackson heard cloth ripping.

Oh crap!

"Carl!" Cheryl pleaded. "Help me."

"I'm trying," Carl said. He yanked Jackson's leg even harder and heard the sound of ripping cloth.

"You're ripping my sweater," Cheryl said. She started elbowing Jackson in the ribs.

Jackson had enough. He reached down and unbuckled his belt, pulling it out of the belt loops.

"Watch those hands, Buster," she said, trying to elbow him again.

"Get your creepy hands off my sister," Carl said. He grabbed Jackson's other leg, so he had both of them in his hands, and lifted him completely into the air.

He finally yanked Jackson so hard that he flew through the air and crashed heavily to the ground. "Now you're going to get it." He stormed towards Jackson.

Jackson scrambled to his feet and held his fists up defensively. "Just try it." He could feel blood dribbling from his nose and running into his mouth.

Carl circled around Jackson, looking for an opening.

Jackson heard his mom call to him, "Hold on, Jackson! I'm calling the police."

Carl looked up to the house. "Cheryl, what did she say?"

"She's calling the police," Cheryl said.

Jackson wiped a sleeve across his nose. "Now you're in trouble."

"What?" Carl said. He suddenly looked worried.

"My mom's calling the police so you and your goofy sister will be arrested for trespassing and assault."

"Hey, who are you calling goofy?" Cheryl asked, planting her fists on her hips.

Carl turned to her. "That'd be you. You practically started this." He glanced towards the house, a worried expression on his face. He turned back to Jackson. "Okay, okay. Let's just cool down a bit." He held up his hands. "Listen, could you please talk to your mom and tell her we'll work this out ourselves?"

Cheryl started towards Jackson. "And who are you calling goofy?"

Carl grabbed her by the arm. "He's calling you goofy, but you'd better cool it, unless you want to deal with the police." He released her arm. "With your luck, they'd probably send Officer Mercer, the guy that lives around the block from us. Then *everyone* in the neighbourhood will know."

"He's an idiot," Cheryl said.

"Maybe, but he's the guy you'll have to deal with," Carl said.

Cheryl exhaled noisily. "Oh, all right." She looked at her sweater. "Hey, look at my sweater. There's blood all over it."

Jackson held up his hands. "Oh, I am so sorry I bled all over your sweater."

"You don't sound too sorry," Cheryl said, scowling at him.

"Well, you almost broke my ribs!"

"Okay, okay. Let's everybody calm down," Carl said. He turned towards Jackson's mom and waved. "Let's see if we can resolve this peacefully. I see your mom's still keeping an eye on what's going on."

"She doesn't like conflict," Jackson said, unclenching his fists. "It'd probably be an idea to shake hands."

"I guess," Carl said.

As they shook hands Jackson asked, "So, what is it you guys are doing out here?"

Carl glanced at his sister who then nodded. "We heard a rumour that there was treasure buried in this yard. I didn't believe it at first, so I checked it out with my metal detector."

"Okay," Jackson prompted.

"Well, I found all kinds of junk back here—nails, old farm tools, whatever—until the other day. That's when the metal detector went crazy. It showed that something large was buried here."

"Huh. And I thought you were digging up a grave," Jackson said, chuckling.

Cheryl glanced at Carl and said, "And he called me goofy." She turned to Jackson. "Where'd you ever get that idea, bozo?"

"Harry—the realtor who brought us out here— he told us about it."

"Did he also tell you that one of the science teachers was responsible?" Cheryl asked.

"Yeah, he did."

"Harry's always telling everyone new to town that old story," Carl said, shrugging. "I think it's how he gets his kicks."

"I'll remember that," Jackson said. "Maybe I'll repay him for the story one day."

"Oh, that'd be good," Carl said.

"So what did you find?" Jackson said.

"Just that metal chest," Carl said. "No idea what's in it though."

Jackson nodded, thinking. "I've got an idea. What's say we split whatever's inside the chest in three equal shares?"

Carl looked at Cheryl. "That's not a bad idea. We found it, but on his property, so splitting three ways works."

"I guess," Cheryl said, shrugging.

"Cheryl and I decided that if it's something historically valuable, we would donate it to the museum."

"That's a good idea," Jackson said, nodding in agreement. "I heard some guy in town actually found Viking coins by some river and donated them to the museum."

Cheryl motioned to her brother. "That was Carl who found them."

"Seriously?"

"Yep," Carl said, puffing out his chest. "I was down on the river bank with my metal detector and found a bunch of coins wedged in between some rocks."

"That's cool. Now when school kids go to the museum, they can see something of the local history," Jackson said.

"They even put Carl's name and photo up for everyone to see," Cheryl said.

Carl blushed. "They didn't tell me they were going to do that."

"How about we open this trunk and see what's inside it?" Cheryl said.

"Hey, there're supposed to be a pile of tools in our garage," Jackson said. "Let's take it there, it's probably closer."

"Good idea," Cheryl said. "How about each of you grabs an end."

"Hey, what about you?" Carl said.

"Me? Well, I'll direct the way of course," Cheryl said. "I don't want to get even dirtier."

"Figures," Carl mumbled under his breath.

CHAPTER 13

As they staggered and crab-walked to the garage, Jackson said, "Do you have any idea who buried it?"

Carl grimaced with the weight of the metal chest. "I've heard some talk in town that the old lady was burying stuff all over the place. People figure it was cash and some of her valuables."

"That's what banks are for," Jackson said.

"I'm just telling you what I've heard," Carl said.

Cheryl shrugged. "Maybe she was losing it." Then she motioned to the ground. "Hey watch out. There's a big hole coming up."

"Thanks," Carl said, glancing behind him and slowing down.

"It's weird," Jackson said, shaking his head. "Some people hide stuff in mattresses or in hollowed out books... my aunt buries it in the backyard. What's with that?"

"Yeah, it sure seems like a lot of work for an old gal," Carl said. "Maybe she was losing it. The last time I saw her she looked in pretty bad shape. Mind you she was almost ninety at the time."

"Okay, let's put it down in front of the garage doors," Cheryl said.

Carl looked at Jackson and then nodded in his sister's direction. "She's so helpful at times."

Panting hard for breath, Jackson said, "I hear you."

"Just lower it slowly," Cheryl said, "in case it's full of jewels."

"I'd salute if my hands weren't so full," Carl said.

Jackson groaned as he slowly lowered his end of the metal chest. Then he straightened to rub his back. "Man, that sucker is heavy. I wonder how my ninety-year-old aunt managed to bury this by herself."

"Maybe she was buff, or maybe she had some help," Carl suggested. He looked at Jackson. "Hey, I'm curious. How did she die?"

Jackson shrugged. "I don't know. Heart maybe."

"So you're thinking natural causes?"

Jackson frowned. "I guess. Why are you asking?"

"Well, I was just thinking, if she died due to foul play, maybe there *was* a helper," Carl said. "And maybe that helper helped her into the grave."

"Let's hope it was due to natural causes," Jackson said.

"Why's that?" Carl said.

"Well, if she did have a helper, they might be watching the property to see if anyone dug up some of her stuff."

Carl went pale. "I never thought of that." He looked around for a moment, looking toward the distant fields.

Jackson eyed the metal garage door. It looked awfully heavy. Cobwebs covered everything in a delicate tapestry of silk. At the bottom, a massive padlock secured the door to the ground.

"Jeez, it looks pretty solid," Carl said, eyeing the door.

"We'll have to get the lock off to get the garage door up," Cheryl said.

"Thank you, oh Master of the Obvious," Carl said.

"It's not going to be easy," Jackson said, eyeing the padlock. He wondered when the last time it had been opened. He looked at Carl. "Hey, did you ever see my aunt driving a car?"

"Ah… no. I don't think I've ever seen the garage door up," Carl said.

"Oh."

"Hey, maybe we'll need something like dynamite to blow the lock off," Cheryl said, rubbing her hands together.

Jackson looked over at Carl. "How does she come up with these things?"

"I couldn't begin to tell you," Carl said. "Sometimes it's like a bad dream."

"I can imagine."

Cheryl tapped the side of her head with a finger. "I come up with them right in here."

Carl looked at the padlock for a moment. "I've got an idea. Cheryl, pass me that shovel will you?" He stuck the metal pole of the shovel through the loop of the padlock and started to pry it. He levered it several times before it snapped off and rattled about on the ground.

"Nice," Jackson said.

Carl flexed his arms and said to Jackson. "See, your aunt wasn't the only one that was buff."

"Spare me," Cheryl mumbled. She motioned to the garage door. "Okay, Muscles. Why don't you lift the door up?"

"No problem," Carl said. He made a show of puffing up his chest, then bent over and yanked the stuttering door up with a loud, squealing sound.

When it reached the top, Cheryl said, "I can't see your aunt doing that. It's just too heavy."

"Yeah, it's also pretty noisy. If you did that at night you'd wake the entire neighbourhood," Jackson said.

"Well," Cheryl said, planting her fists on her hips, "let's find some tools and open this trunk."

"Yes sir," Carl said, saluting. He stepped into the darkness of the garage and peered inside. "Jeez, I can hardly see a thing."

"Hey, take a look at this," Cheryl said, ducking inside. She grabbed hold of something and rolled it out onto the driveway. "A wagon."

"Well, now we know how she moved the stuff around." Jackson said. He turned and looked towards the area the chest had been buried. It must have been important to carry that chest all that way out there and bury it. Why not so it was right near the garage?

Jackson walked slowly into the darkened garage and let his eyes adjust to the dark. He paused to brush webbing from his face. He bumped into something and said, "Hey, there's a car in here. It's covered by one of those storage sheets."

"Huh," Carl said, approaching it. "It looks like—wait for it—one of those ghost cars." He laughed aloud, holding his stomach. "That was too much."

"Yeah, yeah," Cheryl chirped. "You're a real comedian."

Jackson turned to Cheryl. "And I thought you were bad." He approached the car, running his hand along the length of it. "I hope it's a Mercedes or a BMW so I can drive it." He lifted up the one side of the storage sheet, sending a cloud of dust billowing into the air. "Oh, it's an old Volkswagen."

"The poor man's Mercedes," Cheryl said, grinning.

"Well if it works, it's fine with me," Jackson said. "Like I was telling you on the way here, after we hit that *thing* we totalled the van. This is better than nothing."

"I guess," Carl said.

"Hey, I found the light switch," Cheryl said from one side of the garage door. She flipped them on and flickering light filled the garage.

"All right, now let's find some tools and open that chest," Cheryl said.

Jackson continued along the length of the car. In some ways the garage resembled a tomb. The windows had all been painted black so no natural light could get in. Maybe his aunt was a little paranoid after all. But then, are you paranoid when you *are* being watched?

"You're going to have a heck of a time cleaning this place out," Carl said, pulling stuff out of his hair. He gazed up at the webs criss-crossing the ceiling. "It looks like it hasn't been opened in years."

"Wow, look at all the newspapers," Cheryl said, sauntering into the garage. "Your aunt must have been one of those hoarders you see on TV. They're stacked everywhere."

"So?" Carl said. "Maybe she likes to keep up on current events."

"Oh yeah? Cheryl said. "Look at the piles of them. She must have kept every newspaper or magazine she ever bought. There has to be thousands of them in here."

"That's kind of weird," Jackson said, shaking his head in disbelief. He gazed at the stacks of newspapers. They'd been stacked almost two meters high and ran down the entire length of the garage. It was going to be a nightmare cleaning this place up.

"Dangerous place if someone dropped a match," Carl said. This place would go up in minutes."

"Hey, I can see a work bench at the back of the garage," Cheryl said. "I bet there're tools back there."

Carl said, "Okay, let's check it out."

"Ah, I'll wait by the entrance," Cheryl said. "I've got allergies to dust."

Carl and Jackson squeezed between the shrouded car and the tall stacks of newspapers and slowly worked their way towards the workbench.

"Look at all the webs back here," Jackson said. He brushed away handfuls of webs that dangled from the ceiling in long ribbons. He took a couple more steps and rounded the front of the car, pausing directly in front of the workbench.

A tangled mass of webs was layered over everything like curtains.

Near some of the wall-mounted tools, he could see the shrivelled carcass of a mouse entombed in webbing. In one place, it looked like something as large as a rat had been wrapped up.

"This looks like something out of a Stephen King novel," Carl said. "Come on, let's get what we need and get out of here."

"Yeah, good idea," Jackson said. Then a flicker of movement caught his eye. Along the length of the workbench, he saw something snaking through the dense webbing.

If it was a spider, it was huge.

"Hey, there's a hammer and chisel," Carl said, pointing to the right side of the bench.

"Great, might as well grab them," Jackson said.

"Sure," Carl said, slipping past him. He paused for a moment and then grabbed the tools, pulling them and cobwebs away. "Come on, that should do it."

Back outside, Carl dropped the tools on the pavement, and crouched down to examine the lock. "Okay, let me try something."

He put the chisel on the lock and starting hammering it relentlessly. After about five minutes, the padlock flew off and rattled its way across the driveway. Carl sat back and wiped away the sweat running down his face. "There," he mumbled as he tried to catch his breath.

"Took long enough," Cheryl said.

Carl looked at her with a 'you've got to be kidding look' and said to Jackson, "Would you please open the lid?"

CHAPTER 14

"That's it?" Jackson said. "Just a bunch of old newspapers?" He sat back on his heels, shaking his head in disbelief. "I think you guys were right. My aunt *was* losing it."

"You've got to be kidding," Carl said. "We've been looking for this chest for weeks and that's all it holds. Newspapers?"

"Looks like there're some old magazines in here as well," Cheryl said, rifling through the stack of papers in the trunk.

"Whoopee," Carl said. "We can sell them at the second hand bookstore as coming from the collection of a madwoman." He realized what he'd said and looked at Jackson, "Oh, sorry about that."

"No problem," Jackson said, staring down into the contents of the chest. It didn't make any sense. If his aunt thought the contents were valuable, he could see burying them somewhere. But a bunch of old papers? What was that about? Maybe she had lost it.

Cheryl remained silent, still engrossed as she rummaged through the assorted stack of newspaper pages and magazines.

"I wasn't expecting to find more Viking coins," Carl said, "but I sure didn't think I'd be digging up…this."

"That's weird," Cheryl said, staring at a newspaper in her hands.

"That's an understatement," Carl mumbled.

"No, all these papers seemed to be marked up," Cheryl said.

"What are you talking about?" Jackson said, leaning over for a better look.

Cheryl turned them around for Jackson to see. "Look at this—most of these old newspapers have articles highlighted by a red marker pen."

Carl brightened. "Hey, are they some kind of clues leading to the big treasure trove? You know, circle a word here, a word there, and they spell out directions."

"I'm not sure about that," Cheryl said, scanning the top paper.

"Then what are they about?" Jackson said.

"They're all about stuff happening out by the Tor," Cheryl said. As she flicked through the underlying papers, she nodded her head. "Yeah, these are all the same."

"What do you mean?" Jackson said.

"Anything dealing with weird phenomena happening out on the Tor has been circled. Some of these papers are almost ten years old." She sat back, eyes darting over a newspaper article. "This article refers to people seeing some kind of weird lights circling around the Tor."

Carl groaned. "Oh no, not another UFO nut." He glanced at Jackson and grimaced. "Sorry, again."

"Sure." Jackson reached down into the chest and decided to check out some as well. He pulled out a handful and sat back. As he flicked quickly through the pile, he saw how articles in the magazines had been circled by a red felt marker. "I see what you mean. She was kind of obsessed with the Tor."

"Obsessed is the word for it, all right," Carl said, grabbing a stack of papers and magazines in his hand as well.

Cheryl nodded. "Yeah, she certainly was fanatical about it." She looked at Jackson. "Was she always like that?"

Jackson shrugged. "I don't know. I barely remember meeting her."

Carl scratched his head, still flicking through a stack. "I don't remember reading about any of this stuff in the papers."

"That's because the only thing you read are the funnies and the sports page," Cheryl said.

"Hey," Carl said with indignation, "they're important too."

"Yeah, they are," Jackson said, nodding.

Cheryl shook her head. "You guys need to read things other than just sports."

Carl ran a hand over his face. "Cheryl, have you read anything about this stuff in the papers?"

Cheryl thought about it for a moment. "I heard about it from a few people at school. It's some kind of urban legend, kind of like the Sasquatch. Only a few people see them, but most don't believe."

"Hey, listen to this," Jackson said. "This article says that at least a dozen people watched a series of lights move along the slope of the Tor and then disappear."

"A dozen people? That's a lot," Carl said. He frowned. "I wonder if your aunt was one of the twelve."

"Maybe," Jackson said. "It would kind of fit, wouldn't it?"

"I wonder what those lights were." Carl said.

"UFOs, I guess," Jackson said.

"Neither," Cheryl said. "This clipping in the paper says a scientist explained it as an atmospheric phenomena. It was ball lightning."

"There were twelve of them?" Jackson asked. "You usually only get those things when there's some kind of major electrical storm."

"Says here it was a clear night," Cheryl said, looking up. "That was a counter statement to what the scientist had said."

"Hey, this should be good," Cheryl said.

"What's that?" Jackson said.

"This magazine has a cover story about the Tor." She flipped the magazine open and thumbed to the article. "Wow!"

"What is it?" Carl said.

"Check this out." She turned the magazine around so they could see it.

Jackson stared at a breathtaking photo of the Tor. In the backdrop—behind the rugged slopes of the Tor—he could see a thin crescent moon. Encircling the base of the hill was a thick fog.

"Cool photo," Carl said. "But what's the big deal?"

"Check the bottom right of the photo, just above the fog."

Jackson leaned to the left to get a better look at the photo. He looked to where Cheryl had hinted and saw two luminous spheres glowing with an eerie light.

Carl chuckled. "It's amazing what you can do with Photoshop."

"I don't know about that," Jackson said. He looked closer and saw that the spheres were slightly tear-shaped, as if they were moving quickly. The other thing was that he could see the glow of the two spheres on the surface of the fog bank. "It looks pretty real to me."

"Ah," Carl said, waving a hand, "that's someone's idea of a joke."

Cheryl shook her head. "My brother, the skeptic."

Jackson glanced at his watch. "I'd better get going. My mom wanted me to help do some clean up in the house. It's a pretty good mess."

"Okay," Carl said.

"I've got an idea," Cheryl said. "How about we divvy up all the papers and magazines into thirds, search through it later, and get together to see if we've found anything."

"Sounds good," Carl said.

"Yeah, maybe we can find out what my aunt was up to," Jackson said.

"What time do you want to meet?" Cheryl said.

Jackson thought for a moment. "How about noon? We'd probably be taking a break around then."

"Good enough," Carl said, scooping up a stack of papers in both hands. "Hey, I've got an idea. Why don't you come over to our place for lunch?" He shrugged. "It would kind of be an apology for the way we acted."

"Okay, see you 'round noon," Jackson said. As Cheryl and Carl turned to go, Jackson said, "Do I need your address?"

Carl turned, rolling his eyes. "I thought Cheryl had already done that."

"Ah, no."

"Hang on." Carl pulled out a scrap of paper from his pocket and scribbled it down.

"There you go," he said, turning and scowling at his sister. He exhaled loudly, and mumbled, "The hired help nowadays."

CHAPTER 15

Jackson leaned over the makeshift table he'd set up in his bedroom. Yes, his own bedroom. He paused and pumped his fist into the air. Finally, his very own room.

It had been a busy day, especially meeting the brother and sister who should have been named Pete and Repeat. They were a bit odd, to say the least.

He straightened the ancient door he had suspended over two sawhorses. It was crude, but it would do the trick. The magazines he had taken were scattered over the length and breadth of the door.

There was an organization to it, though. Newspaper articles were off to the left, while magazine articles were laid out on the right. In between, and closest to him, were a number of aging photographs. He would look at those later. Jackson grabbed hold of a gooseneck lamp, bending it so that its light illuminated the work area in front of him.

He glanced out his bedroom windows, admiring the view now that he'd pulled away all the plywood that had sealed and protected the glass.

Outside it was late dusk, and the moon was riding over the outline of the Tor.

Jackson directed his attention down to the articles he had been reading.

Some of them reminded him of the old *X-Files* series. The article he was currently looking at was entitled *UFOs buzz the Tor. Invasion?* Another one was titled *The Unexplained Mysteries of the Tor.* As he flicked through the magazine, he noticed it made a lot of references to Area 51 in New Mexico, and how alien visitors had probably landed in Boswell.

He shook his head. Man, oh man. What was his aunt into? Some kind of weird cult?

He checked out another magazine. This one also compared the incident at Area 51 to Boswell. What was going on at the Tor?

He remembered reading about Area 51. A saucer had apparently crashed there and the military had denied anything about it. There weren't any aliens in a flying saucer, there was only an off course weather balloon that had crashed on the outskirts of town.

Sure.

As he leafed through magazine after magazine, he wondered how his aunt had ever become so wrapped up in this stuff. Had she seen something herself? And why had she buried all this stuff in the back field?

He rubbed his eyes, trying to keep awake.

One more magazine, he thought. That would do it for the night. This one was a bit different. It talked about glowing balls of light seen zipping around the base of the Tor by someone with binoculars. He shook his head. The Tor seemed to be like some kind of magnet for all things weird, wonderful, and wacky.

He walked over to the nearest window and stared out over the so-called wastelands.

The sky to the west was a smear of maroon along the horizon. Even the mist was touched with the colour.

What in the world were people seeing out there? Some kind of weird atmospheric phenomena?

He staggered over to his bed and collapsed on it. As he closed his eyes, dozens of questions flitted through his mind. Especially the one wondering what it was they hit the other night.

CHAPTER 16

Jackson matched the address Carl had given to him with the sprawling two-story house before him. It was almost directly behind their place, and looked like it was slowly being modernized.

He'd barely banged on the door when it was thrown open.

"Ah, you must be Jackson," the older woman said, motioning him in. "Come in, come in. Carl said we were having a guest for lunch."

"Thanks," Jackson said.

"I'm Pat Clarence, Carl and Cheryl's mom," she said, shaking his hand.

Jackson started to take off his shoes.

"Don't worry about that," she said, directing him from the foyer. "This house is in a constant state of construction, so there's sawdust everywhere."

"So I see," Jackson said, looking around.

The layout looked quite similar to his house, though a lot messier. Carl's mom was right. There was sawdust everywhere.

Jackson shook his head in disbelief. "How do you keep it out of your food?"

She chuckled. "It's hard, I admit, but we try to keep the door to the kitchen closed at all times."

"I see," Jackson said. He could imagine choking down a sandwich at lunch, trying to ignore the sawdust in it and trying to be polite.

"So, you're fairly new to Boswell," she said heading down one of the hallways. Painting cloths were everywhere, with half-a-dozen cans of paint resting on a plastic sheet.

"Yeah, just arrived yesterday," he said. "We inherited our aunt's estate."

"Sorry about your aunt, though I don't think I ever met her. She kept to herself for the most part," she said.

She motioned to what had to be the family room. "Make yourself at home. Carl should be down shortly. I'm just about to pull some cookies out of the oven."

In the background, he heard the soft ringing of a bell.

"Well, perfect timing," she said, retreating back the way she'd come.

The family room was striking. A massive rock fireplace was the centrepiece of the room, running from ground floor up to the vaulted ceiling.

Sofas were scattered everywhere, so he headed over to a battered old one poised next to a series of bookcases built into one of the walls.

There had to be over five hundred books stuffed into every nook and cranny. From behind him, he could smell the sweet aroma of baked cookies wafting through the house.

Carl's mom returned to the family room with a plate of warm cookies and a glass of milk. "Here. Enjoy." She looked around, shook her head. "I'll run up and let Carl know you're here. You never know what that boy's up to next."

He bit into one of the cookies. "These are really good," he said, talking around a mouthful. As she climbed the curved staircase, Jackson took another cookie.

"Come on up," Mrs. Clarence said, motioning him from the second floor landing. "He's in his room, busy doing something."

"Sure," Jackson said, grabbing the plate of cookies and glass of milk and heading upstairs.

Hands full he used his forehead to bang on the door. A moment later it swung open and Carl waved him in. "Come on in. I'm just working on one of my models." He was barely inside when Carl closed and locked the door behind him.

"Sorry, that goofy sister of mine has a bunch of her goofy friends over as well."

"Ah," Jackson said, nodding in understanding.

"Grab a chair and relax," Carl said, grabbing a couple of cookies off Jackson's plate. Jackson picked a battered, but comfortable looking chair and sunk into it. He looked around and nodded. "It's pretty nice."

"Thanks. It's a refuge from my sister."

"I see," Jackson said, looking around.

On an old desk, a number of plastic models were in various stages of construction. He could see models of Frankenstein, Dracula, and one of the ships from Star Wars—a TIE Fighter, he thought they called it. There was even a model of a German World War II Tiger Tank. He remembered doing the same model last year.

"Looks like you keep busy," Jackson said.

"Oh yeah. I've got lots of interests. How about you?"

"Lots too," Jackson said, checking out a dozen old movie posters thumbtacked to the wall. The best one was a beat up version of H.G. Wells *War of the Worlds* with one of the Martian tripods using the heat ray on London.

Other posters were from *Star Wars*, *Terminator*, and the *Alien* movie with the caption: *In space, no one can hear you scream.*

He was obviously a big science fiction buff.

"I like the old Hammer horror movies," Jackson said. "Especially the old black and white versions."

"Yeah, me too," Carl said, sitting up. "They were classics." Carl motioned to the wall. "Hey, how do you like my poster collection?"

Jackson looked at them and nodded appreciatively. "Yeah, it's pretty good. I like the one of the Martian war machines from *War of the Worlds*. That was always one of my favourites.

Carl nodded. "Yeah, it's a classic. Hey, if you ever need a new book to read, give me a shout. I've got plenty."

"Yeah, so I see," Jackson said, turning to check out the bookshelf.

It was a homemade job, mainly white painted cinder blocks and some old planks. There had to be hundreds of novels stuffed into every available space.

"As you can see, I'm into science fiction. How about you?" Carl said.

"Mainly horror," Jackson said. "Right now I'm reading one called *Zombies from Mars*. The cover alone really creeps my mom out."

"Really?" Carl said. "Maybe I can borrow it after you finish it. I'll leave it out for my mom to see."

"Sure. No problem." Jackson got up and wandered about the room, especially checking out the books. He turned and gazed out Carl's window. "You know what? You've almost got as good a view of the Tor as I do."

Carl got up and joined him at the window. "Well, I'll tell you one thing, it's never boring, but I can't say as I've ever seen luminous lights on the hill."

"Yeah, that sounds pretty farfetched," Jackson said. "It's strange that there are so many stories about it in the local papers."

"Ah, probably just fillers," Carl said, waving a hand dismissively.

"And that mist? Harry said that it's always there."

"Well he's right about that. It's there right through the year," Carl said. He turned to Jackson. "You ever see those movies *The Mist* or *The Fog*?"

"Yeah, of course," Jackson said. "Why?"

"Well, sometimes it's like that. It's so thick you can barely see your hand in front of your face."

"Really?"

"Oh yeah. That's when they usually close all the schools," Carl said.

"Oh? Cool."

"Not really," Carl said. "That's when some people get really scared. They think they see things moving around in the fog."

"What? You mean like other people?" Jackson said.

Carl shrugged. "No one really says too much about it. But I'll tell you something, when that mist drifts up to town, no one goes out into it."

"The sulphur fumes, right? At least that's what Harry says."

"Well, there's that, all right. It's just that people think they're being followed."

"Maybe it's the Creeper," Jackson said with a grin.

"Or maybe it's something like what you hit on the outskirts of town," Carl said.

Jackson's grin faded away. "I never thought of that." He mulled it over, thinking about the thing they'd hit. "So the fumes aren't really poisonous?"

Carl shrugged. "I don't know. We talked about that in science class, but Mr. Markey said it might be in certain places. He said it would be best to carry an oxygen supply, just in case."

Jackson nodded. "I'll remember that."

"Hey, do you want a closer look at the Tor?"

"Are you serious? Go way out there?"

"Not quite. I've got something better," Carl said. He walked to the right of the large picture window and gestured to a small, tripod-mounted spotting scope. This will make you think you're practically flying over the Tor."

"All right. That's more like it," Jackson said.

Carl swung the scope around a bit and peered through the eyepiece for a moment, and then backed out of the way. "Okay, go for it."

Jackson positioned himself behind the eyepiece, bent over and focused slowly. Gradually the image swam into view and finally sharpened.

It was a bleak and barren landscape, something like the desolate images of Mars he'd seen on TV. Steam vented up from dozens of places, pluming into the sky.

"You know what? Sometimes when I'm looking at the Tor through the scope, I swear I can see things moving around out there," Carl said.

"Really? What kind of things?" Jackson turned to ask.

Carl shrugged. "Hard to say. Usually it's only a glimpse of vague shapes moving around in the mist. Not all the time, just once in a while."

Jackson felt his eyebrows arch up. "Really?"

Carl nodded. "Just don't tell anyone that or they might think I've gone off the deep end."

"Ah, sure." Jackson moved the scope carefully following the barren rocky slope of the Tor. "I can't see a single bush or tree."

"Nothing lives out there. It's like the surface of the moon. Some of the kids at school call it the dead zone."

"I can see why," Jackson said. "Does anyone have any idea what happened out there? Why it would be so deadly to any kind of life?"

"Most people figure it's the sulphur gases."

"What about you?" Jackson asked.

"I think it looks more like someone's detonated a nuclear device out there," Carl said.

"Yeah, that's what I thought at first. It looks pretty weird. I've only been here a couple of days and already I'm thinking it's odd."

"Odd's the word for it, all right." Carl snapped his fingers. "I just remembered something."

"Yeah?"

"Talking about weird, you've got to see the aerial photograph of the area that I found jammed between the pages of a magazine!" Carl said.

CHAPTER 17

Carl hurried to his desk and shuffled through a pile of magazines. "Don't worry, it's in here somewhere." He moved a lamp to the other side of the messy desk. "Ah. Here it is." He put the large photo print in the centre of the desk and directed the light of a desk lamp on it. He moved back out of the way. "Okay, tell me what you think."

Jackson sat down at the desk and peered at the print. "Well, the detail is sure pretty good. I'd say this was taken from maybe a few hundred meters directly overhead."

"That's pretty good, Sherlock. What else?"

Jackson returned his gaze back to the print. "I'm sure there's something in particular that you want me—"

"What is it?" Carl said.

Jackson squinted at the photo print. "It just looks like there's something on the summit of the hill."

"Here, maybe this will help," Carl said, passing him a large magnifying glass.

Jackson took the glass and focused on an area of the Tor. The shot was taken almost directly above the hill, and for a brief moment, he thought he was looking down at an extinct volcano. It certainly had that look to it.

Outcroppings of pewter-gray rock rose from the cone like vast fungal growths. The slope of the hill looked steep, but it was the summit that drew his attention. It was completely flat.

It looked like someone had taken a high-powered laser and cut the top off leaving a flat surface.

"Anything?" Carl asked.

"Hang on, I'm still looking."

Then Jackson caught sight of something dead centre of the summit. There was a faint, circular depression with linear markings radiating out from it like bicycle spokes.

"That's weird," Jackson turned to say.

"How so?"

"Well, it looks like some kind of circular foundations on the summit of the Tor."

Carl nodded knowingly. "That's exactly what I thought."

"It could have been some kind of tower, but how is that possible?" Jackson said. "It'd be difficult to build anything up there." He turned to Carl. "How wide do you think the summit is?"

Carl thought for a minute and then shrugged. "I don't know, maybe twenty or thirty meters."

Jackson tried to visualize that diameter. It would certainly hold a pretty good-sized building. Especially something the size of a small tower, like the ones he'd seen in a history book, once. He thought it was called a 'keep.'

Carl was on the same wavelength. "So it could be a large tower?"

Jackson nodded. "That's what I was thinking." He looked at the photograph again. "What a defensive position it would have had. It'd take forever to climb those steep slopes."

"No kidding," Carl said. "Imagine someone throwing boulders down on you or filling the air with arrows."

"Yeah, it'd be almost impossible to get up there in one piece," Jackson said.

Jackson sat back, staring at the photograph of the Tor. "If there is a tower up there, I wonder how old it would be."

Carl ran a hand through his hair. "Well, the coins I found were definitely Viking and the museum dated them to AD 700-800."

"You're kidding. That's over a thousand years ago," Jackson said, shaking his head in amazement. "And the Vikings travelled all this way, just for gold?"

"Well, gold is a pretty good motivator. Look at what the Spanish conquistadors did to the Aztecs in Mexico."

"Yeah, that's true," Jackson agreed.

"And apparently there used to be some pretty good deposits of it around Boswell," Carl said.

Jackson motioned to the photograph of the Tor. "It'd be the perfect place for a fortress, but then how would they have gotten past all that stuff out on the wastelands? Especially the mists and the sulphur gas floating around."

Carl shrugged. "Who knows, maybe this area was completely different a thousand years ago."

"Yeah, you might be right."

Carl picked up the photo and stared at it for a moment.

Jackson turned to look at him. "What are you thinking?"

"Well, I was just thinking if it was a Viking outpost of some kind, wouldn't it be cool to see if there were artifacts or coins buried there?" Carl said. "All I'd need would be my trusty metal detector and some time to prospect."

"Yeah?" Jackson said. He picked up the photo and stared it for a while. "I wonder when this was taken."

Carl motioned to the print. "There's some writing on the back. Check that?"

Jackson flipped it over. "So I see. Looks like it was done in 1963."

"1963? That means it was taken over fifty years ago." Carl squinted at the photo for a moment. "I wonder what the summit would look like today."

"There's one way to find out," Jackson said.

"What's that?" Carl said.

"Go on Google Earth and get a recent satellite view of the area."

"That's good, let's do it," Carl said. "My computer's just over here."

Jackson followed Carl to the opposite side of the room where he pulled out a chair and sat down at a tiny computer station.

He watched Carl type quickly and then sit back to wait. "It's not the fastest computer in the world, but it gets the job done. Here we go," he said typing again.

A view of the Earth appeared on the screen and Carl made a few more key strokes until they zoomed in and appeared directly above town."

"Not a whole lot around here, is there?" Jackson said.

"Not really."

He moved the cursor until it was directly over the Tor. "Here we go. Let's zoom in and take a look."

As Jackson leaned towards the monitor he could almost swear they were falling downward. "There're more details," he said.

"I'll drop us down to an altitude of three hundred meters above the summit of the Tor and hold it there," Carl said. "Then, I'll move it down slowly until we can match the view in that photograph."

"Good idea," Jackson said, nodding his head.

Jackson watched as Carl moved the cursor to the right side of the screen and slowly scrolled down, causing the summit of the Tor to appear to grow larger and larger.

Jackson grinned. "It looks like we're dropping out of orbit and looking for a landing site."

"Yeah, it kind of does, doesn't it?"

They watched in silence until Jackson said, "Whoa, we're getting close."

"Okay, I'll hold it there for a second." Carl glanced at the readout on the side of the screen. "Altitude is almost three hundred meters above the summit."

Jackson glanced from the photo they'd found to the image on the screen. "Looks like a pretty good match for size."

"Do you want me to print the Google image from the screen?"

"Yeah, good idea."

As Carl printed it up, they waited, watching the printer spew out the print.

"Okay, let's see," Carl said, placing one print beside the other.

"They're different," Jackson said immediately.

Carl nodded in agreement. "Yeah, in the Google image there aren't any markings at all. Figure that one out."

Jackson thought about it for a moment. It *was* a puzzle. "There's got to be an explanation. I just can't think of one right now." He let out a breath. "Can I borrow your magnifying glass for a second?"

"Sure."

Jackson took it and examined both prints carefully. The Google image showed a completely barren surface with none of the markings they'd seen in the older version.

As he switched back to check the photo they'd taken from his aunt's stash, he said suddenly, "There's a dark depression in the middle of that circular structure."

"What? Let me check that out," Carl said. He took the magnifying glass and positioned himself directly over the aging print, examining it in silence for a long minute.

"You're right," Carl finally said. "It looks like a clean, smooth surface, except for that dimpled depression in the middle of the circle."

"Huh. In the older print it looks like a tiny, dark hole," Jackson said.

Carl leaned back, frowning. "If there was a tower on the Tor, maybe it was some kind of basement or storage area," Carl said.

Jackson inclined his head. "It's possible. Or maybe it's just the remains of an old fire pit."

"Well, in the satellite view it's definitely filled in, whatever it is," Carl said.

"Yeah," Jackson said, running a hand through his hair. "I wonder if there was more than one shot taken."

"What do you mean?"

"Well, I can't see someone hiring a plane just to take one photo. No, if you're going to pull out all that money and time, you'd want to take lots."

"You're right," Carl said, nodding. "That makes sense. Question is, where are the remainder of the photos? In a private collection or just stored somewhere?"

"I don't know."

"There's an even bigger question. How did your aunt get hold of the print and why bury it in a field?"

Jackson gazed out the window towards his house. The spot where Carl and his sister had found the chest was evident as a brown smear where they'd filled in the hole. Another question was did his aunt bury other photos somewhere in the field? Was she trying to hide them from someone?

"Hey, there's a faint stamp mark on the back of the print," Carl said, angling towards the light.

"What do you mean by 'stamp mark'?"

"You know, some businesses mark their product by stamping their business name on something they've sold."

"Right," Jackson said.

Carl squinted at the faint ink work on the back of the photo. "It looks like it says GeoSystems."

"That could be helpful."

"Oh yeah," Carl said. "Especially since the business is still running."

"You're not serious?"

"That business has been running for years doing specialized photography," Carl said.

"So it's still there?" Jackson said.

"Hey, my mom's heading into town tomorrow to do a bit of shopping. Feel like coming along?"

"You know, it sounds like a plan," Jackson said. "I'll check with my mom and see if it's okay. I definitely want to check this place out."

"We'll be leaving around ten."

"Got it." Jackson headed for the door, and then paused and turned around. "I told you about the notebook, right?"

"Notebook, what notebook?"

"I guess not," Jackson said. He rubbed the back of his neck. "I found a small notebook stuffed inside one of the UFO magazines. I think it belonged to my aunt."

"What's in it?"

Jackson hesitated. "I'm not sure."

"What do you mean?"

"I think it's written in some kind of code," Jackson said. "It's just a bunch of letters and numbers."

Carl frowned. "Are you serious? That's definitely weird." He shook his head. "So your aunt writes coded messages in a notebook and then buries it in her backyard."

"That's right."

"Did you try to decipher it?" Carl said.

"Oh yeah, but it's just a bunch of gibberish to me. Here, take a look for yourself." Jackson pulled it out of his pocket and passed it over to Carl.

It was a cheap, lined book that had a beat-up cover.

"It looks in pretty rough shape." Carl turned the book over in his hand. "It almost looks like a kid's diary."

"Yeah, the kind that your grandmother gives you on a birthday," Jackson said.

"Not my grandmother. I get underwear and socks." Carl opened it and flicked through the pages. Frowning, he said, "You weren't kidding, were you? It must be important because she keeps repeating the same three sets of letters over and over."

Viga ctg eqokpi

"Maybe she's just listing her favourite TV stations and programs," Carl said, "but it's weird because it looks like it's Russian."

"Sure. And then she buried them so no one would know what programs she was watching."

"I was only giving an example," Carl said.

"I can't figure it," Jackson said. "What's with all the secrecy? Maybe she was paranoid."

"You're not really paranoid if they really *are* after you," Carl said.

Carl stared at the code, finally flipping through the following pages again. "Well, it's not all the same. Nothing is repeated." He looked at Jackson. "You need a code breaker."

Jackson shook his head. "Sure, maybe I'll check the yellow pages and see if they're any in town." He hesitated, wiping a hand across his face. "Whatever she's written in code has to be so important she didn't want anyone to know about it."

Carl inclined his head. "Hey, I think I know someone who is good and breaking word puzzles and codes."

"Who?"

"Cheryl," Carl said.

"Your sister?" Jackson spread his hands. "Why didn't you say that in the first place?"

Carl shrugged. "I just thought of it now. Do you want me to ask her?"

"Sure."

"Okay," Carl said. He opened the door, stuck his head outside. "Hey Cheryl, can you come up here for a minute?"

"What for?" Cheryl's muffled voice called back.

"We've got a code that needs breaking," Carl said. He turned to Jackson. "That should bait the hook and bring her running. She loves decoding stuff."

A moment later, Jackson could hear the pounding of heavy footsteps on the stairs.

"Okay," Cheryl said, approaching the door, "what's this about a code?"

Carl motioned her inside the room and closed the door behind her. He nodded to Jackson. "I'll let Jackson explain."

After he had related where he found the notebook, he passed it over to Cheryl who opened it and flicked through a few of the pages.

"What do you think?" Carl said.

"Hang on, let me think for a minute." She paged through the notebook, her brow furrowed in concentration. "Weird, it's all the same. It's just page after page of the same sequence of letters."

Carl glanced at Jackson who just shrugged.

"Just looks like another language," Carl said. "Can you tell us anything?"

"It looks like some kind of a substitution code," Cheryl said.

"A what?" Jackson said, looking at her with a blank expression.

"A substitution code," Cheryl said. "As a matter of fact it looks like an Augustus Code."

"A what?" Carl said. He looked at Jackson and shrugged.

"An Augustus Code. It was developed by the Roman Emperor Augustus Caesar. It just substitutes a letter for the one following it."

"Say what?" Jackson said.

"Are you making this up as you go?" Carl asked.

"Of course not," Cheryl said. "I'll give you an example." She thought for a moment, wrote down 'Carl,' then after it wrote 'Dbsm.'

"What's that about?" Carl asked.

"I simply substituted the letters that came after the letters of your name," Cheryl said.

"Okay, now I see. So if we went backwards from what you did to Carl's name, we could figure out what my aunt said," Jackson said.

"Exactly," Cheryl said. "There's only one problem."

"What's that?" Jackson said.

"From where the vowels are, I say your aunt was jumping two letters instead of one to form the phrase. So to decipher it, we go back two letters," Cheryl said.

"Okay, why don't you do it, Cheryl?" Carl said. "This stuff is starting to give me an awful headache."

"Yeah, yeah," Cheryl said. She picked up a pen and started writing. 'Vjga ctg eqwokpi'

Jackson cleared his throat. "Okay, the first letter, if I jump back two letters, should be T."

"You've got it," Cheryl said. "Keep going."

Cheryl started to write as they called out the letters. T-H-E-Y A-R-E C-O-M-I-N-G.

"That's what she wrote over and over? They are coming," Carl said. He spread his hands. "What's that supposed to mean?"

"I don't know," Jackson said, "but it sure must have been important to her."

"*They are coming*," Cheryl said. She looked at them. "Just what is it that she thinks is coming?"

"I don't know," Jackson said, "but it sure sounds ominous."

CHAPTER 18

The Thorndale Building was a moss-covered structure perched at the corner of Maple Street and Higgins Ave. Jackson couldn't figure out why they named streets after trees. There weren't any in sight.

It was strangely quiet, especially on a normally busy shopping day. Jackson looked around. There was nothing moving.

"Well, what do you think?" Carl asked, breaking into his thoughts.

Jackson shook his head. "It looks like a ghost town. And this is even *Saturday*." He turned to Carl. "And you say this used to be the city centre?"

"Yep. It used to be quite a thriving business area at one time," Carl said. "Eventually everything moved in that direction," he motioned with a wave of his hand. "That's where the shopping is now."

"Amazing." Jackson looked wistfully at the empty streets with wind-blown newspapers scuttling along the cobblestones like tumbleweed.

"What happened?" Jackson asked, kicking away a page of newspaper that the wind wound around his ankle.

"Earthquake," Carl said. "A number of years back they had an earthquake and they discovered a fault line running under this area. There wasn't a lot of damage, but you know how people worry about things."

Jackson nodded to the three-story brick buildings around them. "There doesn't seem to be a lot of damage."

"Just some minor cracks along the streets, that was about it," Carl said. "Nothing too bad."

Jackson looked around. "It looks like it must have been a nice area in its time."

Carl tried to wipe dust from his eyes. "Well, city hall is trying to revitalize the area by investing money and upgrading buildings to earthquake standards. So we'll see."

"Sounds expensive," Jackson said.

Carl nodded. "Yeah, it is." He motioned to the building directly across from them. "That's the place we want, right there. GeoSystems is on the third floor."

"Let's hope it's open," Jackson said, adjusting a strap on his backpack.

Jackson moved to the edge of the sidewalk and started across the street. A brisk wind was blowing clouds of dust along the avenue. He hoped this would pan out.

"The business we want is at the back of the building," Carl said, turning from the wind and shielding his eyes from the dust.

As they hurried across the street, Jackson asked, "How does a place like GeoSystems keep in business?"

"Well, they have changed with the times. Although they still print up photographs from negatives, they do most of their work from digital sources. I think they do a lot of work in tandem with the university."

"Really?"

"Yeah, they help out in documenting archaeological digs, geological imaging, and they sometimes still do aerial photography. I think they recently did stuff with that Ground Penetrating Radar."

"Huh?" Jackson said.

"Detects objects underground so they can photograph them."

Jackson slowed to look at him. "How do you know all this stuff?"

Carl grinned. "I checked out their website this morning."

Jackson laughed. "Good one. For a moment there, you sounded like a genius."

"Hey, maybe I am," Carl said. "It's just that no one's realized that yet."

Jackson wiped dust from his eyes. "I just hope the weather's not always like this."

"Almost never," Carl said. "This summer has been one of the strangest we've ever had."

"Great. Just when we decide to move to town," Jackson said.

He blinked away the dust from his eyes and looked at the weathered façade of the Thorndale building.

The front windows were coated with a heavy layer of soot and dirt. Two massive windows near the roofline resembled the dark, soulless eyes of a killer from a horror movie he'd seen last year.

"Looks like they need a major clean-up down here," Jackson said, shaking his head sadly. "Sand blasting the exterior of these buildings would do wonders for their looks."

"No arguments there," Carl said. He inclined his head in the direction of the Thorndale building. "Well, let's try the door."

"Sure," Jackson said.

They climbed a set of moss-covered steps and paused in front of a massive oak door.

Carl leaned forward and tried the front door. "It's locked."

"Huh." Jackson checked out a panel to the left of the door. "Hey, let's try the intercom system." He pushed a button under the GeoSystems label.

A moment later, a coarse voice came through the tiny speaker: "Can I help you?"

"We're here to talk to someone from GeoSystems," Jackson said.

"That'd be me," the deep nasal voice intoned. "Can I help you?"

"We wanted to get some information about a photograph we found," Jackson said. "It's of an aerial shot from directly over the Tor."

There was silence.

Jackson turned to Carl. "Maybe he's closed for the day."

"I'll check," Carl said. He stepped up to the speaker. "Hello? Are you still open?"

"Oh sorry, got distracted. Come on up. We're at the back of the building, on the third floor."

"Great, thanks," Carl said.

The door buzzed and they pushed it open, entering into an expansive foyer.

"Wow, this is something," Jackson said, closing the door behind them. He wiped his feet on a mat and started towards the stairs.

The floor was made of finely polished oak planks that led to a polished stone stairway.

Carl looked around. "I don't see an elevator anywhere."

"Well," Jackson said, looking up at a curving flight of stairs leading to the upper floors. "It looks like we're climbing stairs, so we might as well get started."

They worked their way up two flights of stairs and were puffing for breath by the time they reached the top.

"You'd be in great shape… if you climbed these… a couple of times a day," Carl said between gulps for air.

As they came out onto a carpeted hallway, Carl motioned to the right. "There we go, we just have to follow the sign."

Jackson paused to look around. Three chairs encircled a small, round table that was stacked with architectural magazines. They had yet to see another person. "It looks like we're the only ones up here."

"Yeah," Carl said, looking around. "Maybe business isn't so hot."

Jackson cocked his head. He couldn't hear anything other than Carl's gasps for air.

"Maybe most stores are closed for the weekend."

"Yeah, maybe," Carl said, trying a door along the way, but it was locked.

"There it is, at the end of the hallway," Jackson said.

Carl nodded. "I know. I just thought I'd see if any of the other doors are open."

They got to the GeoSystems door and it swung open with a noisy squeal.

"Hello," Carl said, stepping into the office. There was only stony silence. "Hello," he repeated, "is anyone here?"

"I'll be right out," a muffled voice said to their left.

Jackson looked at Carl. "I think he's in another office." He shrugged his backpack off and placed it on the floor. "Might as well sit down and wait." He plopped down into a rickety old chair and crossed one leg over the other.

Carl sniffed at the air. "Something smells odd in here."

"Maybe you were sweating more than you thought," Jackson said, grinning.

"Funny, very funny." Carl looked around. "No, it's got a chemical smell to it."

Jackson lifted his head. "Yeah, I think you're right."

He looked around at the expansive room. A long countertop stretched from one side of the room to the other, dividing the room into a couple of sections. Behind the counter, a series of large, framed black-and-white prints of the Tor filled the wall.

One print in particular caught Jackson's eye. It was a view of the Tor in winter. The slopes were dressed with what looked like a fresh dusting of snow, while above the cone-shaped hill, a full moon hung in a clear winter sky. He nudged Carl with an elbow. "That's pretty nice, isn't it?" Jackson said.

"What's that?" Carl said.

"That print on the wall," Jackson said, gesturing to the print.

Carl nodded. "Yeah, I guess."

"You guess?"

Carl shrugged. "Well, when you've grown up in Boswell, you see a thousand different pictures of the Tor. So, after a while, it's no big deal."

"I suppose," Jackson said. He moved forward to take a closer look at it. "I wonder if they've got any extra copies for sale." He leaned forward over the countertop, arms resting on the polished wood.

"I'm sure you can buy a copy somewhere," Carl said, folding his arms impatiently.

The door to their immediate left swung open, and a tall, imposing figure stepped into the light.

"Hey guys, how are you doing," the old guy said, throwing a stack of papers onto the countertop. He came up to where Jackson was and said, "Name's Coop. Now, how can I help you?"

Jackson wondered if this was one of the cleaning staff. He had long gray hair combed back behind his ears, and sported a bushy beard and moustache. He looked like an old prospector, just back from the boonies.

Jackson cleared his throat. "Umm, we'd like to speak to someone about a photograph we found. It has a GeoSystems stamp on the back and it looks pretty old. We wondered about the history of it, and if there were any others like it."

"Really?" he said. He looked from Jackson to Carl. "Okay, let's take a look at it."

As Jackson opened his backpack and rifled through it, Carl said. "It's an aerial shot taken from directly over the Tor. It gives a bird's eye view of the hill."

"Interesting. I'd like to see it."

Coop spun the print around and examined it for a minute. Finally he nodded. "I remember this. We were hired to do a whole series of them by a Japanese research team."

"Really?" Carl said. "Why was that?"

Coop shrugged. "Some kind of a geological survey they said. They wanted a profile of the area." He thought about it for a moment. "As I remember, they were talking about the possibility of a new energy source."

"Like what? All that steam coming up through volcanic vents?" Jackson said.

"Do you remember anything else?" Carl said.

Coop tilted his head back and stroked his beard thoughtfully. "No, they were awfully secretive. I always got the feeling they were looking for something else."

"I bet it was gold," Carl said. "Maybe even Viking gold."

"I think we took something like thirty of forty shots of the Tor, all of them of the summit and surrounding area."

"Huh," Jackson said. "It's strange they didn't want to land out there and check it out more closely."

"That was the plan," Coop said. "Unfortunately, their copter crashed the next day when they tried to do it."

"They tried to land out there?" Jackson asked.

"Yep, but they got caught in some fierce crosswinds and crashed into the wastelands. I think the quicksand sucked them under. That's why people don't try to go out there—too many deaths."

"Do you know where the other prints in the series are?" Jackson said.

Coop ran a hand across his face. "I think we might have a few copies in our storage area."

"Do you think we could have a look at them?" Carl asked.

Coop had a thoughtful look on his face and then shrugged his shoulders. "Oh, why not? I think those prints have been sitting in a storage drawer for years."

"You mean no one ever claimed them?" Jackson said.

Coop nodded. "After the helicopter crash, they pretty well pulled out of the area, taking the series with them. We always print up a backup copy at the same time, just in case. That's what they left behind."

"And they didn't come for them?"

"Nope, they were out of here pretty quick," Coop said.

Jackson turned to Carl. "Still makes me wonder what they were looking for."

"Just an energy source, I guess," Carl said.

Coop turned to go. "Well, I'll get those prints for you."

He came back a minute later, sliding a large envelope across the countertop. "You know that when we took these photos there was a lot of UFO activity around the Tor. Maybe that's the energy source these fellows were looking for."

"Yeah. Maybe," Jackson said.

"Well, don't get your hopes up," Coop said. "They look pretty ordinary to me."

"Listen guys, I've got to get going. Why don't you have a look at them and bring them back, say, next week."

"Are you sure?" Carl said.

"We could leave some ID with you so you know who we are," Jackson said.

Coop took a lingering look at each of them and then said, "Nah, you guys look pretty trustworthy. It's okay."

As they left the GeoSystems office, Jackson paused by the sitting area they had waited in.

"What's up?" Carl asked.

"I'm just going to have a quick peek," Jackson said. He dumped the stack of prints from the envelope onto the small table and quickly shuffled through them.

"There!" Carl said, jabbing a finger on one print.

Sure enough, as Jackson brought the large photo print up to an overhead light, he could see the summit of the Tor with a definite circular marking. "This one really shows it all right. This part here," he pointed, "looks like part of a wall."

"Well, that's it then," Carl said. "It looks like there was a Viking tower out there after all."

"Yes," Jackson said, pumping a fist into the air. He heard an odd chirping noise and turned about to see Carl pulling out his cell phone.

"It's Cheryl. She says she's found something about the Tor in the library archives," Carl said.

CHAPTER 19

Rain hissed against the windows and a groaning wind slapped heavy branches against the wood siding. Every few minutes, the lights in the rec room flickered off and on, threatening to go out permanently.

"I hope this isn't the weather you usually get in summer," Jackson said, letting the curtain fall back into place. "This is the second storm in just a few days."

"Tell me about it," Carl grumped. He turned away from the window. "At least it's supposed to be nice tomorrow and the rest of the week."

Jackson glanced at his watch. "What time does Cheryl get home? I'd like to see what she found."

Carl glanced up at the clock over the fireplace. "It should be anytime now. My mom left to pick her up half an hour ago."

"Okay."

"She must have found something out," Carl said. "That's one handy thing about having your sister work at the library. She gets to go into areas that are restricted to us mere mortals. I wouldn't be surprised if—"

Just then, a bright wash of light swept past the window and illuminated the curtains.

"Here they are," Carl said.

They went to the living room window, swept the curtains to the side and peered out. As the van dome light flicked on, Jackson watched as three figures scrambled out. A moment later they turned to run for the door.

"Oh no," Carl groaned.

"What's the matter?"

"She's got that friend Sarah with her," Carl said, shaking his head. "She's a pain in the butt."

"Looks like she plans on staying," Jackson said. "I think she's got a sleeping bag with her."

Carl groaned again. "Oh, great."

"What's the problem?" Jackson turned to ask.

"I can't get rid of her," Carl said, shaking his head. "I asked her out once on a date, and now she's phoning me all the time. When I'm in school, she's always following me. If I go to the movies, she's there as well."

"That's rough."

"The only time I get a break is when I go into the washroom."

"Jeez," Jackson said, shaking his head.

"I feel like I'm being stalked."

"What are you going to do?"

"I don't know," Carl said.

"Did you tell your parents or your teachers?" Jackson said.

"Nah, they'd probably tell me I'm just lucky to have a girl chasing after me."

Jackson rubbed a hand along the side of his face. "I'll try to think of something." He wondered if some kind of stunt, or some way of shifting her attention to something else, would divert her from Carl. He'd have to think of something.

"That'd be great."

A nugget of an idea started to form in Jackson's mind. "Hey, do you know her phone number?"

Carl stared at him for a moment. "Why do you think I'd have her phone number? She's warped!"

Jackson held up a hand. "Whoa. Let me try that again. Can you *get* me her phone number?" He paused a heartbeat. "And without her knowing?"

Carl frowned. "What are you up to?"

"Nothing yet. I just need her phone number, and without either her or your sister knowing."

Carl thought for a moment and shrugged. "Yeah. I think I can find it in Cheryl's address book."

"Perfect. Just remember, tell no one."

"Don't worry, I won't," Carl said.

Jackson wasn't quite sure what he was going to do, but something was percolating in his head.

They turned their attention outside, watching the taillights flare bright for a moment, and then die. Two shadowy figures, hunched over against the driving ran, ran up the sidewalk to the front door.

Carl moved to the door and opened it. A gust of wind caught it, banging it against the wall. Cheryl and Sarah staggered into the house, dripping water everywhere. Their arms were full of books, shopping bags, and a sleeping bag.

"Jeez, you guys are soaked," Jackson said, helping Carl close the door."

"I know," Cheryl said, shaking her hair out. She kicked off her shoes and stepped onto the wooden floor. She motioned to her friend and said, "Jackson, this is Sarah. Sarah, this is Jackson."

"Hey," Jackson said.

"Hi," Sarah said, nodding to Jackson. Then she turned and said to Carl in a syrupy, singsong voice, "Oh hi, Carl. I was looking for you in town."

Carl flushed and stared down at the floor. "Sorry, I was pretty busy showing Jackson around."

"Oh," Sarah said, frowning at Jackson.

"Come on," Cheryl said, let's hang our coats up to dry."

Carl locked the door and then made a sick face behind them.

Jackson covered his mouth with a hand, trying to stifle a laugh.

"Come on, Sarah, let's go sit down and dry off," Cheryl said. They both took one of the sofas.

Jackson followed them in, eyeing Sarah thoughtfully. From the way she was eyeing Carl, he'd have to come up with a plan to dissuade her quickly. "Well it looks like you've found a lot of stuff," he said, watching Cheryl pull photocopies out of a wet, canvas bag.

She nodded animatedly. "You bet I did. I found a goldmine of information in a remote corner of the archival section of the library. You could easily write a book on the history of Boswell going back to the Vikings."

Jackson rubbed his hands together. "Great! That's what I want to hear."

"Any old stuff on the Tor? Like stories or drawings?" Carl asked.

"Piles of it. I only brought some of the more important stuff. I photocopied it," Cheryl said.

Sarah shook her head. "She's been talking about it the entire way home. My head has been literally swimming with all that information."

"Uh huh," Jackson said, noticing Carl rolling his eyes.

Cheryl flicked through the stack of papers. "First off, I found a couple of journals written by some of the first pioneers into the valley."

"Really?" Jackson said, impressed. "And?"

"They were pretty interesting."

"Go on," Jackson said.

Cheryl cleared her throat. "Just listen to this:

--as we came into the valley, we could see a thick fog had engulfed a strange, cone-shaped hill set in the middle of a vast bowl. On the summit of the hill were the remains of what looked like a stone tower.

Indeed, with the use of Parson Vickers' telescope, we spied the remains of a rock tower that had partially fallen away.

As we thought we were the first visitors to the area, we are at a loss to explain who could have built such a structure in such a desolate place."

"Wow," Carl said, shaking his head in disbelief.

Cheryl looked over at them. "That was written August 16, 1793."

Jackson looked at Carl and nodded. "Now we know for sure."

"Know what?" Sarah said.

"That there was probably a Viking outpost near Boswell," Jackson said. He sat back wondering if was possible to get out there. "And no one has bothered to go out there?"

"Nah. Not with all that mist floating about out there," Carl said. "Then add in some possibly poisonous fumes—"

"What about helicopters?" Sarah asked.

Carl gave her a look. "We found out that there are some nasty crosswinds blowing across the wastelands. It forced a research chopper flying out there into the quicksand. The entire team was killed."

"Oh," Sarah said.

"That's something," Jackson said. "Did you find anything else?"

"Funny you should ask," Cheryl said, smiling at him.

Jackson could feel his cheeks heat up. "Ah, go ahead."

"According to the first settlers, the natives recounted a legend of a star falling towards the Tor."

Jackson leaned forward. "Did you say a star?"

Cheryl checked her notepad and nodded. "That's right. They said it turned the area from a once fertile hunting area to a vast area where nothing lives anymore."

"Sounds like the 'dead zone,'" Carl said.

"Yeah, it does," Jackson agreed.

"That's not all," Cheryl said.

"There's more?" Carl said. "It's fantastic enough already."

"They said that the star 'hit very close to the cone hill and there was a great wind from it and the ground shook terribly.'"

"There had to have been a meteorite," Jackson said, "and a big one at that!"

"Aren't they worth money?" Carl asked.

"Big time," Jackson said. "I read they pay you by their weight."

"That's right," Cheryl piped in. "Our science teacher told us there are private collectors who will pay a lot for large meteorites."

"I think it would be better to donate it to the museum," Carl said.

"Well, if it's in pieces after it hit, you could sell some and donate some to the museum," Jackson said.

Carl nodded. "Yeah, that would work."

"Well, how would you find those pieces?" Sarah asked.

"Yeah, good question," Jackson said.

"Not a problem," Carl said, motioning to the wall.

As everyone turned to look, Carl puffed up. "With my handy dandy metal detector."

"Really," Jackson said, "that's perfect."

"That's how all of the meteorite hunters find them. With a metal detector," Carl said. "Most of them have iron in them."

"Cool," Jackson said.

Cheryl cleared her throat again. "Of course, I left the best part for last."

"You've got to be kidding," Jackson said. "There's more?"

He didn't know how she could beat that. First there probably was a Viking tower out on the Tor, and secondly, a major meteorite fell near it. What could possibly beat those?

"Come on, Cheryl, give us the rest of it," Carl said.

Cheryl hesitated for a moment and finally said, "There's a route through the wastelands that will get to the Tor."

Jackson felt his jaw drop and saw Carl turn to look at him.

CHAPTER 20

"Are you serious?" Carl asked. He looked at his sister, dubiously. "That's supposed to be impossible."

"I am serious," Cheryl said. "And according to some old journal notes, it's *very* possible."

Jackson wondered what she'd found out. So far, she'd pretty well confirmed that there was some kind of tower on the Tor and that the fall of a large meteorite to the area may have aided in the destruction of the tower.

His head was starting to swim with all the new information. Jackson turned to her. "Now wait a minute. Everyone I've talked to about the Tor said that it's impossible to get out there. Poisonous fumes on the ground, vicious crosswinds that will take a helicopter down. What's changed?"

Cheryl held up a stack of photocopies. "This has."

"What?" Carl said.

"It's some new information," she said.

Jackson rubbed his hands together and leaned forward. "Okay, let's hear it."

Cheryl ran a hand across her face, hesitating for a long moment, and then said, "I found an old map that shows the rivers, streams, and details of the wastelands."

Carl frowned. "That's it?"

"Not quite. It also shows a meandering passageway that will take you to the Tor," Cheryl said.

"Are you sure?" Jackson said.

"Oh yeah," Cheryl said. "Somehow someone mapped their way past all the danger spots on the wastelands."

Jackson sat back, thinking about what she had said.

Carl leaned forward. "Is it a recent map, because I've never heard anyone mention a safe passageway to the Tor."

"Not quite," Cheryl said. "The map is over a hundred years old and may have been made by prospectors."

Jackson said, "So, you're saying it might be possible to go to the Tor and return safely?"

"Maybe. That's if the rivers and quicksand areas are the same as they were back then," Cheryl said.

"Yeah, but rivers can change their course at any time," Carl said.

Jackson leaned forward. "What about the meteorite. Is there any mention of that?" "Yeah," Carl said, turning to face his sister. "What about that?"

"Nothing," Cheryl said.

"Well, let's have a look at this map," Carl said.

Cheryl moved around to the other side of the table and squeezed in between Carl and Jackson. She placed a photocopy of a map on the glass tabletop. "There it is."

Jackson bent forward to stare at it, as did Carl.

Jackson followed a path where meandering rivers cut across the wastelands, winding towards the pinnacle that was the Tor. There was no mistaking the rugged contours of the hill.

"What's that written on the summit?" Carl asked, squinting at the tiny print.

Jackson stared at it for a long moment and then said, "I think it says Tower Hill. Yeah. Yeah, it does."

"I think you're right," Carl said.

Jackson studied the dotted line zigzagging across the wastelands, at times even doubling back on itself.

Sketched on the faded map were features of what looked like lakes, bisected by a narrow ridge that ran across the map.

"Look at that," Carl said, stabbing a finger at the ridge. "Looks like a highway across the wastelands. Huh. I wonder what those are."

"What's that?" Cheryl said.

Carl pointed to several dark markings scattered throughout the map.

Jackson shrugged. "It might be some kind of rock formations."

"Odd though," Carl said, studying the map. "There're four of them and they look like they're located on the four points of the compass."

"Yeah?" Cheryl said.

"You know what?" Jackson interrupted. "It looks like it would be possible to walk out to the Tor by following this marked pathway."

Carl nodded. "That's if the details sketched on this old map are the same as today."

Jackson nodded and looked at Carl. "And there's only one way to find out, isn't there?"

Carl winked at Jackson. "Yes, that's right."

CHAPTER 21

Jackson stared out across the wastelands, glad that the storm had finally cleared away, leaving the skies strikingly clear. Carl came into the room.

"So are you allowed to stay for a sleepover?"

"Yep. Your mom went over and talked to my mom and its okay."

"Great!" Carl said. "So what do you want to do? Watch some horror movies or pull some pranks on Cheryl and Sarah?"

Jackson turned towards Carl. "Oh yeah? I'm sure Sarah would love the attention."

"Oh, yeah." Carl waved a hand in the air. "Forget I suggested that. I do have some good news, though."

"Yeah?"

Carl whispered. "I was able to get hold of my sister's phone book and get Sarah's phone number. I've got it right here." He pulled a scrap of paper out of his pocket and handed it to Jackson. "What are we going to do with it?"

"Nothing yet," Jackson said. "I'm still working on it. I'm not sure what I'll do."

"Okay, okay," Carl said. "But you will let me know what you're planning, right?"

"We'll see." Jackson glanced at the number on the paper and then jammed it into his pants pocket. No way was he going to tell anyone what he was up to. He'd done that once and it had really backfired on him. No, he would keep whatever he was doing to himself. Right now he only had a niggling feeling of what he wanted to do. He'd let it brew in his head until he had a firmer idea of a plan.

"Well, I'm glad to see it's cleared," Carl said.

"Yeah," Jackson said. As he gazed to the south, he could see a fat, gibbous moon. It cast an eerie sheen on the Tor and the fog that perpetually surrounded it.

"Are you thinking about the tower that was once on the Tor?"

"Yeah, kind of," Jackson said. "I was wondering how difficult it would be to get out there. I bet there's some Viking stuff out there."

"A good chance of it," Carl said.

"We've got everything we need to get there," Jackson said. "The most important thing, of course, is the map. We just need some equipment."

"What kind of equipment are you thinking about?"

"Well, some kind of breathing stuff in case we did come up against sulphurous fumes. Hiking gear, maybe—"

"Oh, we've got all that stuff," Carl said, waving a hand.

"Are you serious?" Jackson said, turning to face him.

"Oh yeah. My dad's a volunteer with Search and Rescue. They keep a lot of their equipment and gear in our basement."

"You're kidding me?"

Carl shook his head. "Nope. Remind me to show you some time."

"Hey, how about now?"

"Ah, when my parents aren't home would work better," Carl said.

Jackson nodded. "Okay. I'll keep that in mind." As he turned to look back to the Tor, he realized what a great photo it would make. "Hey Carl, do you have a camera I can borrow?"

"Sure. We've got a few of them."

"I was just thinking how great a shot of the Tor that would be. I could get it blown up and hang it in my bedroom."

Carl chuckled. "Sure. There're only about a million similar photos on the web or hanging in some of the art shops in town."

"Yeah, I know, but this would be *my* shot. My photo."

"Yeah, I suppose," Carl said. "Me, I been looking at that barren hill for so many years it doesn't mean that much anymore." He turned and headed for the bookshelf, starting his search for the camera there. After a moment, he turned. "Found it!"

"Great!"

"Come on, let's go out on the patio deck," Carl said.

Jackson was just going over the camera controls when he heard Carl say, "Jeez, look at that, will you."

"What?" Jackson said, looking around.

"The Tor! The Tor! Look at it!" Carl pointed.

Jackson turned and gazed at the deepening darkness creeping around the solitary pinnacle. He stared at it, wondering what the big deal was.

Then he saw them. Tiny pulsating lights drifted down the right side of the Tor.

"Lights. I see lights moving on the Tor," Jackson said.

"So you see them, too?" Carl said in a strained voice. "I'm not just imagining them?"

"No. I see them, too," Jackson said. He lifted the camera to his eye, took two shots, and then touched the screen to zoom in and took a few more.

Jackson swallowed. He counted five of them, glowing like luminescent pearls as they crept down the slope of the Tor.

Two of them moved laterally, drifting across the breadth of the hill.

"Five. I count five," Jackson said.

"Hey guys, what's going on?" Cheryl said, coming up behind them.

Carl pointed to the hill. "Take a look!"

Cheryl came up behind them, and stared out across the wastelands. "What's the—oh whoa! I can see them. They're not just stories—they're real!"

"We should get dad's video camera to get a permanent record of this."

"I'm on it!" Carl said, running back into the house.

"That's amazing," Cheryl said, leaning on a guardrail. "For years we hear about those things and finally we see them."

Carl ran back into the room. "I've got it. Are they still there?"

"Yeah, they've just moved down towards the fog."

Carl fussed with the camera, finally getting it on to the record mode. "All right, I'm ready."

Jackson saw a red light wink on. "Okay, you're recording now."

"Good."

Jackson watched them descend the flank of the Tor, slowly dropping closer and closer to the fog.

After a few minutes, Jackson watched them sink into the fog bank like pearls dropping into water.

"They're disappearing," Cheryl said.

Carl continued to record for a few more minutes and then finally turned the camera off. He shook his head. "I don't believe it. We actually saw them."

Jackson kept his eyes on the luminous balls, watching the pale glow of the spheres fade, as they were lost in the fog. A pang of anxiety suddenly hit him. He'd seen one of those things before… just before they'd hit that thing that had been standing on the road. One of those luminous balls had floated about the struggling figure.

Carl rewound the tape for a bit, and then pressed play. "We've got them on tape."

"I can't wait to show this to the guys at the science club tomorrow," Carl said.

"The science club?" Jackson said.

"Yeah, that's nerd incorporated," Cheryl said. "Where all the geeks hang out."

CHAPTER 22

Jackson shook his head. How in the world did he ever let Carl talk him into coming here? Cheryl was right. It looked like the meeting of the local nerd club. Nerds Anonymous. Most of the guys wore black, thick-framed glasses. A couple of guys even wore bowties. Jeez Louise, these guys needed a life.

Jackson had always loved science, but these guys looked kind of different. He wondered, *do I look like that?*

He eyed the exit door. If he ran for it, Carl might not even see him leave. The problem was, how would he get home? The plan was for Carl's mom to pick them up after her bowling game.

"Don't even think about," Carl said, appearing out of nowhere. He sipped at a can of pop, passing a second can to Jackson.

"What?" he said in an innocent voice. "What are you talking about?"

"You know what I mean," Carl said. "You were thinking of making a run for it, weren't you?"

"Me? No, I was just checking out some of the exhibits."

"Right. Well, unless you plan on walking home, you may as well relax and enjoy yourself."

Jackson nodded and stuck his hands into his pockets. "Yeah. Sure." He glanced up at a clock, shook his head, and figured he might as well.

The room had a vaulted ceiling with a couple of large, model airplanes suspended from it. At the opposite end of the room, a scale model of a three-stage rocket hung from the ceiling.

Carl motioned to the left. "Hey, let's go grab a seat and see what they're doing."

"Sure." Jackson found a seat and sat down.

He figured there were about twenty teens and a couple of teachers, for sure. One guy's face was beet red, and Jackson wondered if he was having a seizure. He was shouting something, but no one was listening.

The kid next to Jackson nudged him with an elbow. "Hey, are you new here?"

"Yeah, with Carl."

The kid nodded. "Okay. Name's Rodney," he said putting his hand out.

"Hi, I'm Jackson. We just moved to town."

"Oh, well then, welcome."

"Thanks," Jackson said. Then he had an idea. "I can't believe that Carl…" He shook his head.

"What do you mean?"

"Carl told me the girls in Boswell think he's the hottest guy in town." Jackson said.

"What? That guy must be full of himself," Rodney said, shaking his head in disbelief. "Where is he? I'll bring him back down to Earth."

"Hey, hey. Don't go blabbing that or he'll know it came from me," Jackson said.

"Oh yeah, right," Rodney said.

"Okay, so he's not the hot guy he thinks he is," Jackson said.

"No, that title belongs to David Bradford, the football captain."

"Really?"

"Yeah, that guy thinks he can walk on water," Rodney said.

"Well, Rod, that's good to know."

"It's Rodney."

"Oh yeah, right," Jackson said. "Sorry, Rod*ney*."

Jackson sat back. He now had Sarah's phone number and the name of the coolest guy in town. At least he thought so, anyway. A plan was beginning to form in his head.

He was startled as a shrill voice screamed, "All right everyone. Quiet please!"

Carl sat down next to Jackson and leaned over. "That's Mr. Stanley. He teaches chemistry and math."

Jackson looked at Mr. Stanley. He was rail thin and nervous. Jackson could see sweat pools under his armpits. "He looks pretty uptight."

Carl grinned. "You should see him when he really gets worked up. You'd think he was going to have a coronary."

Rodney leaned forward and eyed Carl for a moment. "Hey, Lover Boy. How's it going?"

"Screw off, Rod," Carl said.

"Hey, wait a minute!" Rodney said.

Jackson held up a hand. "You'd better cool it, Rodney. Mr. Stanley is glaring at you."

Rodney sat back in his seat, fuming.

"You boys back there be quiet," Stanley said.

Just then, a shrill whistle echoed through the narrow confines of the room.

"That's Mr. Rutledge," Carl said. "He teaches geology."

Geology, Jackson thought. Now we're getting somewhere. He sat up, trying to see over some of the taller guys sitting in the row in front of them.

Mr. Rutledge cleared his throat and pointed to two guys wrestling in the front row. "You two," he pointed. "You're out of here."

"What?" a blond kid said.

"I said, 'you're out of here.' Now leave!" He pointed to the door.

Faces glowing red, the two downcast youth hurried towards the door, never looking at anyone.

Carl whispered to Jackson. "I think they're going to decide what kind of project we're going to do."

"Yeah?" Jackson said, leaning forward over the table.

"All right," Rutledge said coolly, "let's get started."

A dozen heads bobbed in agreement, and conversation dwindled to a low murmur.

Rutledge waited a moment and then announced, "Okay. Everyone into their assigned groups."

Jackson sat up, "Group? I don't belong to any group."

"Don't worry," Carl said, "what they usually do—"

"Any new visitors, please come over here," Rutledge said, looking directly at Jackson.

Carl pushed his chair back and stood up. "Come on, I'll introduce you."

They headed over to the two teachers and Jackson noted that there were two other guys who were new as well.

"This is Jackson. He's just moved to town with his family," Carl said. "We're neighbours."

Rutledge nodded to Jackson, and asked, "How did you get tangled up with this character?"

As Carl's face turned beet red, Jackson said, "Just lucky I guess."

"Fair enough," Rutledge said. "You must like science or you wouldn't be here."

"Yes, sir. Especially geology," Jackson said.

"Good," Rutledge said. He had piercing eyes and wore his hair slightly long. He towered well over the other teacher by a head. "Why don't you join Carl's group, they need all the extra brainpower they can get."

"Ah, sure," Jackson said.

Rutledge cleared his throat and said, "All right everyone, let's get started. We've got a new project tonight,"—he paused dramatically—"especially considering our rocket almost crashed into the school last week."

A sweaty blond kid leaned close to Jackson, nudged him, and mumbled, "Yeah, it almost took out part of the roof."

Rutledge turned. "A problem, Cunningham?"

"Nope. Just giving the new guy a heads up on what happened."

"Okay, just keep it down." Rutledge moved off to one side of the room where a large tarp had been fastened over an object the size of a Volkswagen Bug. It was roped down with Don't Touch signs hanging from the dangling ropes.

Jackson shuffled along with the rest of his group, wondering what the heck he was getting himself into.

"All right," Rutledge said, motioning for everyone to stop. "Anyone have an idea what's under the tarp?" He waited, looking around for a response. "The first person that guesses it right wins a free lunch when school starts."

There was chorus of groans and jeers, and someone made a vomiting sound.

Rutledge folded his arms and grinned. "Oh, come on guys, the lunches aren't that bad."

Someone at the back of the group made more vomiting sounds.

"Okay," Rutledge said, holding up a hand. "Forget the lunch. Any guesses?"

One kid waved a hand. "How about a body bag?"

Rutledge shook his head slowly. "That's pretty lame, Simpson. Anyone else?"

A tall kid with bright red hair and a bad case of dandruff said, "A small car?"

Jackson nodded. That's what he'd been thinking.

"Good guess, but not good enough," Rutledge said. "It looks the right size, though." He paused, looked around. "Anyone else?"

"How about a clue?" someone suggested.

"All right then," Rutledge said. "A little hint." He walked over to the tarp and gave it a hard push. Whatever was inside moved a few meters and then returned to where it had started.

"The school cheerleaders?" A gangly, freckled kid said. He grinned, obviously proud of himself.

Rutledge shook his head. "In your dreams, Beckham."

Jackson ran a hand over his jaw, thinking about it for a long moment, and then waved a hand in the air.

"Yes," Rutledge said, pointing at him.

Jackson cleared his throat nervously. "How about a balloon?"

Rutledge grinned, and gave him the thumbs up. "Okay guys, give that young man a hand. He's just won a free lunch at school."

From behind him, someone leaned forward and said, "Better buy yourself a stomach pump, buddy. You're going to need it."

Rutledge pointed to the shrouded balloon. "Okay, how about a few of you guys pull the tarp off."

Jackson watched as half-a-dozen teens hurried to the tarp, untying some ropes, and roughly pulling the tarp off, exposing a weather balloon a couple of meters in diameter. It bobbed up into the air, held to the ground by a single red tether line. The balloon resembled a large beach ball with alternate triangles of red, blue, and green striping.

"Cute, isn't it?" Carl said, nodding at the balloon.

"Yeah, every kid should have one," Jackson mumbled.

Rutledge motioned to one of the teens. "You there, Andrews. Can you undo that last line?"

"Sure." Andrews hurried over and undid the remaining line and let the balloon drift towards the ceiling.

"Don't let it get loose," Rutledge said. "Hold that line steady!"

"Okay." Andrews wrapped the line around his arm and tried to hold the balloon in place. He was able to hold for a couple of seconds before the balloon lifted him into the air. "Hey! Somebody give me a hand!"

There was raucous laughter as the bobbing balloon carried Andrews toward the vaulted ceiling, his feet dangling and kicking two meters off the ground.

"Help me!" Andrews shouted.

"When that balloon is filled with helium, it's able to lift a payload of eighty kilos," Rutledge said in a loud voice.

"Hey Andrews," someone shouted. "You're lucky you're inside. If you were outdoors, you'd be in orbit by now."

"Give him a hand, guys," Rutledge said.

A tall kid jumped up and grabbed hold of Andrews' foot. He too hung suspended off the ground for a moment before his weight pulled the balloon and Andrews back to the floor.

"Thanks," Andrews said, swiping a sleeve across his forehead. "The rope got wound around my arm. I couldn't get loose."

"Okay, that's enough excitement for the day," Rutledge said. "We'll talk about uses of balloons in a couple of minutes. You okay, Andrews?"

"I think so," he turned around. "Kessler is right. If that had happened outside, I'd be a goner."

"Don't they use balloons like that on Mars?" Jackson said.

Everyone turned to look at him.

"Explain what you mean," Rutledge said, turning to face him.

Jackson felt his cheeks heat up. He cleared his throat. "Well, doesn't NASA use balloons like that to photograph the terrain as it's carried along by the Martian winds?" "Exactly," Rutledge said, nodding in agreement. "Well done!"

Jackson looked at the floor and mumbled, "Thanks."

"Okay everyone, let's move over there," Rutledge said.

Jackson stared at the balloon, an amazing idea forming in his head.

"Hey," Carl said, nudging him with an elbow, "you okay?"

"Yeah. Just thinking about something," Jackson said.

"You look like you'd zoned out for a bit," Carl said.

"I just had an idea," Jackson said, staring at the balloon. "A brilliant one at that, if you ask me."

"Okay..."

Jackson turned to Carl. "Do you think Rutledge would let us borrow the balloon for a weekend?"

Carl's eyebrows arched up. "Are you kidding me? What are you planning on doing, taking a ride on it?"

"Almost," Jackson said. "Let's talk to Rutledge and see what he says."

Carl looked at him blankly. "Well, okay, seeing as he's coming this way."

"What?" Jackson spun around.

Rutledge came up to them, sipping at a drink. "Well guys, how's it going?"

Carl motioned to Jackson. "He's got an idea he'd like to run past you."

"Really?" Rutledge said, sipping again. "And what would that be?"

Jackson cleared his throat and took a breath. "Would it be possible to borrow that weather balloon for the weekend?"

Rutledge did a double take, glanced at Carl, then at Jackson. "You realize that you can't go for a ride on that balloon, don't you?"

"Yes I do," Jackson replied.

"So you want to do what with it?" Rutledge said, motioning for Jackson to continue.

"I was thinking of carrying out a scientific experiment," Jackson said in a flurry of words. "I'd like to get some information about the Tor."

Rutledge stared at him, waiting. "I think I'd like to know what you're going to do with it first."

Jackson said, "Maybe I should explain…"

CHAPTER 23

"All right," Jackson said. He cradled the video camera in his arm and pressed the record button. He waited until a steady red light winked on, and carefully let the camera hang lens side down from the balloon. "Okay, start letting the cable out."

"All right," Carl said, shaking his head. "I still can't believe Rutledge let you borrow the balloon." He turned and began to unwind a spool of cable, watching the wind buffet the balloon for a moment. "Hey, is the camera recording?"

"Yeah, it's working," Jackson said.

Jackson watched the balloon lift into the sky. It had taken a couple of days, but they'd finally found a spot where the winds blew constantly in a south-easterly direction. It happened every morning between eight and ten. If it happened like that today, in theory, the weather balloon would head directly towards the summit of the Tor.

As the balloon receded from them, Jackson could see the steady red light of the recorder sway back and forth in the wind. He turned and waved to Carl. "It looks good, just keep unwinding the cable."

"Yeah, yeah," Carl said. He was bent over and unwinding the cable from a large steel spool.

Jackson shielded his eyes with a hand and watched the helium-filled balloon grow smaller. So far, everything was going according to plan. The balloon and suspended camera were headed on a direct line to the Tor. Hopefully there was enough cable to make it there.

He walked over to spool, grabbed a handle on the opposite side, and helped Carl play out the cable. "So far it's looking pretty good. If the wind keeps blowing in that direction, it should pass very close to the summit."

"We should be so lucky," Carl grunted, slowly playing out more cable.

Jackson looked around. They'd set up on a small hill of grass, nothing but green meadows behind them. In front of them was nothing but desolation.

It was as if every plant or animal had been scrubbed from the wastelands with a giant scouring pad. Jackson could see where animal tracks had gone up to the edge of the wastelands, and then moved off, retreating from the dead zone. Jackson couldn't even spot an ant nest.

Looking towards the Tor, he could only see the top half of the hill. The base was covered by a heavy blanket of fog. It was eerie.

In some places, he could see wisps of mist swirl and drift about like feathery tentacles, chasing other wisps of mist, before sinking back down to the main bank of fog.

They almost acted like living entities… or ghosts.

He wondered how long this had been going on.

"It's weird out here," Jackson said.

"It's pretty well always like this," Carl said, looking up as he unwound the balloon cable. "You know what? One of the teachers who's done some research on the area said that birds won't even fly into it."

"Are you serious?" Jackson said.

Carl nodded. "Yeah, they have some instinct that tells them to keep out."

"Huh," Jackson said.

Jackson looked at the balloon. It was slowly growing smaller and smaller as the cable wound it out. It was still running dead straight towards the peak of the Tor. If it continued, it should pass very close to the summit.

Jackson watched the balloon stutter and start to thrash about frantically. "Wait a minute," he said, holding a hand up.

"What is it?"

"It must have hit a strong wind," Jackson said. He kept watching and then said, "Okay, let's keep going."

"Okay," Carl said.

Jackson squinted at the tiny multi-coloured dot in the distance. "Where'd you leave the binoculars?"

"You're practically sitting on them."

"Oh." He searched around, and found them next to a boulder.

As Jackson pressed the binoculars to his eyes and focused on the balloon, the putrid stench of sulphurous fumes wafted through the air. His eyes suddenly watered.

"Oh that's awful," Carl said, covering his mouth and nose with a hand.

"No kidding," Jackson said, wiping a sleeve across his eyes.

It was gone as quickly as it had come, and Jackson tried to focus on the balloon once again.

"We don't have a lot of cable left," Carl said, checking the spool.

"It's okay, I think we're at the summit," Jackson said.

Carl cupped a hand over his eyes to check. "Yeah, looks like we're right over top of it. It's a perfect placement."

Jackson let the binoculars pan down over the rugged slope of the Tor, and then continue down to the layer of fog.

As he refocused, he could see pillars of steam pluming into the air from where there were volcanic vents.

Between banks of dense fog, he could see steaming rivers of black mud oozing through the wastelands. It was like looking at Mordor from *The Lord of The Rings,* where there was only blackened rock. Carl's description of the place as a 'dead zone' was a pretty good one.

A bubbling, hissing sound caught Jackson's attention, and he turned in time to see a vent discharge a blackened mass of mud and steam into the air. An eerie, rasping scream whistled across the rocks as the geyser slowed and finally stopped.

"Weird stuff, eh?" Carl said, straightening and wiping a sleeve across his forehead. He shielded his eyes and squinted at the distant dot of the hovering balloon. "I think that's as far as we should go. Any further and the cable will go off the spool, and then we'll be trying to explain what happened."

Jackson nodded in agreement. "Yeah, I think you're right." He pressed the binoculars back to his eyes and on the bobbing balloon. "It looks pretty good from here."

Carl checked his watch. "I think we can only record for another ten minutes."

"All right, let's reel it back in," Jackson said. "It'll give us a second pass over the Tor."

Carl nodded. "You know, it's too bad we didn't have the balloon in the air when we saw those glowing spheres."

"Yeah. And to think that Mr. Rutledge thought it was only a rare case of ball lightning," Jackson said.

"Well, I've heard that explanation before."

As they reeled it in, Carl said, "This is hard work. Next time, get a spool that has a motorized return on it."

"Good idea. Right now, I think we should really put our backs into it. It looks like there's a major storm coming in. Look at those clouds moving in," Jackson pointed.

They worked hard at the winch, seeing the balloon grow progressively larger as they pulled it in.

"Hey," Carl said, nodding in the direction of the balloon, "The record light's still on. That means we've almost got a couple of hours of recording on it."

When they wrestled the balloon to the ground, Carl pulled the plug letting the helium hiss out.

As the first fat droplets of rain fell, Jackson said, "All right, let's get this gear packed up before it really comes down."

CHAPTER 24

"Is it ready yet?" Carl asked again. He sat cross-legged on the floor, leaning back against the sofa, sipping at a can of pop. He glanced at his watch again. "This seems to be taking forever."

"Well, *you* can always hook it up," Jackson said. "I mean, it is your TV and video camera."

Carl waved him off. "Nah, I'm terrible at doing that kind of stuff. I always mess up."

Jackson was in the middle of connecting the camera to the LCD screen and there were wires snaking everywhere.

Jackson plugged in the last connection, did a quick check, and thought that should do it. "You know, we can also download it to your computer, as well. Then you can always access it."

"Good idea. Let's see if it's worth saving first," Carl said.

"Fair enough," Jackson said, nodding. He sat up and turned the screen on. "All right, we're ready to roll."

Carl reached for the remote and hit *play*. A blurry image jiggled and danced across the screen, followed by a staccato flickering of images and weird sounds.

"Must be some old stuff on there," Carl said. "Let's hope it settles down."

The images slowed and finally they could see a shot of his feet, and then one of the two of them working about the windlass and pulling some cable out.

"Now we're getting somewhere," Jackson said.

"Jeez, I look pretty good," Carl said, leaning forward. "Working out with those weights has really made me look buff."

"Yeah, right," Jackson said, shaking his head.

The video flickered a bit more and then became steady. The image showed the ground receding as the balloon gained altitude. In the background, Jackson watched the two of them grow smaller and smaller as the balloon drifted towards the Tor.

"Man, this is working out pretty well," Carl said, rubbing his hands together excitedly. "If we put a musical track to it we might have an award winning documentary."

Jackson smiled. "Hey, that's not a bad idea."

He watched as blackened rocks rolled past on the screen. If there was any plant life down there, they certainly couldn't see it.

"That's pretty desolate," Jackson said.

"Yeah, looks about as habitable as the surface of the moon," Carl said. "What do you figure, the camera's maybe a hundred meters in altitude?"

"Yeah, I'd say that's a pretty good guess," Jackson said. "I can't wait to see what the Tor looks like."

"Want me to put it on fast forward for a bit?" Carl said

Jackson thought about it for a moment. "No, let's just let it play through in case something interesting comes up."

"I don't think we have to worry about that. It's just a dead zone," Carl said.

After a few minutes, Jackson leaned forward. "Hey, what's that?"

"Huh? What are you talking about?"

"Just pause it for a minute," Jackson said. "I saw something." He got up and went to the TV screen, pointing to a dark shape. "See it? It looks like something standing out there."

Carl scrambled to his feet and approached the screen. He leaned over, squinting at an odd shape. "Looks like some kind of rock formation."

"You're probably right. Where's that map Cheryl brought?"

"On the coffee table, next to those aerial photos that Coop guy gave us," Carl said.

"Perfect," Jackson said. He scooted over and picked up the map as well as a few of the photos. He sat back down, examining both closely. "It's hard to see, it's so small."

"Want a magnifying glass?" Carl said.

"Yeah, that'd help."

Carl vaulted over the back of one of the sofas and rummaged through a couple of drawers in a small desk. "Got it," he said, returning.

Jackson took it and started a slow pan over one photo and then the other.

"Well?" Carl said.

"Here. You tell me," Jackson said, passing him the glass.

Carl leaned over the aerial photo, slowly and carefully panning over the area. He looked up at Jackson. "It looks like either one tall rock or a bunch of rocks stacked on top of one another."

"Exactly what I thought," Jackson said, "but somehow it doesn't look natural."

"What do you mean?"

Jackson took the magnifying glass and pored over the photo once more. "All the rocks around it are black as coal. That rock, or stack of rocks, is more of a sandy colour."

Carl thought about it for a moment and then nodded his head. "You're right. Maybe it's just a freak of nature or something that's been moved there."

"Also amazing that it happens to be on the north-south line," Jackson said.

"Huh," Carl said. "Maybe just a coincidence."

"Come on. Let's see if the rest of the video shows anything."

They pressed the play button and watched the remainder of the recording.

"Hey, check that out," Carl pointed to the screen. "It looks like a mini geyser."

Jackson shifted position and saw a small hill the shape of an anthill spewing a muddy spray of water and steam into the air. A veil of mist drifted away from the vent and snaked out over the barren landscape. "That's cool."

"Well, for a guy interested in geology, you couldn't have moved to a more interesting place to live."

"Yeah, I'm starting to see that," Jackson said.

"Hey, looks like we're coming up to a heavy bit of fog," Carl said. "I can barely see the ground."

Jackson looked up from examining the map, the journal, and one of the photos. "According to these, there should be some kind of bridge across a river."

"Something there in that clearing," Carl said, leaning forward. He pointed to the right side of the screen. "It looks like an arch of rock."

"Yeah," Jackson said, looking from the screen down to the map. "So far it's dead on. What we see on the screen is the same as what's on the old map."

"That's cool."

Jackson watched a cloud of fog drift slowly and methodically across the screen.

"It looks like the bottom of my dad's barbeque," Carl said. "It's black and everything looks all burnt up."

"Okay, now it looks like we're starting up the lower slope of the Tor," Jackson said. Carl shook his head. "This is kind of exciting! It's like we're actually flying over the wastelands in a balloon."

"Yeah, kind of does, doesn't it?" Jackson said.

Jackson watched the rugged, black features of the Tor slowly slide past. There were crevices everywhere, but not once did he see the slightest hint of green as though there was some kind of plant life growing there.

"Hey, check that out," Carl said.

"Check what out?"

"Just to the left of centre," Carl said. He hit the pause button and ran up to the screen. "Watch that area."

Jackson leaned forward and watched a feathery wisp of fog creep out of a crevice and slide upwards towards the summit. "Man, that's weird!"

"Isn't it? It looks like it's alive."

Jackson nodded. The ghost-like wisp of fog came to a blockage of rock and then turned and moved laterally across the rock face. "Yeah, it does." The wisp of fog continued, winding snake-like around pinnacles of rock, slowing down in some places and then accelerating wildly in others.

"There must be some strange wind patterns out there," Carl said.

"No kidding." Jackson motioned to the screen. "You know, that slope looks climbable. It's not that steep."

"It's just the possibility of running into a pocket of poisonous gas that concerns me," Carl said.

Jackson folded his arms, staring at the screen. "If you were able to get hold of some kind of respirator to breathe with, you'd be okay."

"You're right," Carl said. "And I know where to find some."

"A store in town?" Jackson said.

"No, our basement," Carl said. "Remember? I was telling you about all the gear my dad's got in the basement."

"Oh yeah, that's right." Jackson said. "That would be a big plus."

Fissure lines ran vertically up the side of the Tor, some of them going so deep that the bottom was in perpetual darkness, even though the sun was almost overhead.

"Hey," Carl pointed, "doesn't that look like a cave?"

Jackson stared at the ebony black hole and said, "Yeah, it does." He watched as the camera slid along the sharp features of the Tor and then he said, "Hey, did you see that?" He pointed.

"What?"

Jackson scooted up closer to the screen. "It looked like something moving."

"It can't be," Carl said. "Probably just more fog drifting around."

"Rewind it a bit."

"Hang on."

Jackson waited as Carl slowly rewound the track and hit play once more. "Okay, let's have a look."

They watched an area that looked like a deep cleft in the rock face. Jackson jabbed a finger towards the screen. "There! See it?"

Carl nodded. "You're right." He stared at the screen in astonishment. "It looks like some kind of… of…"

"Movement? Like a dark shadow gliding out of the darkness."

"It's got to be just a bit of fog shifting about," Carl said.

Jackson didn't know what to think. He certainly didn't think it was a small patch of fog. No, it looked like something had lifted itself out of the shadows and ducked back down out of sight. Something as black as ink.

They rewound it several times, but were no more certain than the first time they'd seen it. They let it play past, noting at what time on the recorder they'd seen the anomaly.

"All right, here comes the summit," Carl said, motioning to the screen.

The summit inched into view.

Jackson could see the camera bob around violently as the wind buffeted the balloon. Tiny clouds of dust swirled across the summit. They waited for the image to steady.

"There's something!" Carl pointed.

Jackson saw dozens of faint markings drift into view, straight lines radiating out from the centre like the spokes of a bicycle wheel.

Finally, the faint outlines of a circular impression came into view.

"There it is," Jackson said in a rasping voice.

"And look to the right of that impression," Carl said, "just past the lip of the summit edge."

Jackson saw a pile of square-cut rocks that had tumbled down the slope.

"We were right," Carl said in a hushed voice of excitement. "There was a tower on the summit. Look, you can see where the blocks have rolled down that slope. The area must have been hit by an earthquake."

Jackson squinted at a dark impression dead centre of the summit. "Huh. It almost looks like an opening."

"Or a fire pit," Carl suggested.

"I don't know," Jackson said, still staring at the feature. "It could be an entrance to a cave or a storage area."

Carl leaned back, shaking his head. "Wouldn't it be something if there was a basement under there and a cache of weapons—"

"And coins, perhaps," Jackson offered.

"Yeah," Carl said. "Viking gold!"

Jackson turned to look at Carl. "Of course you realize that there's only one way to find out for sure."

A faint smile crept upon Carl's lips. "I know. Believe me, I know."

CHAPTER 25

Jackson exhaled a plume of steam into the cool morning air and checked his watch. *Jeez, Carl should have been here by now.* He rubbed his hands together trying to warm them as he gazed at the eastern sky.

The pre-dawn sky was a rose blush, and he could see a bright planet flickering on the horizon. *Probably Venus,* he figured.

To his right, ghostly tendrils of fog were on the move, moving like writhing snakes and sliding into small ravines.

He pulled out the cell phone his mom bought him and took a photo. Who knows, maybe he could sell one if he got one that was unusual. Like a shot of Bigfoot.

A sudden vibration from the phone told him he had an incoming text. He quickly accessed it.

Be there in a sec. Carl

About time.

He hoped the message he'd left on Sarah's phone would get her attention off of Carl. He grinned, thinking about it. When Sarah retrieved the message, she'd find that David Bradford, star quarterback of the school football team, was trying to get hold of her.

What better way to divert her attention to someone else, he thought.

There was a rustling through the underbrush, and he turned to see Carl approaching.

"You took long enough," Jackson said, shaking his head. "I thought you'd slept in."

Carl nodded and glanced behind him. "Yeah, that's because Cheryl wanted to come with us."

Jackson checked the tall grass behind Carl, but couldn't see anything. "Are you kidding me?"

"Afraid not," Carl said. "Don't worry about it, though. She's not coming." He paused. "At least she said she wasn't."

"Good."

"I had to make a deal with her, though."

"Hey, don't tell me you've set me up on a date with her," Jackson said.

Carl waved him off. "No, no. I wouldn't do that. I just had to agree to keep her in the loop."

"Okay, what does that mean?"

"That we keep her involved by letting her know what we're doing," Carl said.

"That's all?" He thought about it for a moment. "So if we're eating lunch, we've got to let her know that?"

Carl grinned. "Not quite. If we see something weird, we let her know. If she sees something weird going on, she'll let us know right away."

Jackson nodded. "That doesn't sound so bad."

"Then there's the second part of the deal…"

I knew it, Jackson thought. Here it comes. "Which is?"

Carl exhaled loudly. "That *I've* got to take Sarah out on a date."

Jackson's eyes widened. "You're kidding?"

"I wish I was. Did you come up with anything to get her off my back?" Carl said.

"Maybe," Jackson said. "It might work itself out in time."

"Well, don't take too long," Carl said. "I feel like a guy about to face a firing squad."

"Okay, okay." He thought about it for a moment and then asked, "What kind of weird things were you thinking we might run into?"

Carl shrugged. "Things moving around in the fog."

"Wait a minute," Jackson said, "I thought you said they were just rumours?"

"Well yeah, but you never know," Carl said.

"Yeah. Maybe," Jackson replied.

"And if Cheryl sees something coming our way, she'll let us know ASAP."

"That's good."

Carl looked at Jackson. "Did your mom believe you about our camping trip?"

"Yeah, I just told her I'd be somewhere in the back fields," Jackson said.

"Perfect." Carl shrugged off his backpack and set it down. Unzipping a flap and opening it up, he said, "I also brought along some extra stuff."

"Yeah, like what?"

Carl pulled out some sealed plastic bags, handing a couple to Jackson.

Jackson turned them over in his hands, examining them, wondering what they were.

Carl said, "They're respirators for breathing. Remember I was telling you about them? I brought an extra tank as well."

"That's a good idea," Jackson said.

"I also brought ropes, water, dried fruit, and some flashlights. I even brought my digital camera."

"Yeah, me too." He lifted a respirator and studied it. "How much air does a tank hold?"

Carl shrugged. "I'm not sure, maybe three or four hours." He zipped everything back in place and put his pack back on.

Jackson nodded. That was pretty good. He'd never seen anyone as prepared as Carl was. It looked like he'd thought of everything.

Carl opened a flap on his jacket, pulled out a copy of the map, and unfolded it. "We're right about here," he said, tapping a finger on the paper. "I've marked it with an X."

"Just like a treasure map," Jackson said. "It's fitting. Let's just hope that the features on the map are the same as they are today."

"We'll soon see," Jackson said. He threw his backpack on and adjusted one of the straps. "Well, ready to go?"

"Yeah, the faster we do, the sooner I'll warm up," Carl said. He led off first, slowly weaving a path through thigh-high grass that was slick with dew.

The sun was blood red as it rose higher into the sky, illuminating the Tor with a pink hue. Jackson slowed to take a photo of the sunrise over the Tor. Who knows—maybe he could sell it to some tourists, especially now that he was considered a local.

Carl glanced at the map and then looked up. "Looks like we should be able to follow that ridge there," he gestured. "It looks like it'll take us deep into the wastelands, so we should be able to follow it for as far as it goes."

"Sounds like a plan," Jackson said. "If things get out of hand, we head back at the first sign of trouble."

"That's right," Carl said.

They walked along the top of the ridgeline, Jackson thinking it was almost like they were travelling along the spine of a dinosaur.

On both sides of the ridge, mud bubbled and hissed, steam rising from the surface.

They'd walked for more than an hour before they stopped to check the map.

"Take a look at this," Carl said, pointing to the map. "This ridge runs pretty well parallel to the Tor and then turns sharply and heads directly towards it."

Jackson nodded. "It's like travelling on a highway. Can we get there by keeping to the ridge?" Jackson said.

"That's right. Once we leave the ridge, we will have to cross some of the wastelands," Carl said.

Jackson looked across the breadth of desolation and wiped a sleeve across his face. He felt like he was continually sweating.

In the distance he could see thick pockets of fog gliding across the barren rock. To his left, a pillar of steam and mud shot into the sky as a geyser blew up from a vent. "I wouldn't want to be standing over one of those things when it went off."

"Yeah."

They continued along the ridge, walking on the highest part as much as they could. On the one side, where the rock met the river of mud that slowly oozed past, the black rocks were coated yellow.

"Look at that," Jackson pointed. "Sulphur deposits."

So far, for as long as they'd walked, they hadn't seen any evidence of plant life. Not even one of the hardiest or one of the most primitive had made a toehold across the wastelands. Like Carl had said earlier, it was like crossing another planet—one completely devoid of life.

It was tricky walking along the ridge; everything was coated by a slick covering of slime or ooze.

Every few minutes, Jackson paused to take a photograph. He looked back at Carl when he heard a loud chirping sound.

"Just my phone," Carl said, fumbling it out of his pocket.

"Who is it?" Jackson asked, wondering if Carl's mom was checking up on them.

"Cheryl. It's a text from her." Carl looked around. "She said there's fog closing in on us."

"What?" Jackson looked around. "There it is!"

From a couple hundred meters behind them, Jackson could see a long finger of fog rushing along the opposite side of the ridgeline. It seemed to have virtually come out of nowhere and was rapidly coming towards them. "Look at the speed of that thing!"

"Come on, let's get moving," Carl said.

They picked up the pace, jogging when they could, trying to put some distance between them and the approaching mist. Even at this distance, Jackson could smell the acrid stench of sulphur fumes.

The contours of the ridge were beginning to change, Jackson noted. Instead of the almost railroad-straight line, it was now starting to curve and undulate in a loose, meandering route. If anything was going to slow them down, it would be the change in the shape of the ridge. There was no other alternative, though.

On either side of the ridge was a bubbling sea of mud. Large bubbles of air glooped up to the surface, and Jackson could feel the heat from it making him sweat.

Carl motioned to Jackson. "Do you have your mask ready?"

"No, not yet," Jackson said, tugging the mask out so he could access it.

"I've got a feeling we might need it if these fumes get any stronger," Carl said.

"Okay," Jackson said.

They picked up the pace again. Jackson wrapped the elastic from the mask around the back of his head. If he needed to, all he had to do was pull the mask over his face and turn on the air from the tank.

Steam from volcanic vents hissed into the air, covering the rocks with a fine mist. Jackson and Carl had to slow down a bit, as the rocks were as slippery as ice.

Jackson slowed to traverse a narrow cleft in the rock and used the time to take a few more shots with his camera.

"That fog is really catching up to us," Carl said, gazing back at the path they'd taken.

"Let's move then!"

They started jogging again, their arms stretched out for balance.

To their right, a massive shape slid out of the mud, rolling over as it wrestled with something clinging to it. The two shapes writhed on the surface for a few seconds, and then sunk back under the surface of the mud.

"What was that?" Jackson asked.

"Don't know, and I don't care to know," Carl said. "Let's just keep moving as fast as we can."

Jackson's heart pounded in his chest and his lungs heaved for air. He started running as fast as he dared, glancing back over his shoulder every few minutes. After fifteen minutes of hopping from rock to rock, and running whenever they found a flat section of rock, Carl waved to him.

"Let's... Let's take a... break," he said.

"Sure." Jackson turned and saw that the fog had veered off, almost moving in a perpendicular path away from the ridgeline.

"Hey," Carl called to him. "Check those out."

Jackson followed Carl's pointing arm to a large boulder.

"What?"

"At the base of that rock. It looks like some kind of crystals," Carl said.

Jackson scrambled down the slick rock face and headed towards some very large, yellow crystals. He'd never seen anything like them before.

"Must be some kind of sulphur crystals," Carl said.

"Yeah," Jackson said, pulling a jack knife from his jacket pocket. He opened up a blade and started to pry off a long, hexagonal crystal the length of his hand.

When he'd finally pried it off, he stuffed it into a large bag with some tissue paper. He collected two more and stuffed all three crystals into his backpack.

"These are amazing. Thanks," Jackson said.

"No problem." Carl slid down the flattened rock and pulled out his camera. "I might as well take a few shots as well."

"Hey, let me put my jackknife down for scale," Jackson said.

"Good idea," Carl said. "I'll take a few more when you're out of the way."

"This will look good in my rock collection," Jackson said.

"Do you have a lot of them?" Carl asked.

"Probably somewhere over a hundred," Jackson said. "There're in the back of our van."

"Wow. No wonder you want to be a geologist," Carl said. "Hey, let's take a break up there by that pinnacle of rock. It looks like its high enough to give us a good view of the surrounding terrain."

Jackson nodded in agreement. "Sure."

The high point was a long, cylindrical slab of blue-gray rock that angled sharply upwards. It looked like it was at least five meters higher than any other part of the ridgeline.

CHAPTER 26

Jackson watched a thick wall of mist roll towards them like a tsunami. It was moving incredibly fast. He saw the warm mist grow denser.

"Jeez, look at the speed of that stuff," Carl said. "There must be a strong wind behind it!"

Jackson wiped a hand across his sweaty forehead. It seemed to be getter hotter out here.

"I don't think I've ever seen fog move that fast," Carl said.

Jackson took out his binoculars and swept across the front of the approaching fog. "Hang on. It looks like the fog is not coming towards us."

"Are you sure?"

Jackson nodded. "It looks like it going to sweep along the ridgeline a little bit further on."

Carl took the binoculars from Jackson and studied the fog for a long moment. "I think you're right. It'll come close to us, but it looks like it'll hit the ridge further up."

"Let's take a break and let it pass," Jackson said.

"Sounds good," Carl said, passing the binoculars back to Jackson.

Jackson undid his waist belt and shrugged his backpack off, leaning it against a large rock. He rubbed his shoulders where the straps had dug in and watched the fog slide across the sun-baked landscape.

Grabbing his canteen, he took a sip, and then another. "We're going to have to watch how much water we drink," Jackson said, wiping his mouth with the back of his hand. "I doubt if we'll find any water out here from the looks of it."

"Even if we did, I don't know if I'd want to chance drinking it," Carl said. "Who knows what could be in it."

"Well, if it's anything like the rest of the wastelands, it'd probably taste of sulphur," Jackson said.

"Yeah, you're probably right," Carl said, pulling out his canteen.

Jackson got his camera out and started to take a series of photographs. He took a few and then noticed wisps of fog peeling off from the main bank and slithering off along narrow crevices.

"That's weird," Carl said, watching the progression of the wisps. "You'd think they were alive."

"I know." Jackson turned to Carl. "You were saying earlier that sometimes, in the fall, the fog gets especially thick and even manages to creep into town."

"That's right."

"Has anyone ever seen wisps of fog like that," he nodded towards them, "break off when they enter the city?"

Carl frowned, thinking about it for a moment. "I don't think I've ever heard of anything like that happening. Haven't read about it in the papers, either." He looked at Jackson. "Of course, that's one of the nice things about living in the country—we're out of the way and out of the loop."

"Yeah, I suppose."

"I've got an idea, though. Let me send a text to Cheryl. It'll let her know we're all right, and she can check out your question about those wisps as well."

"Perfect."

As Carl pulled out his phone and started to text, Jackson decided to check out the main fog bank that was continuing its rush across the wastelands. He remembered Carl mentioning something about shapes moving in the fog and thought he'd check it out.

Jackson refocused on the fog and slowly swept his binoculars along it as it moved across the wastelands. It was dense. Really dense.

It had to be at least a kilometer in length and probably about half that in width. It was probably only four or five meters high, but looked so thick it was almost impenetrable.

He swept along the side of it, looking for anything unusual.

Jackson heard a low beep come from behind him.

"Got a text from Cheryl," Carl said, punching buttons.

"Did she find out anything about the fog?" Jackson said.

"No," Carl said. He held up his phone and shrugged. "It doesn't make any sense."

"What do you mean?" Jackson said.

"Cheryl said there's something coming our way," Carl said. "She said it looked like a tiny black shadow."

"A black shadow?" Jackson said. He looked around and checked the sky. "There's not a cloud in the sky."

"Let me check with her," Carl said, tapping out a text again.

They waited, both of them uneasy.

"Maybe she was joking," Jackson said.

"Cheryl?" Carl said. "She's doesn't joke. She—hang on, here's her reply." He shook his head and looked at Jackson. "She says 'There's a dark object approaching from the south. It's fast and it's heading your way.'"

Jackson shielded his eyes with a hand and looked south. "I don't see anything. It's as clear as can be."

"She just sent another text," Carl said. "Listen to this. 'It looks like it's flying directly towards you. Maybe a kilometer out and closing fast.'"

Jackson ran a hand through his hair. "Maybe we should take cover... just in case."

"Sounds like a plan," Carl said. He grabbed his backpack and scattered belongings and looked for a place to hide.

"Let's go on the north side of the ridgeline," Jackson motioned. "See if we can find somewhere to hide."

Carl shook his head, scrambling down the slick slope. "It's probably just a bird."

"Yeah." Jackson pointed. "Over there. It looks like some kind of overhang." He looked behind him, but he still couldn't see anything."

They had just got into place, hidden under a sizeable overhang, when they heard a distant thrumming sound.

Carl looked up. "If that's a bird, it's got to be a big one."

Slowly, the distant hum grew louder as it approached.

"Now I'm glad we took cover," Jackson said. He cocked his head, trying to figure out what it was.

"Sounds more like a giant wasp," Carl whispered.

Jackson nodded, eyes looking overhead. "I thought nothing was supposed to be able to survive out here."

"That's what we've all been told for years. The weird thing is—"

"Shh!" Jackson hissed. "It's here!"

CHAPTER 27

A black orb the size of a chair shot past them and swung out over the wasteland. The thrum from it was like an electric motor whining at high speed.

Jackson leaned back and watched. "Don't move," he hissed to Carl.

Carl nodded in agreement. "What is *that*?"

Jackson shrugged. He didn't have a clue.

The orb came to a complete stop near one of the volcanic vents that was discharging steam. Jackson studied it as it hovered. It looked like there was some kind of protective band around the sphere, because he could see that vapours of steam from the vent couldn't touch it. The hair on the back of his neck rose and he felt his mouth go bone-dry. Whatever that thing was, he doubted he would find it in any of his nature books. The orb doubled back a bit, taking up position not too far from where they hid. He glanced at Carl and saw that his eyes were wide.

As Jackson watched the orb, he thought he saw the outer skin ripple, like waves flowing across it.

"Look at it," Carl whispered.

Jackson held up a hand and hissed, "Quiet!"

The sphere hovered there, and the heavy thrumming continued, rising and falling in crescendos. He thought of taking a picture, but he was frozen with fear. The last thing he wanted to do was draw attention to them if the camera beeped.

The thing started moving again, skimming low over the top of the ridge. Any closer and he would be able to reach out and touch it.

He glanced at Carl and saw his back was pressed up against a flat rock. He was keeping perfectly still, but his eyes were bulging. Jackson's heart pounded so loud he was afraid the thing would hear it and drop down to check it out.

As it drew closer, Jackson could see furtive movement inside the sphere. Nothing obvious. More like something squirming as if something was trying to get out. He saw a vague shape pushing the outer skin.

The sphere wasn't as solid as he'd first thought. Now it looked organic, as if the outer skin was a thick, black tissue, like the mouldy skin of an orange.

The hovering shape came closer. Jackson suddenly had the terrible sensation that he had to clear his throat. He swallowed and tried not to think about the tickle in his throat.

The shape was hovering almost directly above them, the thrumming so loud that Jackson felt like covering his ears. The last thing he wanted to do, though, was move.

He hoped Cheryl wouldn't try to text them now. The last thing they needed was a loud buzz signifying a message had arrived. Jackson tilted his head back, watching the orb slowly glide pass. He tried the Jedi mind trick: *Move on, nothing here. Move on.*

The sphere continued, its shadow moving across the rocks.

With the sun on it, he could definitely see a shadowy shape squirming inside, sometimes pushing the skin of the sphere outwards.

Move on…

Then with a sudden burst of speed, the thing accelerated and sped off towards the fog bank.

Jackson sat up, watching it race over the wastelands until it was engulfed in the thick fog and disappeared from sight. He finally coughed into his hand.

Just then, Carl's phone chimed, letting them know he had an incoming text.

Jackson let out a breath. He hadn't realized he'd been holding it this long.

"Jeez, what was that thing?" Carl said, watching the sphere disappear into the distance. He changed position, grimaced, and started rubbing the back of his leg.

"What's the matter?" Jackson said.

"A massive cramp. I was starting to get it when that thing flew overhead. I didn't dare move."

"Good thing." He eased himself to a standing position, and peered toward the moving bank of fog. "Maybe you should change your cell to vibrate rather than chime like that."

"Yeah, good idea," Carl said. He fiddled with the cell for a moment and then looked at Jackson. "What was that *thing?*"

Jackson shook his head. "I don't know, but I started thinking about those globes we saw on the slope of the Tor the other night."

"Yeah, they were kind of like that, weren't they?" Carl said. He ran a hand across his face. "Man, that thing was scary."

"Do you think we should head back?"

"No way," Carl said. "We're just getting warmed up."

Jackson took another look at the fog bank. "Well, whatever it is, it's staying in that fog bank."

Carl looked at the fog bank and nodded. "That's fine with me."

Jackson had his copy of the map out and was examining it carefully. So far, everything was in-sync with what was on the antique map. He thought things would have changed over the years, but they hadn't.

"Well, I think we just keep an eye on that fog and make sure that thing doesn't return," Carl said. He thought for a moment, eyebrows knitted together in a frown. "You know what that thing reminds me of?"

"What?"

"Some of the drones the military uses," Carl said. "I remember watching a documentary on them, and they showed them flying around, photographing everything."

"You think what we saw was some kind of military drone?" Jackson said. "It looked like it was alive, to me."

"I think it's a possibility. Who knows what kind of stuff the military comes out with?"

Jackson thought about it. Carl was right; it was a possibility. The military always uses out-of-the-way places to test things. Why not Boswell? It was a small town in the middle of nowhere. He turned to Carl. "Is there any kind of military base near here?"

"Funny you should ask," Carl said, wiping sweat from his face. "There's a base maybe five to ten kilometers from here."

"That's interesting," Jackson said. Carl had a point. It could very well be a drone, but deep down, his gut told him otherwise.

"Hey," Carl said, waving a hand in front of him. "Didn't you hear me? I think we should keep moving."

"Yeah, you're right." He consulted his map again and then looked up. "According to this, that rock column should be somewhere in front of us."

"The one we saw in the video?" Carl asked.

"And on the ancient map, as well," Jackson said. He looked around, surveying the bleak landscape.

There was nothing but black rock that had a roasted look. The large fog bank off to their left was now following the ridge to the north. If they kept going, he figured, the way should be clear.

Carl cleared his throat. "You know, even if we wanted to head back home, I don't think we could."

"What do you mean?"

Carl pointed behind them. "Take a look at that. It looks like a huge fog bank coming towards us fast."

Jackson turned and saw a swirling mass of white, churning as it moved along the ridgeline. It was heading directly towards them. "I see what you mean. And that thing is approaching *really* fast."

"Yeah," Carl said, tightening the straps on his backpack. "We'd better get moving. There're things in there I don't want to see again. Besides, I'd like to take a closer look at that hill and see if we can climb to the top."

Jackson shaded his eyes from the sun. "Well, it's sure gaining on us. We'd better move it."

They climbed back up to the top of the ridgeline and hurried along the central portion. They ran for a while and then paused to check behind them. The fog was still gaining on them.

Jackson half expected one of those spheres to come buzzing out of the fog after them. The last one he'd seen had scared the crap out of both of them.

The ridgeline was flattening out, dropping down to the level of the wastelands. Jackson could see that the other fog bank that had been ahead of them was slowly vacating the area, leaving only wisps of mist snaking along the ground.

Carl gestured to the landscape ahead of them. "Hey, look at that. I think I can see that rock tower in the distance. That's the one we saw in the video and the map."

Jackson tried to catch his breath while he gazed ahead. Through layers of shifting mist he could see a pillar of grey stone rearing out of the ground like a giant tombstone.

"Jeez, that thing is a lot bigger than I thought."

Carl nodded in agreement. "It sure is."

"Well, let's check it out. We've got to pass by it anyway," Jackson said.

As they hurried towards the rock formation, layers of mist drifted past them like ghosts. Carl slowed as they drew near the fog-shrouded monolith. "Jeez, that's tall. It must be at least three meters tall."

"Yeah." Jackson cleared his throat. "Did you ever see the movie *2001 A Space Odyssey?*"

Carl turned to him. "A long time ago, why?"

"There's a stone slab in that movie that reminds me of the stone they found on the moon."

"I'll have to watch it again," Carl said, staring at the rock.

"Let me take a few shots of it," Jackson said, pulling out his camera. He took one of wisps of mist slithering around the base, partially obscuring it. He motioned to Carl.

"Hey, why don't you go over and stand beside it. I'll use you for scale."

"Sure."

Jackson waited until Carl was in place and took a few shots with the massive stone slab towering over his head.

It had to be at least three meters in height, tilted to one side like something that should be on Easter Island.

"It looks strange," Jackson said, lowering his camera.

"If you think that's strange, you'd better come and check out the markings on the front of the slab."

"What?" Jackson hurried over to the slab, glancing up to where Carl pointed.

As Jackson drew closer, he squinted at the weathered surface.

Along the perimeter, Jackson could see what looked like vines engraved on the stone. They ran over the top and down both sides. The engravings were faint, worn by the passage of time.

"Check the stuff in the middle of the stone," Carl said.

Jackson looked at the stone again and saw a series of markings, like some kind of writing chiselled into the stone.

"I'm pretty sure those are runes," Carl said. "They're an ancient form of writing that the Vikings used. I saw some of them on the coins I found."

"Jeez," Jackson said, shaking his head in disbelief. "So the Vikings really were out here."

"That's strange," Carl said, looking at his fingers.

"What? The large stone in the middle of nowhere?"

"No. The stone feels like it has an electric current pulsing through it," Carl said.

Jackson stepped forward and laid his hand on the stone. A second later he jerked it away. "Jeez, you're right. That *is* weird!"

"Tell me about it," Carl said. "What's even weirder is that it comes in pulses."

"What do you mean?"

"Lay your hand on it for a minute, and you can feel pulses vibrating through the stone every few seconds."

Jackson put his hand back on the stone and left it there. "You're right," he said, taking his hand away. "There's a pulse every few seconds." He stepped back and stared up at the monolith towering over them. "Go figure."

Carl said, "Let's get some pictures of the runes. We can send them up to Cheryl as an attachment to the texts. She's pretty good at languages, so maybe she can give us an idea of what it says."

"Good idea," Jackson said. He used the zoom features to get some close-ups of the ancient writing. He wished they knew what they were about. Maybe they were some kind of grave marker for a warrior or a king.

He took one more photo that showed the entire span of writing, then lowered his camera.

"I wouldn't put that away yet," Carl said.

"Yeah?"

"There's a weird face carved on the opposite side of the slab," Carl said.

"Seriously?"

"Oh yeah," Carl said.

Jackson came around to the opposite side of the slab and stared up at a hideous face carved into the top of the rock.

"Jeez," he said, taking a step backwards.

"My sentiments exactly," Carl said. "If this is a grave marker, he must have been one ugly guy."

Jackson stared up at a monstrous face that looked like it had come from someone's nightmare.

Two huge, hollowed out eyes stared off into the distance. The nose was an outcropping of stone, shaped by chisel work. The mouth was, more than anything else, a contorted grimace.

Jackson took more pictures and then stood back to stare at the face.

"If that's the face of the warrior buried here, they should have left it blank."

Carl nodded in agreement. He looked around at the sprawling landscape. "Why put it way out here?"

Jackson shrugged. "Maybe this is where he died."

"Yeah, that's possible, but it must have been a major effort to move that stone slab out here," Carl said.

Jackson nodded. "Yeah, that's true."

Carl turned and followed the direction of the giant's staring eyes. He shielded his eyes with a hand. "Huh. It looks like it is looking directly up to the Tor from here."

"Maybe the face was looking towards the ancient tower at the summit," Jackson said.

"Yeah, but why?"

"The runes may give us the answer, and besides, I—" There was a *buzz* and Carl fumbled his phone out of his pocket. "It's Cheryl. She's sent a text"

"Hey, maybe she's found out something about the runes," Jackson said.

Carl turned and looked back the way they'd come. "Not quite. She says there's something coming behind us."

"What? Not another one of those spheres." Jackson turned and searched the wastelands they'd passed through. Heavy layers of fog drifted, and he couldn't see anything.

There was a second *ping*.

Carl read the text. "She said there's something big heading towards us. He looked back into the swirling mists. "Come on, let's move it!"

CHAPTER 28

Jackson stopped to catch his breath and he could hear Carl gulping air beside him.

"You okay?" Jackson asked.

Carl nodded. "Yeah. See… anything?"

Jackson shook his head. "Not a thing." He studied the route they'd travelled after leaving the ridgeline. They'd crossed a large expanse of ancient lava beds. Now, the fog was steaming up the slope of the Tor, lapping at the base like an incoming tide.

They were virtually marooned on an island surrounded by a dense fog. He could smell the pungent reek of sulphur in the air.

Jackson turned to Carl and asked, "Do you think Cheryl could have been wrong?"

Carl grimaced and shook his head. "I don't know. If she said she saw something, I'm pretty sure she saw something."

Carl turned. Shielding his eyes from the sun, he gazed up at the upper reaches of the Tor. "It's a lot steeper than I thought. We're going to have our work cut out for us to get up there."

"Yeah," Jackson said.

"I can see why they would have built a tower on the summit. It's the perfect place for a fort. It's a steep climb to get up to it, and you could roll boulders down on intruders' heads."

Jackson looked up at the route before them, wondering now if they could actually make it all the way. Somehow they would have to follow the natural spiral of the Tor, slowly angling their way around it until they got to the top. He just hoped they could find another way that was easier.

Pulling out his camera, he thought he may as well take a few more photos as part of his ongoing diary. He snapped a few more and sent them to his home computer.

He turned to Carl. "Are you okay?"

Carl leaned against a rock and nodded. "Yeah. I guess I'm not in the shape I thought I was."

"Well, we'll take our time. If it gets too hard, we'll head back."

"If we can," Carl said. "That mist is still following us."

Jackson turned towards the direction of town. It was a spectacular view. He could see the windows of houses and offices shimmering in the sun like molten gold.

"Hey, we haven't heard from Cheryl in a while," Jackson said.

"Yeah, I was just thinking that. I'll send her a text." Carl tapped out a message and quickly sent it.

A minute later, his phone *pinged*.

Carl opened it and read it quickly. "She says she can barely see us even in the telescope."

Jackson chuckled. "I'm not surprised."

"Huh," Carl said, still reading.

"What? What is it?" Jackson asked.

"She said that there's still something moving in the fog. She says, it looks like a tiny ink blot moving about, and it's headed in our direction."

Jackson moved over behind a large outcropping of rock. He pulled his binoculars out and started to scan across the front mass of the mist.

"There it is," Jackson said.

Carl hustled over, pulling out his binoculars. "Where?"

Jackson lowered his binoculars and pointed to a tiny dark smudge to the right side of the approaching fog. "Right there."

Carl pressed his binoculars to his eyes and scanned the fog front. "I see it. Cheryl's right—it does look like a blot of ink."

"Yeah. I wonder what it is." Jackson said.

Carl watched it for a while, carefully refocusing on it. "I don't know if I really want to find out."

"Maybe it's one of those spheres we saw." Jackson said.

"I don't know. It looks a lot larger than that," Carl said. He studied it for a few more seconds. "Whatever it is, I think it's using the fog for cover."

Jackson looked at the steep slope of the Tor. "Let's keep going. Maybe we can lose it in the rocks somewhere."

Carl turned and gazed at the steep slope. "At least it will get us above the level of the fog."

"Let's keep going, then," Jackson said.

They turned and started up the slope, Carl leading, picking their way over rough terrain.

It was slow going, climbing over huge boulders that must have fallen from above. Jackson kept one eye on the summit, ready to take cover if some rocks came hurtling down.

Carl paused to catch his breath, and turned towards him. "It looks like there's a narrow pathway up there, just to the left of that tall pinnacle of rock."

Jackson climbed up beside Carl. He could see a narrow path that wound its way around outcroppings of rock.

Yeah. Maybe it's the way to the summit."

Carl continued. Breathing hard, he paused to wipe sweat from his forehead, then continued up the slope. "Jackson you'd better come see this!"

Based on the tone of his voice, Jackson quickly climbed, scrambling up over loose shale and sending it tumbling down the slope.

"What is it?" Jackson said, coming up beside him.

"Look up there. I can see a cave," Carl said.

Jackson stared up the ravine, wiping sweat from his eyes. At this distance, all he could see was a narrow ribbon of black.

"Let's get closer," Carl said.

As they scrambled up the ravine, they could see the cave mouth was a narrow oval, maybe three meters in height, but only a couple of meters in width.

"Look above the cave mouth," Jackson said.

The cave was part of an enormous face, Jackson realized. The cave was just the gaping mouth.

Above that, two chiselled holes were the eyes that stared back over the wastelands.

"This is incredible," Carl said. "As in National Geographic incredible!"

Jackson stood there, silent, his mouth gaping open.

"We've got to get some pictures," Carl said, "because no one is going to freaking believe this."

"Yeah," Jackson said, pulling his camera out and starting to take a few shots.

The nose was a jagged outcropping of rock, crooked and bent to one side.

"Look at that," Jackson pointed. "There're hand and footholds chiselled into the rock. We climb those and we're into the cave."

Carl took a step forward, gazing up at the yawning mouth above them. "I wonder how far back that cave goes?"

"Hopefully it'll take us up to the summit," Jackson said, staring at the face. "You know, it kind of looks like the face on that stone column we passed."

"Yeah, it does, doesn't it?"

"Remember how that old map showed four of them?" Jackson said.

"That's right. It did," Carl said, nodding. "I wonder if they've all got faces on them."

"And what do they mean?" Jackson said. "Well, let's check out the cave first."

"You go first," Carl said. "I'm not much of a climber."

Jackson shrugged. "No problem."

He started off, slowly fitting his feet into the toeholds and then pulling himself up with the handholds.

He took his time, carrying only a coil of rope over his shoulder. When he got into the cave, he could pull everything up after him.

It took him a few minutes until he was able to grab hold of the lip of the cave—or the lip of the mouth—and pull himself up into the cave.

He collapsed onto the floor of the cave, breathing hard, his arms shaking from the exertion. He was going to have to start working out again.

"You okay?" Carl called up.

Jackson crawled over and peered down. "Yeah. It was a tougher climb than I thought."

He uncoiled the rope and threw it down. "All right, tie the backpacks on and I'll pull them up first."

After they were up, Carl tied the end of the rope around his waist. "Okay, I'm coming up."

Like Jackson, he collapsed onto the cave floor, heaving for breath.

Carl finally sat up and then howled out in pain.

"What is it?" Jackson asked.

"I sat on something sharp," Carl said.

"Probably just a rock," Jackson said. He pulled out his flashlight and thumbed it on, shining it over the cave floor.

"Oh jeez!" Carl said, scrambling to his feet. "Bones! Thousands of bones!'

As Jackson played his light beam across the ground, he could see they'd been sitting on a deep layer of bones. They stretched back for as far as the light would shine.

Jackson shook his head in disbelief. There was virtually no life at all on the wastelands, and yet here they were, sitting upon thousands of bone fragments of every size and shape.

What was going on?

CHAPTER 29

"This is so weird," Carl said, backing up until he was against the cave wall. "What could have done all this?"

Jackson shook his head. "I don't know, but there has to be a predator that killed these things."

"You mean like a mountain lion?"

"I don't know. It has to be something like that," Jackson said. He used a foot to push aside the yellowing bones, amazed at the depth of the pile. "It doesn't make any sense, though."

"What do you mean?"

"Well, look at the location of this cave. How could anything climb up that sheer rock wall? We had to use ropes to get up here," Jackson asked.

"I don't know," Carl said. He played his light over the mound of bones. "This had to have taken place over many years. There must be literally thousands of bones here."

"Maybe it was the Vikings."

Carl looked at him strangely. "Come again?"

"Well, we pretty well know there was a Viking tower on the summit, right?"

"Yeah, that's what we've been thinking," Carl said.

"Suppose they were under siege by a hostile force," Jackson said. "After they ran out of food, they probably would eat whatever was available."

Carl eyed the heaped bones, stirring a foot through them again. "That's totally gross. I can't imagine eating mice and rats."

"Well, if you had to do it, you'd do it."

"But why stack them here? Why not just chuck them out of the cave?" Carl said.

Jackson thought about that. It didn't make any sense. "I don't know."

Carl frowned. "Unless there's a predator around here that no one has seen before."

Jackson ran a hand through his hair and exhaled. "Nothing makes any sense out here." He stirred a few more bones aside with his foot. "And from the colour of these bones, I can tell it happened a long time ago."

"How do you know that?"

"The colour. The older the bone, the more yellow it becomes," Jackson said. He pushed some of the bones aside with his toe. "The ones down here are *really* old."

"That's right," Carl said. "I remember we covered that in science class." He moved to the opposite side of the cave, bones cracking and crunching under his weight, his light beam playing over the bone bed. He paused for a moment and looked at Jackson. "Do you know what's really weird?"

"What's that?"

"There isn't a single skull in all these bones," Carl said.

"What? That's impossible."

"Take a look," Carl said. "I can't find any."

Jackson swept his bright beam back and forth across the surface of the bones, even checking deeper by stirring some of them to the top with his foot. "Huh, you're right. There aren't any." He took a step and repeated his search there. Nothing. "That is weird!"

"I wonder if that thing that buzzed us on the wastelands had anything to do with this," Carl said.

Jackson looked at him for a moment. "You mean that military drone?"

"Yeah," Carl nodded. "But what if it's not a drone, but some weird life form that hasn't been seen before?"

Jackson shook his head. "If that's true, it's really creepy."

"There's no way a military drone could have done this," Carl said. "No, this has been going on for a long, long time."

"Let's check the rest of the cave, maybe see how far back it goes," Carl said. "And see how far back these bones go."

"All right," Jackson said, probing the back of the cave with his flashlight beam. "Let's do it."

The layer of bones went as far back as their lights would shine. It looked like a tsunami had swept a mass of debris in, depositing it after the wave retreated.

The cave grew narrower as they worked their way deeper, and it felt like they were walking into the gullet of a monstrous animal. The ceiling dropped sharply, and the sides narrowed in.

Carl swept his light over the cave walls and then probed the ceiling.

"If that roof drops any lower we'll be on our hands and knees," Carl said.

"I know." Jackson turned to Carl. "You're shorter than me, maybe you should go first."

"You've got to be kidding!" Carl said. "It was your idea to come out here."

"Oh, all right," Jackson said. "I'll go first."

"If you insist," Carl said. He bowed and motioned him forward with a dramatic sweep of his arm.

Jackson shook his head and started down the shaft. He crouched low, crunching over more bones, slowly working his way deeper into the cave.

He kept sweeping his flashlight beam from one side to the other, illuminating clouds of dust pluming into the air. Jackson waved a hand in the air, trying to clear the dust away.

"Hang on a minute," Carl said.

Jackson stopped dead in his tracks and turned about. "What is it?"

"I've got a text coming in," Carl said, looking at his cell. "The signal's pretty weak, but it's from Cheryl."

"What does it say?"

Carl looked up at him, his face tense. "She says that thing that was following us is right below us."

"What? She can see it?"

"Yeah, she said it's partially hidden by the fog, but it's heading up the ravine."

"We'd better take a look."

As they hurried back to the entrance, they stopped and stared down at the narrow ravine.

"There!" Carl pointed.

Jackson watched as heavy fog poured into the ravine.

He followed Carl's outstretched arm and saw a flicker of movement from deep within the mist. The movement was a blot of black moving, changing shape, and fluxing as the fog poured towards them. There was something about its movement that was familiar.

Carl rubbed a hand across his face, looking worried. "What do you want to do? See what it is? "

Jackson's thoughts were racing. "I think we'd better hide." He turned and directed his light to the rear of the cave. He didn't know how far back it went, but there had to be somewhere they could scrunch into. A crevice, maybe.

Or maybe there would be a rock they could hide behind. He didn't know why, but he had a bad feeling about what was coming.

Carl gazed down into the fog-shrouded ravine. "What is it?"

"Do you remember I was telling you about the thing we hit on the outskirts of town?"

Carl nodded. "Yeah, so?"

Jackson swallowed. "I think that's it coming up the ravine. It's got that same weird, hobbling gait."

"Oh, crap!"

CHAPTER 30

Carl stepped back from the cave mouth and looked at Jackson. "How about we drop a boulder on its head?"

"What? You can't do that—that's murder!"

Carl thought for a long minute and then shook his head. "Yeah, I guess. Still, it's not a bad idea."

Jackson shook his head, wondering about Carl. "Besides, do you see any boulders lying about?"

Carl turned and looked around. "Ah, no."

"Come on, let's head deeper into the cave. There's got to be somewhere we can hide," Jackson said.

"Or maybe we'll find a big rock," he looked at Jackson. "Just in case."

Jackson led off, hurriedly scrambling over the bone bed, his light beam stabbing the darkness and moving up to lick over the walls and floor.

"Watch your head," Carl said, illuminating the ceiling. He ducked under an overhanging ledge.

The roof descended in a sharp angle, knobby protuberances hanging from the roof like barnacles. The walls narrowed in after a few paces.

Carl came up beside him, his voice tremulous. "It looks like we're heading towards a dead end. We'll be trapped back here."

"Let's keep going," Jackson said.

The cave had a tomb-like quality to it, especially with all the bones strewn about the floor. There was also that dank, musty smell.

They stirred up clouds of fine dust that lingered in the air.

Carl coughed. "Let's hope that thing out there doesn't notice all the dust hanging in the air."

Jackson wiped a sleeve across his mouth. "It might already know we're here."

"Oh yeah." Then Carl nudged Jackson. "Hey, do you feel that?"

"What?"

"I can feel a draft coming from the end of the tunnel." Carl said. "There must be an opening back there."

Jackson came up beside Carl. "You're right. I feel it, too." He shined his flashlight light along the narrow shaft. "There's got to be an opening to the outside back there."

"Let's check it out," Carl said. "And fast."

Jackson stepped forward, crouching low to get past the sloped roof. He got a sudden pang of claustrophobia, but shook it off, focusing on the fact that they had to find a way out. His light revealed a tiny opening at the very bottom of the end wall. The opening was barely the size of a small box.

"That looks pretty small," Carl said, shaking his head. He added his light to Jackson's. "I don't know if I can fit through there."

"You'll fit," Jackson said.

Carl got down on his hands and knees and crawled towards the hole, shining his light into the gap. "It looks like it goes into a larger chamber."

Jackson let out a sigh. "Good. That's a relief."

Carl turned his head. "Do you want to try it first?"

Jackson shook his head. "It's okay, you go ahead."

Carl stared at the narrow opening. "What if I get stuck?"

"You can make it," Jackson said. "We don't have any other options."

"I know." Carl exhaled. "It's just... it looks about big enough to let a cat squeeze through."

"Well... meow, meow," Jackson said, grinning.

"Yeah, funny," Carl grumbled. "It's okay for you. You're skinny."

"You can do it," Jackson said. He studied the gaping hole. "It might be tight, but you can make it. I'm sure of it."

Carl slipped off his backpack and threw it to the ground. He crawled closer to the narrow opening and examined it for a minute. "That's weird. It looks like somebody cut the hole with a boring tool." He ran his hand over the circular wall of the chamber. "It looks completely round and the sides are smooth as glass."

"Don't worry about that now," Jackson said, glancing back towards the cave entrance. He thought he heard a scuffling noise, but it must have been the wind.

"I'll try," Carl said, pushing his backpack in front of him.

"You can do it," Jackson said. He heard another noise and turned towards the entrance. It sounded like a weird, rasping sound.

"You'd better move it. Something's coming up that rock wall."

"What? Are you sure?"

"Yeah, now move your butt! We don't have a lot of time," Jackson said, looking back over his shoulder.

Carl squirmed though the narrow entrance, twisting and turning, grunting and groaning.

A light flickered over the roof of the cave near the entrance, and a noisy scraping sound echoed along the length of the cave.

"Almost… almost… ugh. Hey, I'm through!" Carl said.

Jackson threw his pack into the opening and then scrambled after it. He took a quick look backwards and saw a light blossom across the cave entrance. He turned back and pushed the pack ahead of him, crawling as quickly as he could.

The narrow passage was actually a lot larger than he'd expected. When he got to the opposite side of the two-meter shaft, he took a final look back. A huge shape rose at the cave entrance, blotting out the blue of the sky.

Frantically, Jackson scrambled out from a shallow crevice, grabbed his pack, and ran.

"Come on," Carl hissed, signalling to him.

Carl had his flashlight on, but had a hand over the lens to shield the light. It was pointed at the ground to illuminate the way.

They ran up a steep slope and followed the cavern wall as it turned to the left.

Behind them they heard the loud crash of a rock falling. Then, a chilling scream echoed in the distance.

CHAPTER 31

At the end of the corridor, Carl turned and motioned Jackson over. "You've got to see this."

"What is it?" Jackson said, breathing hard and hurrying after Carl. He turned and glanced over his shoulder, quickly checking behind them. "We've got to keep going."

"Yeah, I know, but this'll only take a minute," Carl said. "Check out the wall."

"What?" Jackson said.

"There's something weird about it."

Jackson hesitated, his hand almost touching the passage wall. He wondered if it was like that column on the wastelands, with that strange pulse of current flowing through it. He took a breath and laid his palm on the rock. "Hey, it's metal!"

"Yeah, go figure," Carl said.

"Metal," Jackson said, shaking his head in disbelief. "Why here, and how?" He turned and let his light lick over the shimmering wall. Blurred reflections ran along the length of the metallic surface.

As he played his light over the inner surface of the pipe, he wondered again, why? The thing was huge, maybe three to four meters in diameter, almost large enough to drive a car through. Why someone had gone to all the effort of putting a pipe here was beyond him. The technology to put a pipe through the solid rock had to be pretty expensive.

Carl ran his hand along a metal pillar that ran from the floor to ceiling. "I wonder what this is for. Some kind of support beam, maybe."

Jackson nodded, suddenly nervous. "Come on. Let's keep moving."

"Where?"

Jackson flashed his light along the surface of the dark pipe. "We'll see where this goes. It has to go somewhere."

"Yeah, I guess." He sighed. "It's not as though we have many choices," he said. He turned and glanced behind him. "Did you hear something?"

Jackson shook his head. "No. Did you have any luck getting in contact with Cheryl?"

Carl shook his head. "Nothing. I think this hill's preventing any signals from getting in *or* out."

"Yeah, you're probably right."

As they hurried up the slick pipe, Carl slowed to run his hand over the sidewall. "Weird. This surface is as smooth as polished glass. Only problem is that there's some kind of secretion flowing down the walls."

"I wouldn't be touching that stuff too much," Jackson said. "Who knows what it could be. Let's just keep going." He took a step and then hesitated. "Hey, I wonder if that thing is still following us. If we're lucky, it turned back."

Carl shrugged. "That'd be fine with me."

There was a scuffling noise behind them, and both of them stopped and turned around.

"Did you hear that?" Carl whispered.

"Yeah, just keep your light pointed to the ground."

They had climbed almost halfway up the slope, Jackson reckoned, and as he stared into the oily blackness behind him, his stomach tightened.

They waited, and then a spray of shimmering light swept across one side of the corridor and then slipped down to the floor. It slowly brightened, telling Jackson that something was approaching, and it was coming fast...

"W—What do we do?" Carl stammered.

"Run!" Jackson said, taking off. "Let's go!"

With Carl right behind them, they ran up the length of the pipe, slipping and sliding over some kind of fluid flowing along the bottom. Panting for breath, they paused when they came to an open door.

Beyond there was darkness so black it seemed to devour their light.

"Are you sure about this?" Carl said.

"We don't have any other choice," Jackson said. "All I know is that I don't want to get caught by that thing that's following us." He turned and saw a light flicker along the walls, shimmering with a kaleidoscopic effect.

"It—it's right there!" Carl moaned.

Jackson backed away from it, his legs feeling like putty.

A huge shape lumbered into view, climbing the length of the pipe, a single light from its head probing the pipe.

"Go," Jackson hissed, giving Carl a push. "Move!"

They ducked through the door and tried to find cover.

Jackson flashed his light and illuminated a slab of rock that looked like a sarcophagus.

"Over there!" Jackson said, flashing his light over the stone.

They ran behind the outcropping and ducked down behind it. Heart pounding, Jackson raised himself slowly until he could peer over the top.

"Do you think it saw us?" Carl rasped, panting for breath.

"I don't know," Jackson croaked. As he watched the mouth of the tunnel, he saw its light shimmer along the sidewall and blossom like a flood light.

It was coming...

Bright light poured out over the rock platform. The thud of heavy footsteps grew closer.

"Get down!" Carl hissed.

Jackson slid down a bit, but found a niche to the side of the rock that would allow him a view of what was coming.

As it was, his heart was pounding so loud and fast it felt like it was trying to burst out of his chest.

Then he thought of something.

"Carl," he hissed. "Is your cell on vibrate?"

"Crap," Carl said, fumbling his cell out of his pocket. "I forgot." He tapped a button and gave Jackson a thumb up.

Jackson nodded back, and tried to relax. His mouth was so dry it felt like it was filled with ash.

Just then, a massive figure loomed into sight, ducking low to clear the ceiling. It stepped out onto the rock platform and stood there, looking around. Was it looking for them?

It was a giant.

It turned in their direction, a helmet light flaring bright and blazing in their direction. They ducked low, waited, and held their breath.

CHAPTER 32

Behind them, a shadow from the rock bobbed against the wall, fading away as the helmet light slid on to illuminate the rest of the rock platform.

With the sound of footsteps shuffling on, Jackson lifted his head and took a peek.

He caught sight of a massive shape limping away, its helmet light swivelling about and probing the darkness.

He knew it had to be the same thing they'd hit on the outskirts of town. The limping gait was identical. Even in the dim light, Jackson could see it wore a spacesuit like NASA astronauts, the only difference being that its suit was inky black. Two air tanks were fastened to the figure's back. Jackson wondered what kind of gas it was breathing.

It obviously wasn't oxygen, or it wouldn't need the tanks. Maybe it was methane or chlorine, something completely inhospitable to human life. Or maybe it was in case of toxic sulphur gas.

It turned and went to a panel, stabbing its finger into a series of coloured lights set into the wall.

With a fluttering of a gloved hand, a deep rumbling started to vibrate through the rock as a massive door slid across the entrance. With a heavy thud, the door closed and the figure turned and hobbled off into the darkness. Only the helmet light was visible until it, too, was swallowed by the blackness.

They waited a long minute until Carl whispered, "Do you think it's gone?"

"I'm not sure," Jackson said, straightening slightly. He quickly scanned the area, wishing he could turn on his flashlight, but realizing it would be a dead giveaway. "I don't see it anywhere."

"Are you sure?"

"I'm going to check that panel."

"You're crazy," Carl said. "Just wait a bit longer."

Jackson squinted into the ebony blackness, watching and listening. His body tensed. He could hear his heart pounding and could hardly get any air into his lungs.

There were two options. Either that thing had moved off or… it was standing in the shadows nearby, watching and waiting.

As he moved out from behind the rock, he felt oppressive darkness like a heavy weight.

Finally his eyes made out a dim light filtering in from the centre of a domed roof. That had to be the Tor's summit.

Jackson warily moved across the rock platform, his light obscured by a hand over the flashlight lens. He approached the door, ran his hand over the metal surface, and then moved over to check the panel with a quick flash of his light.

He could make out nine touch pads set into the panel.

Jackson shook his head. "Great," he mumbled.

Unless they knew the exact sequence of touch pads to be depressed, it was unlikely they'd be able to open the door. A cold wash of fear swept over him. If anything, he would probably trigger an alarm.

Carl slipped up beside him. "What do you think?"

Jackson started. "Jeez, don't sneak up on me like that!"

"Sorry. Can we get back out?"

"Not a chance," Jackson said.

"Nine separate pads?" Carl said. He shook his head. "We definitely won't get out that way."

Jackson exhaled loudly. "So what do we do now? We're trapped up here."

Carl ran a hand through his hair. "Well, maybe we could wait until that thing returns to go back out."

Jackson shook his head. "That might take days… weeks, even. I don't really want to stay down here that long."

Carl shrugged. "Yeah, our parents would kill us."

Jackson nodded, wondering if there was another way out. There had to be some sort of emergency exit, he thought. He turned and gazed in the direction that the creature had disappeared.

"What are you thinking?" Carl said.

"I saw it disappear over there," Jackson said. "Maybe there's another tunnel that way."

Carl stared off into the blackness and swallowed. "Well, I guess there's only one way to find out."

Jackson nodded. "Okay, let's do it."

Carl flicked on his flashlight and swept the bright beam across a rugged plateau of rock.

"Turn that thing off!" Jackson said.

"What's the problem?" Carl asked, thumbing it off.

Jackson shook his head. "You might as well just shout something. That light's bright enough to attract all kinds of attention."

"Oh yeah. Sorry, I didn't think of that."

"Let's just take our time, maybe keep an eye out for its helmet light," Jackson said. "Cover your flashlight with a hand so it gives off just a trickle of light."

"Okay, I'll keep it pointed at the ground."

"Good," Jackson said.

They slowly walked across the rough rock surface, their shielded lights illuminating a rock surface cut by dozens of fine cracks.

Carl leaned over to shine his light down one of the cracks. "Jeez, it goes down a long way."

Jackson grunted an acknowledgement and then paused to look around. His eyes were finally adjusting to the darkness, helped somewhat by the dim light coming through the cavern dome. He gazed at it wondering if it was a way out.

He saw a flicker of movement: shadows shifting and moving around up there.

"Huh, there must be pigeons up there," Jackson said.

Carl followed his gaze and stared up to the dim light. "I don't think so. Everyone knows nothing lives out here." He paused and then added, "Not even pigeons."

Jackson stared at the domed ceiling. "Man, its one massive cavern in here. It looks as big as a football stadium."

"Yeah, it does," Carl said, nodding in agreement. "Who would have thought there'd be something like this inside the Tor?" He turned to Jackson. "Are you sure we can't turn our lights on for a little bit? It's pretty dark."

"No way. Not until we find out where that thing went," Jackson said.

"All right," Carl said, grudgingly.

"The last thing I want to do is draw attention to us."

"Yeah, but we need to see where we're going," Carl said.

Jackson considered it for a moment. The last thing they needed was to fall into a bottomless crevice. "Okay, but let's keep the flashlights shielded and pointed at the ground."

"You've got, it" Carl said excitedly. He covered his flashlight lens with a hand and turned it on, illuminating the ground with a dim light.

They moved forward slowly, stepping carefully over rugged ground until they reached a stone column.

"Holy crap!" Carl said, flashing his light over the ground in front of him.

"What is it? Another—" Jackson stopped abruptly at the edge of a precipice. He backpedalled quickly.

"Good thing we had our lights on, eh?" Carl said. "One more step and we would have stepped into thin air."

Jackson nodded, his mouth feeling as dry as parchment. "Yeah."

Carl looked around. "So where did that creature go?"

Jackson got down on his hands and knees, crawled up to the edge of the cliff and shined his light down its steep face. His light showed the rugged features of the rock for about ten meters before it was swallowed up by the darkness. "I don't know. Maybe it fell off the edge."

Carl shook his head. "Somehow, I don't think so." He knelt down next to Jackson and shined his light over the precipice wall. "It's pretty steep. Strange though, it seemed to know exactly where it was going."

"It did, didn't it?" Jackson said, a tone of incredibility entering his voice. He worked his light along the precipice wall, going past large outcroppings of stone and what looked like shadowed caves. He passed over one feature and stopped. "So that's how he did it."

"How?"

"Take a look at that, just off to the left. There's a metal ladder going down the length of the cliff. It looks like it's been fastened to the rock face." He shined his light over the rusted shape and followed it down until it disappeared into the blackness.

"That's pretty slick. Unless you were looking for it, you'd never know it was there."

Jackson nodded. "Yeah." He eyed the ladder, thinking that they didn't really have a lot of options about what they were going to do. It was either stay where they were and hope someone opened the door again, or go down the ladder and look for a way out somewhere on the cavern floor.

"What do you want to do?" Carl asked, turning towards him.

Jackson let out a breath. "I don't think we have a lot of choices. We either wait up here indefinitely for that door to reopen, or—"

"—or we go down and try to find a way out from down there."

"That's right," Jackson said.

Carl ran a hand through his hair. "I don't know about you, but I think our best bet is to go down."

Jackson nodded. "Yeah, I don't think we have a lot of choices."

They carefully crawled across the rock platform, following the edge of the cliff to where the top rungs of the ladder protruded.

Jackson turned to Carl. "Do you want to go first?"

Carl was silent for a minute, and then said, "Maybe you'd better. I'm actually afraid of heights."

"All right, we'll just take it nice and easy."

"Sure. No problem," Carl said.

Jackson swung himself around and started down, his flashlight beam lancing the rock wall crazily.

"Turn off your light!" Carl said.

"What?"

"Just turn it off. I can see a light down below!" Carl said.

Jackson snapped his flashlight off and stuffed it into his pocket. He held his position and looked down.

"To your left and behind you," Carl murmured.

Jackson swivelled around and saw a dim light meandering around rock columns and then moving across the cavern floor. "Yeah, I see it now."

"It looks like he's looking for something," Carl said. "He's cut back twice now, keeping to that area around that rock column."

"Maybe we should go down now that he's searching for something," Jackson said. He took a tentative step down to the next rung.

"Hold it!" Carl said. "And don't move. We've got company." He flattened himself to the rock and didn't move.

Jackson looked around, not sure what was going on. He thought that maybe a second figure was approaching the ladder. If so, then he was hooped, standing on the third rung. "I—I don't see anything."

"They're above you and coming down fast."

Jackson looked over his shoulder and saw two luminous spheres dropping from the cavern roof like dive-bombers.

"Don't move," Carl hissed.

Jackson nodded and hugged the ladder, frozen in place. His neck craned to the side, he watched the two globes speed downwards, heading directly towards the helmeted figure.

As they sped past, Jackson glimpsed a shadowy shape, squirming about inside the sphere. For an instant, just a heartbeat of time, a wave of terror surged over him as he picked up the sense of malevolence coming from the orb.

CHAPTER 33

"All right, let's get down to the cavern floor as quickly as we can," Jackson said. He glanced down, estimating the distance.

Carl looked down at Jackson from a few rungs above. "Okay, but let's take our time. I don't want to fall."

"Okay." Jackson glanced down to where that helmeted figure had been. Still no sign of him. Whatever those spheres were, that thing in the helmeted suit had taken off in a hurry when they came towards him.

Jackson had been sure that both were together, somehow. Now it looked more like they were mortal enemies. It reminded Jackson of when he first saw that creature and the sphere on the outskirts of Boswell. He realized now that the sphere had been attacking that thing.

But why? Some kind of turf war?

The two spheres still hadn't returned. As he dropped down a few more rungs, he looked towards the yawning mouth of a huge cave. He figured all three had disappeared somewhere within it.

He climbed down another ten rungs of the ladder, his hands sore from gripping the rusty metal.

By the time he finally reached the cavern floor, Jackson's arms were aching from the descent. He waited until Carl touched down, watching him flex his hands.

"Jeez, that was a workout," Carl said. He looked back up the way they'd come, and shook his head in disbelief.

"We'll have to be careful," Jackson said, surveying the vault of the cavern, particularly the roof where the spheres had dropped from. He wondered if there were more of them up there, waiting.

Carl nudged. "Hey, what's that glow over there?"

Jackson turned and saw a pulse of blue light coming from the rear of the cave. He couldn't see a source, just a pale blue light winking on and off at regular intervals. "I don't know. Maybe it's where those spheres come from."

Carl looked skyward. "Somehow, I thought that was high above us. Like perches that birds of prey would use."

"I suppose," Jackson said.

Carl pressed backward against the rock wall. "Hide. There're more of them coming."

Jackson looked skyward and saw more of the glowing spheres drop from the ceiling and start a looping descent towards the cave mouth. Only problem was, these ones looked like they were going to pass by very close to them.

"Get back!" Carl hissed.

Jackson moved back and cringed against the cold rock wall, flattening himself against it.

In the pitch black, the orbs glowed in a dull yellow hue and sped along the ground, looping around columns of rock like TIE fighters from *Star Wars*.

Jackson could see they were heading directly towards them. Now he wondered if those things had somehow become aware of their presence.

"Don't move!" Carl warned in a whispered voice. "Don't even breathe."

No problem, Jackson thought, his breath caught in his throat.

As the spheres drew close, he could smell an awful stench, like that of rotting flesh. It almost made him gag.

The spheres were definitely slowing down, Jackson saw. Something must have caught their attention. Maybe *their* odour, Jackson thought. He slowly turned his head towards Carl and whispered, "Don't move a muscle."

This was the closest that Jackson had ever been to one of these things. Over the pounding of his heart, he could hear a faint buzz coming from the spheres—or maybe he should describe it as a faint hum—like that of a tuning fork vibrating.

The sphere itself—at least the outer membrane—was almost transparent, except that it looked clouded over. Perhaps this was the effect of a different atmosphere inside it. The shadowy movements inside were muted by the effects of the membrane.

It looked like the thing had numerous appendages that there were whip-like. The initial thought that came to mind was an octopus or a squid. The worst part was when the body of the creature inside the sphere pressed up against the outer membrane. Then it looked like the thing was trying to burst out. That's when the grotesque outline of the creature bulged outward with a single yellow, reptilian eye gazing out.

Jackson willed himself to close his eyes, waiting for the things to move on.

A single gunshot, then two more echoed through the vast dimensions of the underground cavern.

Eyes flicking open, he watched in fascination as the spheres lifted off their position and climbed into the air. Gathering speed, the humming sound changing to a heavy drone like that of dragonfly, the two orbs raced off towards the mouth of the cave. With two more loud gunshots, the spheres went even faster, becoming blurs of light as they rocketed towards the cave.

"There's got to be other people down here," Carl said. "Someone's got a gun."

"Yeah, but who?"

"I think we're going to have to find out," Carl said.

CHAPTER 34

Jackson held out a restraining arm to Carl. "Hold on a minute."

Carl suddenly looked panicky, his eyes widening. "What? What is it?" His head swivelled from one side to the other.

Jackson shook his head. "I'm not sure. I just got this strange feeling that something's not right."

Carl turned to him. "That's it? You're trying to tell me your *Spidey senses* are tingling?"

Jackson nodded. "Yeah. Something like that." He looked around nervously. "I get this feeling once in a while and it's usually dead on." He sidestepped past a small pinnacle of rock, keeping one eye on the black maw of the cave.

He knew that was where those spheres had disappeared. Staring at the blackness he wondered if they were just inside…waiting.

"Hey, you okay?" Carl asked.

"Yeah. I was just wondering if those things are waiting for us in there." He exhaled loudly, thinking it had been a while since the last gunshots had echoed through the cavern.

Carl turned and glanced behind him, checking the passageway they'd just come through.

"What is it?" Jackson asked, turning around as well.

"Nothing. It's just you've got me doing it, too," Carl said. He flexed his fingers. "I'm feeling jumpy, too." He motioned to the blue light cascading down the tunnel from an unseen source. "Any idea as to what we're seeing?"

Jackson wiped a hand across his face. "Not a clue. I've been thinking about it but the only thing I can come up with is that it's a beacon."

"A beacon?" Carl repeated.

"Yeah, either to show people the way to come, or…"

"Or what?" Carl asked.

"Or it's a warning to keep trespassers away," Jackson said.

"Great. That's what I didn't want to hear," Carl said.

"I've been watching that light, and it's weird," Jackson said. "It pulses bright for about ten seconds and then fades away to complete darkness for another ten seconds."

Carl shrugged. "Maybe it's just a way of conserving energy."

Jackson nodded his head. "Yeah. Maybe."

Carl took a deep breath. "You still want to go in there?"

"Yeah, I think so."

Carl shook his head. "I was afraid you'd say that."

"Well, we need to find a way back out of here," Jackson said. "We need to tell someone what's going on in here. That it's not as lifeless as everyone thought."

"Yeah, I guess so," Carl said.

Jackson stared at the utter blackness again. The light had faded to nothingness. He waited until a trickle of light gleamed from the distance, telling him the light would be pulsing to brightness once again. "Let's go."

They started slow, entering the giant mouth of the cave, searching everywhere as they walked down the glass-like corridor.

As it dimmed again, Jackson ran one hand along the sidewall to guide himself.

"Let's just take our time," Carl said in a low voice.

"Yeah."

"We could always use our flashlights," Carl suggested.

"No. No flashlights," Jackson said. "The last thing we want to do is draw attention to ourselves."

After thirty or forty meters, Jackson realized that the cave was opening up. The ceiling was disappearing, telling him that they were walking down a long, narrow ravine. He also realized that if those spheres returned, they could simply drop down on them.

Steeply rising walls stretched up some three meters in height to a narrow opening above them. He now felt as though he was walking along a narrow cylinder, but the roof had been ripped away.

"Check out the wall," Carl said, running a hand along it. "It feels like it's made of polished glass."

Jackson laid his palm on the wall and ran it up and down for a moment. "Yeah, I see what you mean. It *does* feel like glass. Like it's been completely polished."

Carl stooped down and found a few pieces that had fallen there. "These will make good souvenirs to bring back."

"Yeah," Jackson said, picking up some as well, "or to add to a growing rock and mineral collection."

"Of course. Something for the junior geologist," Carl said.

Jackson motioned to the right side of the cave. "Let's keep over there so we're not visible if those spheres return."

"Good idea," Carl said, moving closer to the wall. He was quiet for a moment. "I wonder where they come from."

Jackson shrugged. "Maybe some other planet."

"Maybe they've just existed here, in this cavern," Carl said.

"And where did they come from before that?"

"Who knows? Maybe they're survivors from the age of dinosaurs, and this is the only place they've been able to survive," Carl said.

Jackson shook his head. "I don't know about that."

They continued along the sidewall of the ravine, slowly working their way around nodules of rock that had been fused to the floor, and stepping gingerly over glasslike rocks.

Carl held up a hand. "Hold it a minute, there's an opening up there."

Jackson came up beside him and saw what looked like an oblong hole cut into the fabric of space. It was a narrow cave cut into the wall, maybe three meters in height and a meter in width, if you were lucky.

As they drew closer, Jackson saw a pale glow from the back of the cave, like a dim lamp was lit inside.

"Maybe we should check it out with a flashlight," Carl suggested.

Jackson nodded. "Yeah, maybe. I'll keep it shielded, though." He pulled out his flashlight and approached the rift. "If you see anything coming, let me know."

"No problem."

Jackson used his hand to shield the beam of the flashlight, and stepping up to the opening, shined it into the opening.

Dozens of huge crystals ignited into glowing embers when the light hit them.

"Jeez, look at that, will you," Carl said, looking over his shoulder.

"Yeah," Jackson said.

"That's cool," Carl said. He turned and checked behind them for a moment. "Let me take a couple of pictures."

Jackson shrugged. "Sure, why not?"

Carl took out his cell phone and accessed the photo app. He took three shots.

With each photo, the crystals glowed even brighter under the use of the flash.

"That is so cool," Carl said.

Jackson saw movement out of the corner of his eye and turned to see a sphere drifting down the length of the ravine. "We've got company," he said. "Get inside that cavern, fast! And turn off any lights."

"But—" Carl started to say.

"No time to explain," Jackson said, pushing him forward. "Get inside!"

Jackson took a last look at the approaching sphere and saw a luminous glow reflected off the glasslike walls of the ravine.

"Hurry up," Jackson said, squeezing in beside Carl, one shoulder jammed up against a jagged group of crystals. He felt as though he was jammed into a telephone booth.

"Is it still there?" Carl whispered.

"It's still coming," Jackson whispered back. "I can see the glow. We'd better be quiet."

Carl nodded, giving him the thumbs up.

They heard it before they actually saw it, a faint hum that increased slowly in volume. It sounded like a tuning fork that had gone out of control.

A faint glow played along one edge of the opening then slowly blossomed across the mouth of the cave like a sunrise. Jackson pressed back against the rear wall as the sphere swept past.

There was furtive movement inside the sphere as a shadowy shape pressed up against the membrane. His heart was pounding so loud, Jackson hoped it couldn't hear him.

For a split second it slowed, and Jackson thought it was going to enter the narrow crevice where they were hiding. It moved off to the opposite side of the ravine as Carl sucked in a chest-full of air.

CHAPTER 35

They were close enough to see a part of a huge blue globe peeking out from behind a rock wall. The thing was immense, probably the size of a four-story building.

As they watched, Jackson could see the sphere change in brightness—slowly fading from a brilliant, turquoise blue to a pale glow.

"What *is* that thing?" Carl said, his voice croaking.

Jackson shook his head. "I don't know. It looks like a tiny sun."

It didn't even look solid, he thought, but more like some kind of plasma that fluxed in brightness. The shape was almost identical to the geodesic domes he had seen at Science World on a school field trip. The outer shell appeared to be partially transparent, like a fogged glass window. As they watched it, it gradually grew to too bright to even look at.

"Jeez, that's bright," Carl said, turning away.

"No kidding," Jackson said, massaging his eyes with the heels of his hands. "It is like a mini sun."

They waited until the brightness of the ball had faded and they were able to look at it again.

Jackson heard a soft *click,* and glanced over to Carl. Even with all that was happening, he had enough savvy to pull out his phone and take photos.

Carl turned to him. "I'm going to take a couple of video clips, as well. It may be of interest to scientists, and… National Geographic."

"Yeah, probably."

"Take a look at it on the camera screen," Carl said. He zoomed it on the blue ball as it dimmed, allowing them a better look at it.

It was weird, Jackson thought. The outer surface of the globe had a rough, pebbled appearance to it, and glistened like a wet surface.

He thought about it for a moment and realized it was very similar to some pond life he had observed under the microscope in science. What was its name again? It came to him a minute later—Volvox. "It looks like Volvox."

"It looks like a Volvo? What the heck are you talking about," Carl asked.

"No, I said Volvox. It's a kind of primitive microscopic life that lives in ponds."

"Huh?" Carl said, turning to stare at him. "What are you rambling about?"

Jackson tried to explain. "That sphere over there is very similar in shape to some microscopic life I've seen in the science lab."

Carl nodded. "Okaaaay," he said, drawing the word out. "I hate to break it to you, but that thing over there is hardly microscopic."

"I know that, but the thing under the microscope was organic and resembles that thing over there a lot."

Carl gazed back at the massive blue ball. "So, you're thinking this thing could be organic, too?"

Jackson shrugged. "Well, maybe part of it. The thing is—"

"Hey," Carl interrupted. "There's movement over there!"

"What? Where?"

Carl pointed. "Right near the base of that ball."

Jackson turned and looked towards the darkening sphere. It looked like a dying star.

A line of tiny figures were approaching it from the deep shadows. He could see their helmet lights playing over the cavern floor, illuminating pipes and coils of cables or hoses, some probing tall pinnacles of rock. Dust from their footsteps plumed into the air like tiny clouds.

"Let me check something," Carl said, pulling his binoculars out and focusing on the receding figures.

Jackson waited a minute and then said, "Well... Anything?"

Carl lowered the binoculars. "They're all wearing those suits like the other one, but I can't tell what they're up to."

"Are they all headed towards the sphere?"

Carl nodded. "Looks like it, but two of them have swung further to the left and look like they're setting something up on the ground."

Jackson held out a hand. "Let me take a look." He took the binoculars, pressed them to his eyes and focused.

Carl shielded his eye with a hand and squinted towards the brightening sphere. "Looks like they're busy doing something."

"Three of them are setting something up on some kind of tripod," Jackson said. "The others have moved out of sight somewhere."

"I wonder what they're up to," Carl said.

Jackson watched the activity around the tripod. It was still too distant to see exactly what they were setting up, as the three figures were crowded around it. He watched one of them turn and connect a thick cable to the tripod. "I wish we had something more powerful. It's hard to see what they're doing."

"Well, I guess we could always move a little closer," Carl said.

"Yeah," Jackson said, sweeping past the three figures he could see, searching for the others.

The cavern looked as large as a football stadium from their vantage point, and as the sphere brightened, he was able to see massive pillars of rock rising up to the vaulted ceiling.

He counted at least ten of them scattered throughout the cavern. The place was a lot larger than he had originally thought.

Carl tapped him on the shoulder. "We've got company."

Jackson lowered the binoculars and looked around.

"There. Behind us," Carl said, pointed to the ceiling. "And it looks like there're more on the way."

Jackson turned around and gazed up. "Yeah, it looks like reinforcements, doesn't it?"

He could see dozens of the luminous spheres hovering near the very centre of the cavern roof, just a short distance away from rays of muted light. From the darkness, at the opposite end of the cavern, he could see more luminous globes coming. "Let's get to cover. It looks like trouble coming."

Carl shrugged. "I don't know, maybe they're working with those other guys."

Jackson watched the mass of luminous spheres grow in number until there was more than thirty. They were all different sizes, ranging from small baseball-sized globes to the largest that was the size of a medium-sized dog. They were clustered together, almost as if they were keeping warm. "Somehow, I don't think so."

They glowed with a dim, phosphorescent light, looking almost ghost-like in the dim light that was filtering in through the dome of the cavern.

Carl nudged him with an elbow. "Hey, look at the size of that one. It must be the granddaddy of them all."

Jackson had been watching it approach already. It was the size of a desk and glowed with a much brighter glow than the others.

Even at this distance, he could see a dark shadow within the sphere, squirming and moving about.

"It looks like some kind of confrontation," Jackson said.

"Yeah, you may be right," Carl said. "And I sure don't want to be caught in the middle of it."

"Hey, do you think I should take a couple of photos?" Carl asked.

Jackson turned to face him. "Are you kidding?"

Carl held up both hands defensively in front of him. "It's okay. I'll make sure my flash is disabled."

Jackson thought it over. "Well, all right. Just as long as the flash is off. I don't want those luminous balls coming down to check it out, do you?"

Carl shook his head. "No, of course not."

Jackson watched Carl fiddle with the camera

"All right, that should do it." He pointed it towards the cavern roof and took three photos. He waited, and showed them to Jackson. "Not bad, are they?"

Jackson examined the frames. "Shows quite a gathering of spheres, doesn't it?"

Carl nodded, looking down at the images on the camera. "Maybe I'll try a few video clips later on."

"For the TV documentary?" Jackson asked.

Carl smiled. "You bet. Later on I'll get a photo of you as co-discoverer."

"Sounds good," Jackson said.

Carl motioned to the ceiling of the cavern. "It looks like we've got some action. Those spheres are on the move."

Jackson watched as a mass of spheres slowly began a downward descent, picking up speed as they left the ceiling. They split into a wide, winged formation. "Jeez, they look like a flock of birds in flight," he murmured.

Carl backed up so he was underneath a rock overhang. "I think they look more like a pack of wolves closing in for the kill."

"Are you going to get this on video?" Jackson asked.

"Oh crap, I forgot all about it," Carl said, fumbling the camera up to his eye. He made a few adjustments and started to film.

Jackson used the binoculars while Carl was recording. He watched one of the figures turn around, and then motion frantically to the others.

Three of the figures turned and ran, making a beeline for a number of darkened caves behind them. Jackson figured there might be all kinds of tunnels cut into the rock face.

"Look at that!" Carl said, motioning to the left.

One of the helmeted figures appeared to be in panic mode. He was running, tripping and falling, and then scrambling to his feet again, turning to glance back over his shoulder. It was obvious he was trying to make it to cover.

"I hope he makes it," Carl said, shaking his head in horror.

Close behind, Jackson could see three luminous spheres chasing after him, almost nipping at his heels.

A moment later, he could see one of the spheres trying to attach itself to his back.

What the heck is that about? he thought. A sudden flashback ran through his head—it was when they first saw that figure on the highway. Then, one of those dimly glowing spheres was trying to secure itself onto its back.

But why? And for what purpose?

He shook his head. How could he ever forget that?

Jackson tracked the stumbling figure and saw him fall again. The spheres were on him in an instant. Gloved hands tried to push them away, and he started rolling and rolling, trying to keep them off.

Carl was right. Those things were like wolves… or leeches.

Jackson could see the helmet light throwing weird patterns of light on the ground and surrounding rocks as he twisted and rolled about frantically. He finally managed to get to his feet, grabbing rocks and throwing them at the spheres. As the spheres backed off a bit, he turned and ran into the deep shadows. A moment later, the spheres rushed after him.

"I hope he makes it," Carl said.

Jackson nodded and then swung the binoculars back to the main group of suited figures. They were huddled together in a tight group and using pipes, or some kind of poles, as spears to keep the spheres at bay.

It was like watching a movie of ancient Greek warriors in combat. The figures were moving as a group, slowly working their way towards a massive pillar of rock that had a narrow crevice cut into it. They kept close, pipes jabbing out at the spheres as they swarmed above them. After a moment, they squeezed into the crevice one by one and disappeared from view.

All Jackson could make out was a series of pipes protruding from the crevice like porcupine quills.

The spheres didn't seem too keen on pursuing them anymore.

Carl shook his head. "I don't believe it." He turned to Jackson. "Those guys have all kinds of hi-tech gear on and the only weapons they have are pipes? That doesn't make any sense."

"I know. It's weird. Unless for some reason they don't work in this cavern."

"Yeah, but I thought we heard a gunshot, earlier." He nervously ran a hand through his hair. "What do we do?" Carl asked.

Jackson exhaled. "I don't know. Maybe we should wait until all those spheres leave and head towards that pulsating sphere. There's got to be a way out of here somewhere."

Carl thought about it and then said, "Okay, let's wait for about ten minutes. If those globes leave, we'll head after those other guys."

"Good enough," Jackson said.

CHAPTER 36

Carl partially slid down a slight embankment before finally getting his balance.

"You okay?" Jackson asked, coming up beside him.

"No problem. It's amazing how much skateboarding comes in handy. It improves your sense of balance, big time."

"Glad to hear it," Jackson said, peering back over his shoulder. So far they'd been fortunate. Those luminous spheres had returned to their roost at the top of the cavern.

They were like pigeons, in a way, but really vicious ones. Especially the way they had attacked those other guys in the suits.

"You know what?" Carl turned to say. "Maybe that's why they have to wear those environmental suits."

"I think you're thinking along the same line as me," Jackson said.

Carl checked his footing and then continued. "I bet they give some protection against the spheres, whatever they are," Carl said.

"I think so, too," Jackson said. "I just wonder what kind of creature is inside those suits. Is it something like you or me, or something completely alien?"

"Well, at least they have two arms and legs, and a head," Carl said.

"Yeah, but you have to wonder what's behind the helmet faceplate."

"I don't want to know, really" Carl said. He shone his light over a pile of stacked rocks, following a bundle of cables running off into the distance. Suddenly he turned to face Jackson. "Hey, what if one group are escaped prisoners?"

"What?"

"I saw a show like that on TV. I don't know if it was the *Outer Limits* or not, but they had these two different groups fighting it out on Earth. One was cops and the other was a bunch of escaped prisoners."

"Huh," Jackson said shaking his head. "I guess anything is possible." He thought about it for a minute. "That would mean the huge blue globe could be some kind of prison ship."

Carl frowned. "I never thought of that."

"Well maybe if we get close enough we could see what they're up to."

Carl played his light over the ground. "I've got their footprints right here. It looks like they've gone over the crest of that small hill."

"Well, let's keep going," Jackson said, turning and looking around. "I don't like standing out here in the open."

They scrambled up the side of a small hill, following a thick bundle of what looked like electrical cable.

When they drew near the summit, Carl waved him to slow down.

"What?" Jackson said in a whisper.

"Keep low," Carl said. "We'll be the most visible at the summit."

"How do you know that?" Jackson asked.

"Paintballing 101. I've been hit more times than I can remember on the summit of a hill and looking around," Carl said.

Jackson nodded. "That makes sense."

"Okay. Keep down," Carl said, getting down on his hands and knees and crawling towards the hilltop.

Jackson crawled up behind Carl, pausing when he did, and continuing on when he moved again. They paused just below the summit and slowly crept up to the top.

Jackson saw they were looking down into a small valley, walled by sheer cliffs on both sides. In the middle of the valley he could see a couple of small buildings. "Do you see them?"

"Yeah. Maybe that's home sweet home for them," Carl said.

Jackson watched the buildings for a minute and then said, "Doesn't look like there's much movement down there."

"Yeah, looks pretty deserted," Carl said. He motioned to the right. "Look over there. You can see their tracks heading towards those huts."

"And towards that blue sphere," Jackson said. "That's just around that next corner."

"Let's keep going," Carl said. "Maybe we can get some answers inside one of those huts."

"Good idea. We need a few answers," Jackson replied. "And maybe they left some equipment behind we can use."

They carried on, creeping forward in a low crouch, zigzagging back and forth as they wound their way down the hill.

When they got close to the nearest building, they hunkered down behind a mound of dirt. Jackson lifted his head and looked around. To their right, a stack of large pipes was piled to head height. Past that, more cables snaked across the ground, some of them branching across and going to each of the battered trailers.

"What do you think?" Carl asked.

"Looks like a workers' camp."

"I've seen something like this used as a science lab," Carl said.

"Yeah?"

"Last year they had an archaeological dig on at the outskirts of town. They brought in three big trailers: one as sleeping quarters, the others as makeshift labs. They had microscopes and all kinds of equipment inside it." He turned to Jackson. "It was kind of cool."

Jackson wiped away a bead of sweat trickling down his face. It seemed to be getting warmer inside the cavern.

He straightened, checking again to make sure there weren't any luminous spheres floating nearby or dropping from the roof of the cavern. One positive thing, Jackson thought, is that they might be more protected inside the trailer.

"Ready?" he turned to say to Carl.

Carl nodded. "I'll be right behind you."

Jackson grinned. "That's comforting."

Carl tapped Jackson on the arm. "Hey, look at that. There's a fog creeping in. You know what that means?"

"That there has to be an opening to the outside," Jackson replied.

Carl let out a breath. "Yeah, that's kind of good to know."

Jackson watched a tendril of fog wind and creep its way along a ditch. He motioned to Carl. "Come on, let's check out the trailers."

As Jackson walked towards the nearest trailer, he saw a huge gaping hole in the front wall. "Whoa. There's some major damage in this one."

Carl drew up beside him. "Wonder if something happened in there?"

"I don't know."

Carl waved vaguely at the front of the trailer. "Look at it. The metal's been forced outward."

"Yeah."

"There must have been an explosion in there," Carl said.

"Let's take a look inside. We'll go slow and easy," Jackson said.

Jackson pulled out his flashlight and thumbed it on, directing it towards the gaping hole. It was pitch black inside—so dark it seemed to gobble up his light beam.

He swallowed and took a tentative step forward, his heart pounding in his chest.

"Easy," Carl said in a quiet voice. He saw a length of pipe lying on the ground and picked it up.

Jackson paused to look at him.

"In case of trouble," Carl whispered.

Jackson nodded. It was a good idea. He picked one up as well.

He approached the opening tentatively, Carl right behind him.

Jackson played his light over the torn metal along the hole. It was shredded, as if someone had been at work with a giant can opener.

The hole had to be at least a couple of meters in width, wide enough to drive a small car through.

"Ready?" Jackson said.

Carl took a deep breath and exhaled. "Whenever you are."

Pipe held protectively in front of him, Jackson stepped into the black void.

CHAPTER 37

Jackson felt like he was walking into an ancient tomb. His light beam flitted past dust motes floating in the air and illuminated old battered tables lining the far wall.

"I wonder how long this stuff has been here," Carl said.

"A long time, from the looks of it," Jackson said.

Jackson took a couple of deep breaths and stepped over piles of rotting wood and bits of piping. Other than their breathing, it was deathly quiet.

"What's that stench?" Carl asked.

Jackson shook his head. "I don't know." He swung his light in an arc as he looked around. It smelled like meat that had gone seriously bad.

To his left, the flashlight beam played across a long line of environmental suits. Jackson figured there had to be at least fifty or sixty of them.

"Looks like we're in their dressing room," Carl said, looking around. "They've got enough stuff in here to clothe a small army."

"Yeah," Jackson replied, playing his light along the long line of suits. They were all hanging on pegs in the wall, and looked like they varied in sizes.

At one end of the sidewall where they'd entered, at least a dozen suits had been simply thrown into a heap.

"Looks like the same suits those guys are wearing," Carl said. "And look at that, there're dozens of tanks along the far wall."

Jackson slowly moved down to the opposite end of the room, his light illuminating tanks, helmets, gloves, and boots.

"Quite the collection of gear," Carl said. He turned and looked back towards the hole they'd come through.

"What's up?" Jackson said, looking back as well.

"Just making sure one of those glowing balls isn't floating up behind us."

Jackson ran a sleeve over his face, wiping away sweat. "Good idea. Keep it up."

Carl held up his length of pipe. "At least we have something to use for protection, and if we—" He left the thought unfinished.

Jackson turned to look at him. "What is it?"

Carl nodded in the direction of the torn away opening. "It looks like blood smeared over the torn metal."

Jackson took a walk back and examined it closely. "I think you're right. One of those guys must have caught his suit on the sharp edge and cut himself."

"Hey, there're a lot of specimen jars and stuff over here," Carl said. "Come here and check it out."

"Yeah?"

"They've got rock samples," Carl said, rummaging through one of the boxes. "It looks like some old prospector was looking for gold or silver." He pulled one out. "Huh, looks like silver." He stuffed it into a pocket. "I'll get it checked out when we get home."

He continued along the table, looking at the rest of the stuff.

"What are you looking for?" Jackson said.

"Just looking to see if they left any old Viking artifacts lying about," Carl said.

Jackson swept his light further along the wall of the trailer, illuminating a line of huge aquariums set end to end.

"You've got to be kidding," Carl said. "They kept fish in here?"

"I don't know. Maybe they grew their food in there," Jackson said.

Carl put down the box of rock samples he was checking out and walked towards the huge glass tanks. These things are filthy. You can't see anything inside," he said, sweeping his light over the glass.

He leaned his length of pipe against the supporting table and tried rubbing the front of the tank. "It looks all fogged up," Carl said.

Jackson came over and added his light to Carl's. He bent over and tried to see inside, but it was impossible. He rubbed a hand over the glass, but it didn't help.

"Maybe it's fogged on the inside," Carl said. He stepped closer to the coffin-sized glass tank and tried to get his hand inside to wipe down the glass.

"I don't know if you should be doing that."

"Huh, that's weird. The top is locked down so you *can't* get inside," Carl said.

"There must be a reason for it," Jackson said. He looked inside the tank and saw ripples of white drifting past like miniature clouds. "You know what? The glass isn't fogged. I think there's some kind of gas in there."

"Gas? What kind of gas?"

"Haven't got a clue," Jackson said. "It could be poisonous if they've got a locked lid on it."

Carl was just straightening up when he said, "Hey, wait a minute. I think I saw something moving in there."

Jackson clapped him on the shoulder, and grinned. "Nice one. You almost had me there for a minute."

Carl staggered back from the tank, pointing to something. "Look!"

"Not sure. I thought I saw a flicker of movement in there."

"Seriously?"

"Yes, I'm serious," Carl said, taking another step back. "You take a closer look."

"Okay." Jackson bent over, peered into the tank, searching. "I don't see anything."

"Well, I sure did!" Carl's voice was tremulous. He motioned to the tank. "What if that's the atmosphere from another planet? And the thing that's in there can only survive in that... that gas."

"I guess that's possible," Jackson said, tapping on the glass pane with a knuckle.

As Jackson peered into the tank, something long and whip-like slithered along the side of the glass like a giant worm.

Jackson staggered backwards, almost falling. "Jeez. Did... did you see that?"

"I told you something was alive in there!" Carl said.

Jackson caught his breath and pulled his flashlight out. Taking a step closer, he shined the light over the glass tank and saw furtive movement.

A moment later, a yellow reptilian eye slid into view and glared out at them. More whip-like shapes flowed into view, coiling and uncoiling like snakes.

CHAPTER 38

"What *is* that thing?" Carl asked.

Jackson shook his head. "I don't know. It looks like a nest of snakes." He watched the slick black shapes slide and caress the glass, hidden for the most part by a dense layer of gas or cloud behind the glass.

The thing was repulsive, Jackson thought, as the tentacles left a thick, oozing fluid on the glass tank.

Jackson's face contorted with disgust. "I don't think it's anything from this planet."

He watched a slug-like shape press up against the glass, whip-like tentacles swirling about it like the mythical hair of Medusa.

A yellow reptilian eye gazed out at them with the cold, detached regard of a shark looking for its next meal.

It looked like a predator.

"Jeez," Carl said, shuffling backwards a step. "It's gross!"

"No argument there," Jackson said. "I wonder who put it in there, and why?"

Carl shivered. "I wouldn't want that thing crawling over me in the middle of the night."

Jackson nodded.

Carl eyed the creature in the tank. "You don't think it can read minds, do you?"

"I hope not. It would see the things I'd like to do with it that aren't nice," Jackson said.

Carl flashed his flashlight beam directly at its eye and saw it retreat back behind the cover of the fog. "Huh. So it doesn't like the light."

"That's good to know," Jackson said. He looked at its furtive movement and then said, "You know what? I think it's a thing that comes from inside one of those spheres."

Carl looked at him. "Are you serious?"

"Yeah. And maybe those guys in the environmental suits captured one or two of them and were trying to study it."

"Whatever for?" Carl asked, shaking his head in disbelief.

Jackson shrugged. "Who knows, maybe some kind research. Maybe those guys in the suits are scientists and they're trying to find out what those things are."

"Yeah, maybe," Carl said, staring at the tank. "Maybe that's why they wear those environmental suits—for protection against those things."

"Yeah, maybe." Jackson flashed his flashlight beam at the aquarium again. "I wonder who those guys in the suits are. Are they human or some beings from another world?"

"And what that pulsating blue ball is? Unless... unless it's some kind of ship that brought those *things* here."

Carl nodded again. "If that's the case, how did they get those creatures out of that protective shell?"

"There's got to be a weakness there somewhere," Jackson said.

Jackson swept his flashlight beam across the rest of the room. He could see a partially shattered tank on another table, with large chunks of glass scattered across the floor.

"It looks like one of them got out!"

Carl looked around frantically, his flashlight beam dancing over the floor, walls and ceiling. "It could still be inside here."

"I don't think so," Jackson said, his light licking over a section of the floor. It illuminated a trail across the dusty floor from the shattered tank to the gaping hole in the front wall. "It looks like it must have broken out of the tank and crawled across the floor."

Carl let out a sigh. "That's good." He swung his light back to the tank, flicking over the creature that had sucked itself onto the front glass of the aquarium. "You don't suppose they were trying to breed those things, do you?"

"I don't think so. Not with the way they were attacking those guys in the suits. I wouldn't be surprised if they were trying to find out what they were, and how to get rid of them," Jackson said.

Carl shook his head. "I can't imagine anyone wanting to deal with those creatures in—"

"Turn off your light!" Jackson snapped.

"What?"

"Turn it off! We've got company," Jackson said, thumbing his flashlight off.

"Where?" Carl asked.

Jackson motioned to where they'd come in. "I saw a light flickering outside."

Carl whirled about to face the entrance. "Crap, what do we do?"

Jackson stared at the hole and saw lights again. "We better find a place to hide." He looked around. "Get over by those hanging suits. That's the best place."

"What about making a run for it?" Carl said.

Just then a bright light flared across the front of the hut, probing in through the hole in the front and licking across the floor.

"Forget it," Jackson whispered, his heart pounding in his chest. "It's too late now."

Jackson motioned to the far right corner of the room, the furthest spot away from the opening. "Over there!"

They rushed across the trailer, pushing their way past hanging environmental suits, and hunkered down behind a storage box. They were scrunched together behind the waist-high box, peering over the top. All they could do was wait.

From here, Jackson could see they had an excellent view of the entire room.

As the light brightened through the gaping hole, the environmental suits' slowed swinging came to a stop. There was a loud *thump* as a suited figure ducked low and scrambled in under the torn wall panel.

Jackson held his breath as a helmet light licked over the dust-covered floor, showing pieces of broken glass and electrical cables.

Another set of heavy boots clumped onto the floor as another figure entered.

Jackson held his breath as they walked to the middle of the room and paused there for a long moment. One figure motioned to the surviving glass tanks, and they slowly headed towards them.

Jackson slid sideways to watch what they were doing.

He could see there was a lot of animated gesturing between the two. One figure broke away from the other, bent over in front of a tank, and began rapping on the front of the glass.

The reaction from inside the tank was immediate. A huge bulbous shape lunged out of the fog and thumped up against the glass with a loud *thud*. Whip-like tentacles whirled about, slithering over the surface of the glass as it attempted to get out.

The closest figure jumped back, almost tripping and falling over a coil of cable lying on the floor.

They stood staring at the thing pressed up against the glass, watching the tentacles coil and slither over the inside of the tank.

Jackson could see it all, especially when an eyelid opened and a single eye glared out at the pair.

After a couple of minutes, the pair thumped their way out of the hut and left.

Jackson and Carl waited a full five minutes without moving or talking before Carl whispered, "Do you think they're gone?"

"Yeah, looks like it," Jackson said.

"Good," Carl said, trying to get to his feet, "because I'm getting a cramp in my leg." He stood up, partially hidden behind a pair of environmental suits that swayed back and forth.

Jackson nudged Carl with his arm. "I'm going to make sure they're gone." He slid out from the line of dangling suits, pausing for a long minute and staring out through the hole in the wall of the building.

"Anything?" Carl hissed to him.

"Not yet," Jackson whispered, trying not to clear his throat. Why now, of all times, did he have to get a tickle there?

He glanced at the tank and saw that he was being watched by that thing in the tank. *Ugly creature*, he thought.

Finally, he took a deep breath and stepped out from the protective cover of the hanging suits, carefully weaving his way around all the stuff littering the floor of the hut. The last thing he wanted to do was trip over something and make a racket.

Jackson peered around the torn edge of the hole and surveyed the cavern floor. As his eyes adjusted to the darkness, he could start to make out dim shapes.

There were pipes and cables everywhere and, in other places, what looked like posts rearing up into the darkness. At least he couldn't see any other lights.

Turning around, Jackson called in a soft voice, "Okay, you can come out now. It looks like they've gone."

Carl pushed his way out from behind the environmental suits and waved a hand in the air. "What a stink!"

Jackson checked the cavern again. It looked like it was safe to leave.

"Hey, wait a minute," Carl said from behind him.

Jackson turned around and noticed that Carl was checking something on one of the suits.

"You'd better come take a look at this," Carl said.

Jackson thumbed on his flashlight and headed back to where Carl was. "What's the matter? Can't you find your size?"

"Very funny," Carl said. He held up the sleeve. "Check this out."

Jackson shined his light over the arm of one of the environmental suits. Some kind of a ceramic badge sewn into the sleeve. "Yeah… so?"

"Do you know what this is?" Carl asked.

Jackson shrugged. "I haven't got a clue."

"It's a radiation detector," Carl said.

Jackson stepped closer. "Are you sure?"

Carl nodded. "My dad's got a couple stored in the basement. They register exposure to radiation. These badges register how much radiation you've been exposed to."

"You mean—"

Carl nodded. "There's got to be a radioactive source down here. That's why those guys are all wearing these suits."

Jackson got hold of the sleeve and turned it so he could examine it.

"You see this?" Carl said, pointing to a scale on the badge. "If it gets up into the red range, you're in trouble. It means you've had long-term exposure to radiation and are at the danger level."

Jackson shook his head and checked out a couple of other suits. "These all show levels in the safe range. How can that be possible? If they've been stored in this hut for months, you'd think they'd show higher levels."

Thinking, Carl ran a hand over the back of his neck and then looked around the interior of the hut. "I bet this building is lined with lead."

"What"?

Carl held up a hand to explain. "I remember finding out that lead blocks out any radioactivity."

"Who told you that? Your Science teacher?" Jackson asked.

Carl shook his head. "No, my dentist. Anytime they give you an x-ray they'll put a lead apron on you and run from the room."

"That's right," Jackson said. Radiation, he thought. That's why everyone was wearing those suits. He looked at Carl. "If that's the case, what's the source down here?"

"I bet it's that blue globe down here," Carl said. "Whatever it is, I bet it's the source of the radioactivity."

"So we should find a suit that fits," Jackson said, "before we head back out to the cavern."

Carl nodded. "That's probably not a bad idea."

Jackson smiled. "Yeah, and then we will look just like one of them."

CHAPTER 39

"It's tight, but it'll do," Jackson said, stretching the suit sleeve down over his wrist. He pulled one of the gloves on and pulled the end up over the sleeve. There was no way he wanted any skin showing.

They were now completely suited up, except for helmets.

Carl was examining his, turning it over in his hands to peer inside. "Hey, it looks like there's some kind of communication system inside."

"What do you mean?" Jackson asked, coming over.

Carl pointed inside. "See that? There's a mini microphone in here. And up here, there're a couple of small speakers."

"So every member of that group can communicate with each other," Jackson said.

"You've got it."

Jackson stared down into helmet. "I wonder if we should try it. See if we can understand anything."

Carl nodded. "Well, if we turn the system on, we should be able to hear them. It also means that they would be able to hear us."

"Oh, that's right," Jackson said.

"So we switch the system on and hear what they have to say, but don't say anything to give ourselves away," Carl said.

"Good idea." Jackson looked at the line of air tanks at the back wall. "If we go out into the cavern we should use the air tanks as well."

"Probably a good idea," Carl said. "Who knows how much radioactivity there is on some of the dust down here."

"Exactly," Jackson said. "The other perk is that we would look like one of them."

"And if they try to communicate with us?"

Jackson looked at him. "Then we run."

"Only thing is, in one of these suits we'll probably be moving a lot slower," Carl said.

"Yeah," Jackson said. "And we've still got those spheres to worry about."

"Well, I'm going to keep my trusty pipe nearby," Carl said. "It looks like it's what those other guys are using."

"I wonder just who those other guys are?"

"Well, maybe if we can tune in to their conversations, we can find out"

"Let's do it," Jackson said. "Just remember: no talking."

"Got it," Carl said.

They took their helmets and flicked the systems on. Jackson had to force his helmet down over his ears. Then he listened.

There was silence and only the faintest hiss of static.

He turned to Carl and shrugged.

Carl slipped his helmet onto his head and lifted the tinted faceplate.

Jackson pushed his glass faceplate up as well.

While they waited for any sounds, Jackson found a small switch to the right side of his helmet and flicked it on. Immediately, a small pulse of light winked on. As he turned, Jackson could see the powerful light melt away the darkness.

Perfect. It also left his hands free, as he hefted the length of pipe he was carrying. He nodded approvingly.

Carl tucked his pipe under his arm and gave Jackson a thumbs up.

They shuffled their way through the torn hole in the front wall and clomped out onto the cavern floor. Dust plumed into the air.

Outside, Carl motioned to the left where five large pinnacles of stone climbed high into the sky.

Jackson nodded in response. It looked like the perfect place to hide for a while. He started towards them, his helmet beam probing the earthen ground.

They stepped over trenches that seemed to run everywhere, criss-crossing the cavern floor like a checkerboard. Most were filled with cables and lengths of pipe—for what reason he couldn't fathom—and he had to keep a sharp eye out not to fall into one.

The going was slow with all the added weight, and the air from the tank had a stale, metallic taste.

When they finally reached the group of pillars, Jackson reached up and switched off his light. Carl saw what he had done, nodded approvingly, and turned off his own helmet light. No use being too visible.

In the darkness, Carl was pretty well invisible.

There was a sudden burst of static echoing through his helmet, and he could hear a distant, garbled voice. He cocked his head to listen.

"*They're coming back. Looks like maybe eight or nine of them. They're bigger, much bigger than we've ever seen before!*"

A second voice crackled into their helmets.

"*All right, get into a defensive formation! I'll be there as soon as I can. And get off the radio—you know how those things hone in on our transmissions!*"

"*Got it.*"

The line went dead, and Jackson hurriedly switched off his intercom and lifted his visor up.

"Did you hear that?" Jackson asked. He saw Carl fumble his intercom switch off and lift his faceplate, too. "They're human. I bet they're scientists!"

"Yeah," Carl said. He looked at the open cavern above them. "And he said those things should be coming soon."

"I know," Jackson said, checking the cavern roof.

"What was it he also said, that those things were bigger than before?"

"Something like that," Jackson said. "I just wonder how *big* is big?" He continued his search, the blue pulse of the giant sphere fainter here, barely colouring the walls of the cavern. "Some of the ones—"

Carl stepped in front of him and motioned to the left. "I think we've got incoming!"

Jackson followed Carl's outstretched arm and saw a group of luminous spheres approaching, and they were moving fast. "I think we'd better get out of sight."

Carl watched them for a minute. "I think behind one of those pinnacles."

"Let's move then!"

CHAPTER 40

Jackson watched them approach from the darkness. He was sure he could hear a faint hum, like the buzz of a distant swarm of bees. He cocked his head and said to Carl, "Do you hear that?"

"If you're talking about a high-pitched hum, I sure do," Carl said. He was scrunched down at the base of one of the rock pinnacles, peeking around one edge at the oncoming spheres.

Jackson took a quick look and ducked back down. "I count at least a dozen of them."

Carl peered over the edge of a slab of rock. "Where do you think they're heading?"

"Probably towards that pulsating sphere. I have a feeling that's where those men are working. I just wish I knew what they were up to."

"Well, we know they're human," Carl said. "So I can think of a couple of reasons."

"Yeah?"

Carl nodded. "I think they could be some kind of research team that's trying to make first contact, or they're interested in what I think is their ship."

"That's what I was thinking, as well," Jackson said. "Those spheres are more like pit bulls guarding the ship. Of course there's another possibility."

"Okay."

"They're military and they're trying to get hold of alien technology," Jackson said.

"I never thought of that, but yeah, that's a possibility as well," Carl said. "Kind of like the Area 51 thing."

"What do you mean?"

Carl glanced over the rock again and then motioned Jackson to be quiet.

They waited as a swarm of luminous spheres sped past overhead in the direction of the huge blue, pulsating sphere.

When they had passed, Carl continued.

"Apparently after an alien saucer crash landed in Area 51, the military got hold of the technology and used it in their Stealth Aircraft," Carl said.

"Are you sure? I've never heard anything about that."

"You must be the only guy in the world who hasn't heard about that technology. The military got hold of it and used it," Carl said.

Jackson got down into a kneeling position and gazed at the darkness. "Come on, it looks like they're gone. Let's keep moving. We're too much in the open."

"All right," Carl said, taking a quick look and then getting to his feet.

They waited for a moment and then got started.

Crouching low, they followed a shallow trench with more scattered lengths of piping and cable along the bottom. They passed one area where a shovel had been left abandoned, sticking into the side of a mound of dirt.

Carl turned towards him. "What's with all the piping and ditches?"

Jackson shrugged. "I haven't got a clue. They seem to be everywhere down here. Maybe they're trying to install some hot tubs."

"Yeah, right."

They skirted around a series of concrete pillars that had been planted into the ground like posts for a jetty.

Suddenly, Carl stopped and held up his hand.

Jackson drew up beside Carl, looking around. "What is it?"

Carl turned his head and in a low voice said, "There's a body lying in the ditch up ahead."

"What? Are you sure?"

Carl pointed. "There, on the right side of the ditch. I can see part of a helmet."

Jackson squinted into the gloom, unsure.

They continued on.

After a few more steps, Jackson said, "Maybe we should turn on a light."

"Are you serious?" Carl asked.

"Not a helmet light, but a shielded flashlight."

"One of those spheres might see us," Carl said.

Jackson nodded. "Okay, just shield the lens with your hand. There's something wrong here."

"What do you mean?" Carl whispered. "Maybe the guy just had an accident."

"Maybe, but I've got a funny feeling about it," Jackson said.

"You go ahead, then," Carl said.

"Okay." Jackson pulled his flashlight out and, shielding it, played it ahead of them, illuminating the ditch with the partially exposed environmental suit draped along the side.

It was lying face down.

Weird, Jackson thought. *Why would they leave one of their own lying out here?*

He could see the air tank on the back reflecting their flashlight beam with a dull sheen. There was something wrong with the suit, but he couldn't place what.

They took a tentative step forward. Jackson played his light up and down its length as they drew alongside it. It looked like a scarecrow with the stuffing pulled out; it had a deflated look.

Carl drew up next to Jackson. "This doesn't look right."

Jackson came abreast of the still suit and used the pipe he was carrying to prod it.

There wasn't any movement.

"Try it again," Carl said.

He stretched out and prodded again. "Feels weird—like the suit is filled with putty."

Carl gazed at the motionless suit. "Maybe we should just move on."

"What if there's someone injured in there?" Jackson said. He thought about it for a moment. "Let's roll it over."

"Are you serious?" Carl said, giving him a pained look.

"Yeah, we've got to check it," Jackson said.

Carl let out a breath. "Okay."

Carl added his length of pipe to Jackson's. Working together, they were able to flip the suit onto its back.

"There's definitely something moving inside," Jackson said.

There was an exhalation of nasty smelling air from the partially open faceplate.

"Jeez, that's gross," Carl said, holding a hand over his mouth and nose

"Yeah," Jackson said, moving back.

"Let's lift the faceplate all the way," Carl said.

"Why?"

"Well, to make sure he's not dead, of course," Carl said.

As Jackson used the end of his length of pipe to lift the faceplate entirely open, he heard Carl gasp in shock.

CHAPTER 41

The face was grey—a sickly shade of grey, like the colour of a dead fish. But there was something else.

It was the stench of something that had gone seriously bad. It looked shrunken and wrinkled, like one of those Egyptian mummies that had had the outer wrappings peeled away.

"That's disgusting!" Carl said, grimacing and turning away.

"The skin looks like leather," Jackson said.

Carl nodded, "It does look like one of those mummies—all shrivelled up like the heat sucked away all the moisture."

"Nasty. I wonder what happened." Jackson said.

Carl stared at the suit for a while. "You'd think some of his buddies would come looking for him, to try and see what'd happened to him."

Jackson shrugged. "Maybe they've been so busy and on the run they haven't had a chance."

"Yeah, I guess that's possible."

"It's hard to tell how long he's been lying there," Jackson said. He played his light over the rest of the sagging suit.

"Well, we're going to have to—" Carl pointed to the suit. "Hey, did you see that?"

"What?"

"The suit! I thought I saw it move," Carl said.

"Are you serious?" Jackson looked at Carl, trying to tell if he was joking. When he saw Carl's stricken face, he knew he wasn't. He let his flashlight beam lick over the body once more. "I don't see any movement."

"I'm telling you, I saw the suit move!" Carl said.

"Okay, okay," Jackson said, holding his hands up defensively. "Maybe it was just the lights casting weird shadows."

Carl shook his head. "No, it wasn't shadows. It was movement."

"All right, let's take another look," Jackson said. He swept his light along the length of the environmental suit. "You know, sometimes—"

"There!" Carl said, pointing to the prone body. "See it?"

Jackson swept his light back down the suit. He *had* seen something. Probably just gases shifting within the suit, he figured. He played his light over the stomach area, Carl's light beam tagging along, as well. Jackson saw a faint flicker of movement, the suit bulging up slightly, and then moving towards the chest. It had to be gas. What else could it be?

There was a sudden flurry of movement within the suit, and the bulge moved up towards the helmet.

"You see it?" Carl said in a raspy voice.

"Yeah," Jackson croaked. His voice didn't even sound like it was his.

They both took a step back from the body. The movement stopped abruptly near the neck, leaving a small ball shaped mound protruding.

Jackson nervously tried to clear his throat. His mouth felt bone-dry.

The movement began again, the lump worming its way around the neck. He wondered if a rat had somehow gotten inside, but remembered nothing survived out here.

For a long moment, nothing happened. Then, a thin, snake-like shape wormed its way through the open faceplate.

A heartbeat later, two more tentacles slithered out and secured themselves to the outer rim of the faceplate.

"Get back!" Carl motioned. His voice was high-pitched and coarse.

Jackson felt rooted to the spot, his legs like putty.

"Move Jackson!" Carl said, nudging him with an elbow.

Jackson managed a step back as two more tentacles slithered out of the helmet, reaching up as if to savour the outside air. They curled and uncurled, coming down to fasten on the top of the helmet.

A bulbous shape—like a fat slug—squeezed out through the faceplate and lingered there for a moment, as if the movement had been strenuous. The creature oozed its way down the side of the helmet, whip-like tentacles reaching out, fastening onto something and dragging the body forward.

It looked like some nightmarish black squid that lived on land.

"Wha… what in the world is that?" Carl croaked.

Nothing of this world, Jackson thought. *Nothing at all.*

The thing left a black, slug-like trail behind it, as it slid down the helmet. Now Jackson knew what must have happened.

This had to be the thing in the aquarium, the same thing that somehow was able to travel within those luminous spheres.

Jackson was horrified and yet mesmerized as the creature slowly worked its way across the arm. It came to a stop and a single, yellowed eye opened and regarded them with apparent malice.

"Move back, Jackson," Carl murmured, waving a hand.

The thing saw Carl's motion and froze.

Jackson slowly moved back, watching the creature's body pulsate and quiver. He didn't know why, but he thought the thing was readying itself for something. Slowly and carefully, Jackson brought the pointed end of the pipe up defensively. From the corner of his eye, he saw Carl do the same. Now if they could back away from the thing…

Without warning, the creature sprang from the helmet, launching itself into the air.

CHAPTER 42

Jackson swung his pipe to the left as the creature flew through the air. He steadied it as the thing impaled itself on the sharp end. It squealed shrilly and flailed about, wriggling, clawing, and trying to pull itself off the pipe. The main body spasmed, leaking droplets of thick, black ooze to the ground.

Inverting the pipe, Jackson jammed the sharpened end into the ground. The creature quivered a bit more and finally went still.

"Holy crap!" Carl said, clutching a hand to his chest and breathing hard. "I can't believe you did that. You got it in mid-air."

Jackson fought to catch his breath, as well, his heart hammering in his chest. "Just lucky."

"I don't know about that, but thanks," Carl said. "That thing was coming right at me."

"Give me a hand to push that thing off," Jackson said.

"Right."

They were working at getting the dead creature off of the pipe when a brilliant burst of sun-bright light engulfed them. Jackson turned slowly, half expecting a huge luminous ball to be hovering behind them in response to the creature's death cry.

Instead, three shadowy figures stood there motionless, their helmet lights directed towards them.

Carl half-turned toward Jackson and murmured, "I don't like the looks of this."

"No, but they look like they want to talk to us." Jackson looked at the trio and saw one motioning for them to come up.

"I guess we're going to find out what they want," Carl said.

Jackson nodded, noticing that two of the figures appeared to be holding some kind of weapon.

"Do you think we should try and make a run for it?" Carl asked.

"I don't think so," Jackson said. "They're armed, and I don't want to take any chances."

Carl sighed. "Okay."

Jackson pulled his pipe from the ground, shaking off the creature they'd impaled. It flopped to the ground and collapsed onto itself, like a jellyfish on a beach.

The tallest one flipped his faceplate up and said, "Was gibt?"

Carl stared at him blankly. "Huh?"

Jackson turned towards Carl. "I think it's German." He tried to look at the man's face, but it was hidden in shadow.

The man stepped forward. "Sprechen zie Deutsch?"

Jackson flipped up his faceplate. "I'm sorry, no."

The man asked, "English?"

Jackson nodded. "Yes."

He motioned to himself. "My name is Hans, and we're wondering who you are and why you're here?"

Jackson swallowed, glancing at the armed men on either side of Hans. "My name's Jackson and this is my friend Carl."

He swallowed again to moisten his throat. "We're explorers looking for Viking artifacts."

Hans shifted position. "Viking artifacts? Are you serious?"

"Yes," Jackson said. "Carl already found several Viking coins some months back by the river. They're currently in the Boswell City Museum."

A look of disbelief crossed the bearded man's face. He looked at Carl. "Is that true?"

Carl nodded. "Yes. They've been dated to the 12th century by one of the historians at the museum.

"You were very lucky," he said. "How did you find them?"

Carl made a sweeping motion with his pipe. "I used a metal detector."

Hans nodded appreciatively. "Very good."

He looked down the still form of one of their men and then at the motionless creature by the ditch.

"We should get to cover quickly. We're too exposed out here." He gestured to the still form of the squid on the ground. "When one of them is hurt or killed, the others come to the attack."

"They're deadly," one of the other men said.

"Lars has already killed one today," Hans said, looking skyward, "so we can't afford to be in the open for too long." He waved an arm. "Come on, we'd better get back to the base before they come again. They always become active at this time of day."

As they hurried along a narrow corridor, Hans said, "Why do you think there could be Viking artifacts out here?"

"We found some historic records and journals that showed there may have been a Viking tower on the summit of this hill," Jackson said.

"Seriously?" Hans asked. "I've never heard of that."

"The historic records show a drawing of a partial tower several hundred years ago," Jackson said. "Apparently there may have been an event in the past that devastated the area and knocked down what was left of the tower."

"Huh. Dieter will be interested to hear what you have to say," Hans said.

"Dieter?" Carl said.

"He's in charge," Hans said.

Jackson and Carl fell behind Hans, with the other two men following behind them. There wasn't any way they would be able to leave.

Carl glanced at the men behind them and leaned towards Jackson. "I don't like this. I don't like it at all."

"I know," Jackson murmured. "There's not much we can do about it right now."

They weaved around tall pinnacles of rock and crossed numerous ditches before they stopped for a break.

Jackson came up to Hans. "Why are you and your men here? Research?"

Hans looked at him for a minute. "Salvage."

"Salvage?"

"That's what we do," Hans said. "We find things that can be used for salvage and sell them."

"Really?" Carl said. "What's down here that you can salvage?"

"The ship, of course," Hans said.

"The ship?" Jackson asked.

"It's a massive blue sphere that's been stranded here for a very long time," Hans said.

"So that *is* a ship?" Carl said. "What about those spheres we see everywhere?"

"We're not sure," Hans said. "We know they are not of this world. We also found out they breathe nitrogen."

"Are you sure?" Jackson asked.

Hans nodded. "We captured three of those creatures and kept them in glass tanks in one of the huts."

"We saw them," Carl said.

"One escaped, but we were able to determine what they breathed and what they lived on."

"You sound like you're also scientists?" Carl asked.

Hans grinned. "Not quite. We do have a few men of science, but for the most part, our group is what you would call entrepreneurs. We collect items, and we sell them. To whomever can pay the most."

"To businesses?" Carl asked.

Hans smiled. "Sometimes. Sometimes to countries. We can always find a buyer for technology."

"Yeah, but then—"

Hans held up a hand. "Look, Dieter will explain everything to you."

"Okay," Jackson said.

Hans motioned to a battered trailer at the bottom of a wide ravine, partially dug into the side of the cavern wall.

"That's it? Your base of operations?" Carl asked incredulously. He shook his head in disbelief.

Hans shrugged. "It doesn't look like much, but it does the job. It also looks bad because we've been under attack for a while."

"From the spheres?" Carl said.

"Yes," Hans said. "But there's also something else here that we haven't seen yet." He looked at them for a moment. "It's more of a sense that something is watching us."

As they walked towards the trailer, Jackson could see that the metal sides had been battered and buckled in. It looked like someone had taken a giant hammer and smashed in the sides.

"Just what are these *spheres*?"

Hans shrugged. "We're not sure. They are the carriers. Inside is what we call the *riders*. You referred to them as squid, which is quite apt."

"Riders? Why do you call them that?" Carl asked.

"It's what they do," Hans said.

"What do you mean?" Jackson asked. "I don't understand."

Hans looked at Jackson for a moment. "Those spheres try to deliver the creature inside it to a person's back. When it is able to secure itself to a person, it takes over all their nervous system functions and controls them."

Jackson felt his jaw tighten. "They control a person?"

Hans nodded. "We have lost many men that way. Somehow, they are controlled to do work. We think there is some kind of hive consciousness, but we are not sure what controls it."

"That's gross," Jackson said.

"That is what you found in that suit—one of the riders. Once they secure themselves to a host, they are slaves to their master's bidding. We're not sure what the master is, though."

Carl eyed the compound. "So how are you going to stop those things from coming after you? From the looks of it, they've almost destroyed the place."

Hans smiled grimly. "We have some defensive measures in place now. We had some trouble at the beginning when we first arrived, but things are working out now."

"You mean you've got something that stops them?" Jackson said.

Hans nodded. "That's right. We found a defensive item in the ship. It's a protective shield."

"A protective shield?" Carl repeated.

Hans smiled. "That's right. A force shield we've been able to adapt for use."

"Wait a minute. How did you find this ship in the first place?" Jackson asked.

"We traced it on a radiation spike," Hans said.

"A radiation spike? What's that?" Carl said.

Hans paused. "We have a satellite in orbit that detects any kind of weird signatures or anomalies. A few months back, we picked up a burst of radiation that occurred over regular intervals. When we traced it down, we found the radiation spike came from this hill. We were able to find that the spike occurred every eight days, but for a duration of only one hour."

"Every eight days?" Carl said.

"That's right," Hans nodded. "We realized then that we had some kind of artificial source."

"So what is it? Some kind of beacon?" Jackson said.

"Possibly," Hans said. "It could be a homing device for a rescue ship—"

"—you mean like a SOS?"

"Yes, a distress signal."

"I wonder how long this has been going on." Jackson said.

Hans shrugged. "Maybe centuries, or perhaps a thousand years. Who knows?"

Carl shook his head. "Huh. That's not so far-fetched."

"Oh?" Hans said. "Why do you say that?"

"Before we knew how to get out here, we researched some of the town's historic records," Carl said. "In them we discovered that the Vikings may have witnessed something coming down on the wastelands."

Hans shook his head. "Yes, you mentioned the Vikings were here, but why?"

"Gold," Jackson said. "Large deposits of it."

"I see," Hans said, nodding in understanding.

"We also found stone columns on the wastelands with what looks like Viking runes carved into them," Jackson said.

"And as I was saying, the Viking coins I found were dated back to the 12th century."

"Interesting," Hans said, leaning back against the wall. "Nearly a thousand years ago."

"They may have had a tower or some kind of fortification on the summit," Jackson said, "but some kind of catastrophe may have knocked it down. We thought it might have been a meteorite impact."

"Or the impact of some kind of ship crash landing," Hans said, nodding. "That's very interesting." He motioned to the trailer. "Come on. Let us get inside. We have been out in the open for too long already."

CHAPTER 43

An imposing figure in a sleek, black environmental suit limped out to meet them at the front of the trailer. He waved an arm at them. "Come on, hurry! They're coming."

Jackson heard the urgency in the man's voice and turned to look behind them. At the darkened end of the cavern, he could see a number of luminous globes approaching en masse. It looked like there were dozens of them.

"Let's move it!" he said to Carl.

They hurried towards the trailer, hurdling pinnacles of rocks that jutted up from the cavern floor like shark's teeth. Finally, they scrambled up a flight of wooden stairs that led to the trailer door.

"They'll be here in a minute!" Dieter shouted. "Move it!"

They paused when they got to the landing, and Jackson paused to glance back. He saw even more luminous spheres emerging from the darkness. There had to hundreds by now.

As soon as they were inside, Dieter charged in, slammed the door shut, and locked it.

He turned and yelled, "Turn on the field generator!"

Jackson ran to the front window and peered past a set of inset steel bars. He could see dozens of luminous spheres rushing towards them. They looked like giant snowballs flitting through the air. The variety of sizes was amazing—from the size of a baseball to the size of a washing machine.

The massive throb of a powerful generator kicked in and reverberated through the trailer, shaking the trailer floorboards violently.

"Hey!" Carl cried out, grabbing hold of the window frame to keep from falling.

Dieter limped past them, clomping to a branch in the hallway and yelled, "And keep it at maximum strength!"

When Dieter returned to the front door, he gazed past the dirt-smudged window and nodded in satisfaction. "That should hold them."

Dieter turned and studied them for a long moment and then pointed a bony finger at Jackson. "You look very familiar."

"Me?" Jackson asked.

Dieter nodded. "Yeah. I can't place where, but I've seen you before."

Jackson shook his head. "That's impossible. We just moved to this area."

Dieter stared at him and Jackson could see him trying figure out where he knew him from. "No doubt about it. Your face is familiar."

Jackson shook his head. "I don't know how."

Dieter said, "It'll come to me sooner or later." He hesitated. "I never forget a face." "Why is that thing so noisy?" Carl said, looking towards the rear of the trailer. "It sounds like a jet engine ready for take-off."

"Nothing to worry about," Dieter said, turning to face Carl. "That's just the field generator getting the shield up to full strength."

Jackson turned to one of the windows and looked out. He watched as a shimmering blue light cascaded to the ground.

It looked like a giant soap bubble was forming up a short distance away. "It kind of looks like the Northern lights."

Carl nodded. "It does, doesn't it?" He turned to Dieter. "And that's strong enough to protect us from those spheres coming towards us?"

"We'll soon find out," Hans said.

"Where did you find it?" Jackson asked.

Dieter turned to him, his piercing eyes staring at him for a moment. "We found it near that ship you've no doubt seen."

"You mean that giant blue ball?" Carl asked. "The thing that almost fills the entire cavern?"

"That's right," Dieter said. "Pieces of it were scattered across the ground."

Jackson could hear a loud crackling and hissing sound coming from outside, and then a loud hum as the shield formed up.

"Did those spheres come from the ship?" Carl asked.

Dieter shrugged. "Possibly, we just don't know."

Hans cleared his throat. "We tried to communicate with them at first, but they're like rabid dogs. They attack without provocation."

"They look pretty nasty," Carl said, looking back out the window. "It looks like there are hundreds massing out there."

Dieter nodded. "We've never seen that before. They used to attack in small groups or singly, but now they are like wolves. They form up and attack in packs."

"How are you going to get out of here if they keep attacking?" Carl asked.

Hans nodded. "I know. That's the problem. We have to find a time when there's a stoppage in their attack, pack up the generator, and get out of here."

"Something's happening out there," Carl said, looking through the window.

"What?" Dieter said.

"I think Big Momma has come to check out your defenses, as well," Carl said. "Look at the size of that sphere."

Jackson moved to the window and watched a huge sphere approach the shield. The thing had to be as big as a van. It hovered just beyond the edge of the flickering shield.

"That's something we haven't seen before," Hans said.

"It looks like a couple hundred smaller spheres are forming up behind it," Carl said. "It looks like a small army."

Hans shook his head in disbelief. "I don't think I've ever seen so many spheres together at one time. There's something going on."

Jackson swallowed. He wondered where they'd all come from. It was like a gathering of eagles out there. Somehow, it gave him a sense that there was definitely some kind of intelligence at work out there. They were gathering for a reason.

Dieter chuckled. "It's futile. They can't get through our shield, it's much too strong."

"Sure looks like they're going to try," Carl said.

Dieter left and hurried towards the back of the trailer, shouting out commands as he walked. He took a last look at Jackson before ducking around a corner.

Jackson turned towards Carl. "We've got to find a way out of here."

"Are you serious?" Carl said. "We're safe in here."

"For now, but who knows how long that shield will hold," Jackson said. "Besides, I figured out where Dieter knows me from."

"What? Where?" Carl asked.

Jackson looked around, checking to see if any of Dieter's men were nearby. "Remember I was telling you about how we hit this shape on the road as we came into town?"

"Yeah."

"I think it was Dieter," Jackson said.

Carl's jaw dropped. "You've got to be kidding?"

"Keep it down," Jackson said, motioning for him to tone it down.

"Sorry."

"I think that's when he saw my mom and me. When we hit this thing, it flipped up to our windshield, and hung there for a minute just staring at us."

"Jeez!" Carl said, shaking his head in disbelief. "What are we going to do?"

Jackson turned to check the back hallway. "I think we need to get out of here as soon as possible. I've got a bad feeling about this situation. I mean, I don't know if what they're doing here is entirely legal."

"Yeah, I was wondering about that," Carl said, looking around. "So what do we do?"

"We've got to get outside." Jackson said. "If we see an opportunity we got to run for it."

"That won't happen as long as that shield's up," Carl said.

"I wonder how long it'll hold," Jackson said. He motioned to the window. "I mean look at them out there. There're hundreds of them."

"Don't worry, the shield will hold," Hans said, coming up behind them.

Jackson and Carl jumped.

"Jeez, don't sneak up on people like that," Carl said. "You almost gave me a heart attack."

Hans checked the window. "It looks like something's happening out there."

Jackson looked at Carl, wondering how long Hans had been standing there and if he'd heard anything.

"It looks like the biggest one is going to try breach the field," Hans said. He chuckled to himself. "So much for thinking they had intelligence."

The largest sphere moved back a bit and then picked up speed, heading directly towards the field. It crashed into it as an explosion of intense blue light flared from the place of impact. A second later, the trailer shuddered. It felt as though it had moved slightly.

The huge sphere hung on the field like a fly caught on a spider's web, wriggling as it tried to get free.

"What a joke," Hans said. "Dieter's got to see this for himself." He turned and headed to the generator room.

Jackson watched the shield buckle inward and then flex back out as pulses of dazzling blue light shimmered along the perimeter of the force field.

He turned to Carl. "Come on, let's get outside."

"Don't you think we'd be safer inside?" Carl asked.

"I think I'd rather take my chances outside if that shield fails," Jackson said.

"Okay," Carl said.

They carefully unlocked the front door and went outside, easing the door shut after them.

"Come on." Jackson said, "Let's find a place to hide."

CHAPTER 44

As they hurried away, they snapped their helmets back into place.

"Okay," Carl said, sliding his helmet on and securing it to the suit. "Now what?"

"We find a place to hide," Jackson said. He'd grabbed both lengths of pipe from the stair landing when they'd left, just in case.

"Here, you might as well take yours," Jackson said. "No telling when you'll need it."

"Yeah," Carl said, looking in the direction of the shield.

"Let's go that way, towards that small shed," Jackson said.

As they jogged towards it, Carl said, "I hope you're right about leaving the safety of the trailer."

"Yeah, me too."

The shed was just under the curved swell of the shield. As they entered it, they could hear the crackle and hiss of it above them.

"Window over here," Carl said, clearing a couple of boxes to the side. "Hey, it looks like something's happening out there."

"What do you mean?" Jackson said, stepping over some tools and joining Carl at the window.

Carl pointed to the shield where the huge sphere was hung up. "It looks like the rest of the spheres are up to something."

Jackson watched as hundreds of smaller spheres started to launch themselves at the glowing force shield. They, too, became hung up on the shield, but more kept coming. From the darkness, at the far reaches of the cavern, Jackson could see even more appearing.

"That's suicide," Carl said. "They're all getting caught up on the shield."

Jackson shook his head. "I'm not sure what they're up to."

The shield started to change colour and fade. He watched as the light of the shield began to flicker and flux, like a light bulb that was burning out.

"Look at the shield! What's going on?" Carl said.

As more and more spheres got hung up on the shield, Jackson turned to Carl. "I think they're trying to overload the force field. I think they're trying to do it by sheer numbers."

"Well, it may be working. Look at that. The shield is really flickering now."

Dieter and a few others came out the front door, weapons in their hands. They had barely started firing when the field pulsed brightly and flickered out.

"It's down. They actually did it!" Carl said.

Jackson saw Dieter run back inside while the other two were chased by a dozen spheres.

A black, rope-like structure came out of the largest sphere and slithered over the ground snaring one of the men around the ankle. As it dragged him back, more tendrils came out and ensnared him.

"I've seen enough," Jackson said, turning away from the window. "Let's get out of here before it's too late!"

CHAPTER 45

"Can we take a rest?" Carl said, looking back over his shoulder. "My heart's pounding like crazy."

Jackson, breathing hard, bent over and vomited onto the ground. Behind them, they could still hear the faint rattle of automatic weapons firing.

"Come on. Let's go over there," Carl said, motioning to a narrow cleft in the stone.

Jackson nodded, wiping a sleeve across his mouth. They sat down on a small ledge, and pulled out their canteens.

"Still wish we'd stayed in the trailer?" Jackson said, taking a drink.

"No, we'd still be trapped back there," Carl said.

Jackson reached up and turned on his helmet light. "Now, we've got to find a way out of here."

Carl nodded. "The sooner the better. I think we've stumbled into a nest of those spheres."

"I know."

"I've tried getting in touch with Cheryl, but I've still been unable to get a signal through," Carl said. "We've still got to find a way out of here."

Jackson took another sip. "I've been thinking about that. I was remembering how Dieter had told a couple of his men to guard the passage."

"Yeah, so?"

"Well, I saw them hanging around the back of the trailer, so I wonder if the way out is somewhere behind the trailer."

"You're not thinking of going back to the trailer, are you?" Carl asked.

"No, but I'm wondering if the way out is a passage somewhere behind that building."

"Wait a minute, we barely escaped from there, and now you're thinking about heading back?" Carl said. "What about all those spheres?"

"I was thinking if we head towards the cavern wall and follow it, we could loop around behind the trailer and see if there's a way out," Jackson said.

"I don't know," Carl said, shaking his head.

"Well, do you have any suggestions?"

Carl was quiet for a while and then shook his head. "No I don't."

"We've got to get out of here, so let's give it a try," Jackson said.

Carl exhaled loudly. "Well, all right."

They walked for an hour, zigzagging back and forth, skirting around dozens of massive rock pillars and crossing over massive fissures in the cavern floor. Jackson felt like a rat in a maze, desperately trying to find the way out.

When they stopped to rest, Carl pointed to the distance. "Hey, I can see a light flickering over there."

"That's got to be the trailer, or what's left of it," Jackson said, staring at it for a moment. "Looks like it's burning."

"We're not going there, are we?" Carl asked.

"No. If we keep that on our right, we should be able to pass behind it."

"I hope so," Carl said. "I don't want to go anywhere near it."

After ten minutes of walking, Carl stopped and pointed ahead of them. "I think that's the cavern wall."

Jackson gazed into the dark gloom. "You must have good eyesight. I can't see a thing."

"It's there," Carl said, as they continued on.

When they finally reached the sheer wall of the cavern, they turned right and started following it.

Jackson looked up, following the steep face of the rock as it disappeared into the darkness far above. He paused to shine his light over the rock face, illuminating narrow crevices and the openings to caves. Then Jackson had the odd sensation that they weren't alone. He started looking around, backing up a step.

"What's the matter?" Carl asked.

Jackson held up a hand. "Can't you sense it?"

"Sense what?"

Jackson cocked his head. "There's something coming."

"What?" Carl looked around fitfully. "Where?"

"Shh!" Jackson said, holding up a hand for silence. He whispered, "I don't think we're alone."

Carl backed up until he was against the rock wall, his flashlight beam licking over the half-buried rocks and up the surrounding walls of stone.

Jackson moved away from the open ground until his back was against the wall, as well. He wasn't sure how, but he *sensed* rather than saw or heard, that something evil was nearby. A feeling of cold dread slithered through his gut. Heart pounding in his chest, he thumbed his light on.

Carl slid closer towards him. "Do you see anything?"

"No, nothing," Jackson said.

"Are you sure there's something here?"

Jackson nodded. "Yeah, can't you sense it?"

"No," Carl said.

Jackson kept his light dodging about, and then he felt it.

There was a sudden coldness to the air, as if a door to a slaughterhouse freezer had been swung open. The smell was like that of rotting meat.

"It's freezing in here," Carl said, shivering.

Jackson nodded.

Then, he heard a delicate sound, like something was slowly creeping up on them.

It was an odd sound, like sandpaper was being scoured across a rock surface.

"What *is* that?" Carl said, looking around.

Jackson felt dirt and sand cascade down upon his head.

"Hey—" Carl said, looking up. "Above us!"

Jackson turned and swept his flashlight beam across the rock wall. There was something moving above them, clinging to the rock wall and sliding across it like a huge manta ray. It was blacker than the surrounding darkness and seemed to devour their light beams.

It peeled off the wall and fluttered across the rock as if it was gliding across ice.

Jackson tracked it with his light, turning and turning, trying to keep it in sight. The stench was nauseating as the thing literally swam across the rock face.

Jackson picked up the sense of utter, unrelenting malevolence.

He watched it flit upwards until it came to a narrow cleft in the rock. In a blur of movement, it turned sideways, squeezed through a narrow fissure, and disappeared from view.

Carl kept his flashlight beam trained on the narrow cleft. "What *was* that?"

Jackson shook his head. "I think that was the thing that Hans referred to as the 'something else' watching them."

The cold sensation of utter darkness and fear was slowly dissipating. "Come on. Let's get out of here before it comes back!"

They hurried along a narrow passageway that meandered back and forth like a snake's trail through desert sand. They wound their way through sheer cliff faces that had their summit clothed in Stygian blackness.

Carl nudged Jackson with an elbow. "There's something carved on the rock face."

"What?"

"Just ahead of us, above that rock archway," Carl said.

Jackson paused and swept his light across what looked like a Roman triumphal arch. It had runes carved into the stone, running across the archway and down both sides of the support columns.

As they drew closer, Jackson thought they looked exactly like the runes they'd seen on the stone column on the wastelands. He stared at them, wishing he or Carl could read what they said.

"Let me take a few shots with my camera," Carl said. "It'll only take a minute." As he turned on his flash and began to shoot frame after frame, he turned to Jackson and said, "I can't wait until we get them deciphered. It might tell the story of what happened out here."

"Yeah, that would be something," Jackson said. He kept his eyes on the rocks above them, watching in case their intruder returned.

"Come on, we've got to keep moving," Jackson said, taking a last look around. He passed under the yawning archway.

They hurried on, following the meandering passage until Jackson stopped so suddenly that Carl stumbled into his back.

"What is it?" Carl said, coming up beside him.

Jackson motioned to the pathway in front of them. "There's something lying on the ground up there."

"Not again," Carl said, letting his light probe the ground ahead of them.

CHAPTER 46

"What is it?" Carl asked.

"I—I think it's a body," Jackson said.

"What? Are… are you sure?" Carl said.

"Yeah," Jackson said, letting his light beam dance over a motionless figure lying across the narrow passageway.

It stretched from one wall to the other, blocking the way. They would have to step over it to continue on.

"Another body," Carl said, shaking his head. "Remember the last one we found down here?"

"Yeah," Jackson said.

"And the thing that came out of the suit?"

"Believe me I remember," Jackson said. "I'm going to have a hard time trying to forget it." He took a breath. "Unfortunately, we're going to have to get past it."

"Great. Just great," Carl said, shaking his head. "I wonder if it's one of Dieter's men."

"I don't know," Jackson said. "We've just got to get past it." Even as he said it, he thought all he wanted to do was run back the way they'd come. But to where?

"What do you want to do?"

Jackson thought for a moment. They didn't have a lot of options. "I think we have to keep going."

"Yeah, I guess so." Carl looked around. "I just wish we could get out of here. For me, the adventure is over."

"I know," Jackson said. He felt his stomach start to churn again. "I'll go first, you back me up."

Carl nodded, lifting his length of pipe in preparation. "Got it."

Jackson stepped forward, his flashlight beam sliding across the ground and then up over the narrowing walls of the passageway.

After a couple of steps, he swept it over the prone shape on the ground, frowned, and came to a stop.

"What's wrong?" Carl asked.

Jackson had his flashlight beam on the shape, squinting at it. "You know, I'm not sure it's a body after all."

"What?" Carl said, coming up beside him. He directed his light on the motionless shape, as well. "Hard to tell, but I can't see any arms or legs splayed out."

"Exactly. It just looks like a sack that's been left there."

"Yeah, kind of. Or some weird kind of egg sac," Carl said.

Jackson looked at him sharply and then waved his hand in a calming motion. "Let's not jump to conclusions. We'll just take it slow," Jackson said.

"Okay."

As they crept closer, the details started to get sharper.

It was made of a heavy cloth, like a canvas bag or a tarp. Just behind his right shoulder, he could hear Carl breathing fast.

"Careful," Carl said. "Just hold it for a bit."

"Yeah," Jackson said. He swept his light over the object, remembering what Carl had said about it being an egg sac. He got close enough to reach out with his length of pipe and prod it with the end.

Nothing.

He tried it again, but there wasn't any movement.

He took a deep breath, trying to slow his pounding heart. "All right, I'm going to try and roll it over a bit. Get a better look at it."

"Let's both work at it," Carl said, coming up beside him.

"You sure?"

"Yeah," Carl said.

They used the ends of their pipe lengths to roll it, watching as the fabric tore away and discharged what looked like pieces of wood onto the ground.

"What the heck?" Carl said.

"Looks like junk." Jackson moved closer, shining his light on the torn-open sack and some of the contents.

They moved closer, using their pipes to peel away the outer layers of cloth.

"At least it's not an egg sac," Carl said, a note of relief in his voice.

"Yeah."

They moved closer and started to pull the sac apart.

"I think its cowhide," Carl said. "Cowhide made into some kind of carrying bag."

"You may be right," Jackson said. He tore away a piece of the rotting fabric and his light showed a glitter of metal. "Hey, you see that?"

"Metal," Carl said, stepping closer, his light probing the bag. He poked it with his pipe and a couple of swords rolled out.

"Swords?" Jackson said.

"Yeah, and in pretty good shape," Carl said. He pulled away more layers of cloth and dragged the swords clanking across the rocky cavern floor.

They bent and picked them up, holding them in their light.

"Man, these have to be old," Carl said. "Look at this one. There are runes engraved into the blade."

"This one, too," Jackson said, holding the sword in his light. Runes had been incised into both sides of the blade. There was very little rust; it almost looked new.

He used the end of his pipe to pull the rest of the sack apart, but there was only junk—a pair of rotting boots, some rope, and a couple of pieces of half-carved wood.

"Looks like that's about it," Carl said.

Carl lifted one sword and took a couple of practice swings with it. "Boy, the balance of this thing is fantastic."

Jackson held the shorter sword in his hand, marvelling at the lightness of it. "I wonder what the museum's going to say when we show up with these in our hands."

"I'm not sure. I bet it'll make the front page of the local paper," Carl said.

"Oh," Jackson said. "I don't know if I want all that attention before I even start school."

"Yeah, I can see that."

"Come on, let's keep going," Jackson said. "The faster we find an exit, the faster we can get out of here."

They loaded up the swords and some of the wood carvings, stepped over the torn sack, and continued on.

"You know, they could carbon date the chunks of wood and give a pretty good date as to how old they are," Carl said.

They hadn't gone much farther when Carl slowed down, his light bobbing across the ground. "Look at this. There's been a lot of traffic through here."

Jackson came up beside him and saw a large number of footprints criss-crossing the ground. It looked as though an army had marched through.

"Must have been Dieter and his men," Jackson said.

"Yeah, that's encouraging," Carl said. "Maybe we're getting somewhere."

They picked up the pace, hurrying along the passageway that was becoming straighter and starting to widen out.

"Hey, I can see a dim light up ahead," Jackson said.

They hurried on, turning a couple more loops in the passage before Carl stopped abruptly and pointed. "Look! Sunlight!"

Jackson looked up and said, "Sweet!" He could see a ray of sunlight coming from a hole in the cavern wall and lancing across the rock face.

"Let's go!" Carl said, starting to jog.

They hurried along, turned a sharp corner, and came face to face with a basketball-sized sphere hovering in the middle of the passageway.

"Oh crap!" Carl said. "Now what?"

CHAPTER 47

The sphere hovered in the middle of passageway, just about waist-height, humming with a low drone.

"Don't move," Jackson said. "I don't think it's aware that we're here."

"Right," Carl whispered.

Jackson swallowed hard, trying to think of what to do.

Somehow, they had to get past that sphere ahead of them. He could see the glow from it shimmering on the glassy rock walls.

Carl leaned towards him and whispered, "Any suggestions?"

"Move slowly behind me to the left side of the passage," Jackson said. "And when I say *slowly*, I mean in *slow motion*."

"Got it."

From the corner of his eye, he saw Carl slowly move behind him, edging his way to the passage wall. He was slow all right, almost excruciatingly so. When he saw that Carl had made it to the rock wall, he started as well.

He made it in a couple of minutes. His heart pounded so loud he was worried that thing would hear him.

"You okay?" Carl asked.

Jackson nodded. "Barely."

"Now what?" Carl said.

Jackson leaned out past an outcropping of stone and saw that the sphere was in the exact same place. He could see the muted shadow of a whip-like tentacle curling and uncurling restlessly inside the sphere.

Moving back, he said to Carl, "Well, we've got to get past it somehow if we want to get out of here."

"I was afraid you were going to say that," Carl said.

Jackson let out a breath. "I'd rather do it now before more of them come."

Carl nodded. "Good point." He leaned past Jackson to take a peek, and then ducked back to the cover of the rock. "So how do you want to do this?"

Jackson thought about it quickly. "When we go out into the passageway, we keep close together. We don't want one of those things to drop onto us."

"You got that right," Carl said. He gulped in a breath. "Ready whenever you are."

"Okay." Jackson took the newly found sword in one hand and had the sharpened pipe in the other.

Carl did the same. "At least our backs are protected by our backpacks," he said.

"Yeah, you're right," Jackson said. "That's a point in our favour." He turned his head. "Good thinking."

"No problem," Carl said.

Jackson sucked in a deep breath and stepped out into the middle of the passageway, Carl shadowing him closely.

They stood shoulder to shoulder, facing the sphere, swords and pipes in hand.

"Now what?" Carl asked. "It's not moving."

"It will when we start to walk towards it," Jackson said. He took another deep breath. "Okay, let's go slow and easy. Let it make the first move."

"Got it."

As they got within three meters of it, they could hear the humming drone intensify into a loud saw-like buzz.

"Get ready," Jackson said.

It rushed at them, just a blur of white.

Carl got his pipe up, while Jackson threw up his sword defensively.

They ducked and Jackson knew he had nicked the outer skin of the sphere.

After it sped past, they whirled to face it again.

"That's it, keep tight together," Jackson said. He could see the thing was wounded. It was leaking a thick black fluid onto the ground.

"It's bleeding," Carl said, holding his pipe's jagged end towards the sphere.

"Yeah, score one for us," Jackson said.

As the black fluid wept onto the cavern floor, Jackson could hear the hiss as it hit the rocks.

"If we're lucky, it will bleed out," Jackson said.

"Not likely," Carl said, as the humming ramped up again.

"Get ready, it's coming again!" Jackson said, getting his sword and pipe ready.

This time the sphere changed tactics, coming at them low at about knee height.

"Watch it!" Carl shouted, his voice cracking with the tension. He quickly lowered the end of the pipe as it rushed at them again.

Jackson saw it quickly change course, veering up and over Carl's pipe and speeding towards Carl's stomach. Reflexively, Jackson threw his sword into its path. The sword barely missed, but still managed to slice through the translucent outer shell.

"Nice shot!" Carl said, trying to spin away from it. He instinctively turned, as did Jackson, to follow the high looping path of the sphere.

"You've nicked it," Carl said. "Look at it. It's really oozing black stuff now!"

"Watch it," Jackson said. "Things are even more dangerous when they're wounded."

"Okay."

The sphere went high, and then with a quick turn looped back, diving towards their heads.

"Get the pipes up!" Carl said, instinctively aiming the end of the pipe towards the onrushing sphere.

It dodged past both sets of sharp-ended pipes, fluttering a bit as it tried to manoeuver away. It slowed just enough that Carl was able to slice at it with his sword. He sliced the sphere in half, dropping the rider inside it to the ground.

With the momentum of its rush, the rider continued on towards the rock wall to the side of the passage.

The squid stuck to the wall, righted itself, and began to walk along the rock towards them like a big black spider.

Jackson knew those things could jump, especially after the previous encounter they'd had with the one in the ditch.

"Watch it," Jackson warned. "Back up a bit."

The reek of sulphur wafted through the air, a sickening stench of gas and rotting meat.

"What a stench," Carl said, backpedalling a bit.

A single eyelid flickered up, and the squid gazed at them through a yellowed, reptilian eye. Its tentacles bent slightly, lowering the body of the squid to the rock.

"Watch it! It's getting ready to jump!" Jackson said.

The words were barely out of his mouth when the squid launched itself at them.

Jackson had his sword blade up defensively, but Carl impaled the squid with a quick thrust of his sharpened pipe. The creature squirmed and thrashed about, trying to pull itself along the shaft of the pipe towards Carl.

"I don't think so," Carl said, swinging the sword in his hand and slicing the creature into halves.

It dropped to the ground, black fluid oozing from it, hissing as it came in contact with the ground. The squid had two spasms and then went still.

"Nice one," Jackson said, turning to Carl.

"My pleasure," Carl said, poking at the dead squid with the tip of his sword.

"Come on," Jackson said, nodding to the passageway ahead of them. "Let's see if we can get out of here!"

They hurried around two more curves of the passageway and saw rays of sunlight spilling in through an opening in the cavern wall.

"Man, oh man, is that a sweet sight," Carl said, shading his eyes with a hand. "Just what *is* that thing?"

"The sweetest bright thing I've seen in a while," Jackson said.

They hurried through the narrow gap and emerged into the cool breath of a morning breeze. In the dawn sky they could see the moon and Venus riding above the distant mountains.

"Is that ever a beautiful sight," Carl said, stepping outside into the sunlight.

Jackson turned to Carl, "Come on. Let's go home."

Carl hitched up his pants and said, "That's the best idea I've heard in a long time."

CHAPTER 48

Sherriff Tim looked at his notepad and tapped his pencil on the desktop. After a moment, he wrote something down and sat back in his chair. "That's quite a story," he said.

"It's absolutely true," Jackson said. "Every bit of it."

"That's right," Carl said. "As bizarre as it sounds."

The sheriff let out a breath. "The crazy thing is, I believe you."

"Really?" Carl said, glancing at Jackson in surprise.

Jackson leaned forward in his chair, hands clasped together. "Has something happened that we should know about?"

Tim looked at Carl and Jackson in turn. "We caught one of the killers," he said quietly.

"Really?" Jackson said.

Tim nodded. "We found him stealing electrical equipment after he killed the owner of Woodward Electronics."

"And you caught him, you said?" Carl asked.

Sheriff Tim sat forward, elbows on the desktop. "After one heck of a fight, yes. We had to Taser him several times before we finally subdued him."

"Taser? Isn't that when you shoot someone with some probes and shock him with high voltage electric currents? Kind of like a stun gun?" Carl said.

"That's right," Tim said, nodding in agreement. "When he was unconscious on the ground, we noticed a large lump on his back that was still moving."

"That sounds familiar," Carl said, glancing at Jackson.

"At first we thought he was having some kind of a seizure, and that his back was convulsing. When we pulled up his shirt, we found some *thing* fastened onto his back." Tim shook his head. "It looked like something from someone's darkest nightmares."

"So you've seen one of them?" Jackson said. "A rider, as Hans called it."

Tim nodded. "I wish I hadn't, but I did." He hesitated. "We have no idea how many of those things are around, but we think there're a lot more out there."

Jackson nodded. "So what are you going to do? They're using people to repair the ship in a cavern, and to come into town to get the materials they need."

Tim looked at them. "It's just amazing that they've been able to come and go, between the Tor and town, without being seen."

"I heard a couple of them talking," Carl said, sitting forward. "They were talking about some tunnels under the wastelands that stretch from the Tor right up to the outskirts of town. It sound like it would be possible to do that without any problems."

"That makes sense," Tim said. "I wonder how they got to the cavern in the first place. Or even knew there were tunnels."

Jackson shrugged. "Maybe a helicopter? Or, if someone knew about the tunnels…"

"Wouldn't be a chopper," Tim said. "The last helicopter that tried to get out there crashed. Crosswinds on the wastelands are deadly. Besides, if there had been a chopper, people in town would've see it for sure. Tunnels are more like it."

"What about asking the guy you caught?" Jackson said.

"Great idea. Only problem is that he's in some kind of a coma. They've tried taking that thing off his back, but it's secured there as if it were a part of him."

Jackson shook his head. "I wonder where those things come from. Somewhere in space?"

"Well, we're really not too sure they came from there," Tim said.

"Why do you say that?" Carl asked. "We saw the ship."

Tim hesitated for a long moment.

"What?" Jackson said. "You're not telling us something."

"Well, we had some info come in. This may be the result of a secret government project."

"Are you serious?" Jackson said. "You saw those things. Do you really think the government would have made something like that? And why?"

Tim looked at them and then leaned forward over his desk. "I didn't say it was *our* government."

Jackson sagged back in his chair. "You've got to be kidding. Those things live in a nitrogen atmosphere."

"How do you know that?" Tim asked.

Jackson waved his hand expressively. "We smelled a weird odour when the outer shell of the sphere ruptured. And the blood hissed on the ground when it hit it."

"So you're sure it was nitrogen gas?"

"Of course," Carl said. "Either Hans or Dieter told us it was."

Tim sat back a moment, looking at each one of them in turn. "What nationality were these two?"

Jackson shrugged. "I think they were German. I recognized a few words."

Tim wrote that down in his notebook. "German, eh?"

"But why would any foreign government put those creatures in an out-of-the-way and remote place like Boswell?" Jackson said.

Tim nodded. "Phase 1, possibly."

"What?" Carl said.

Tim let out a breath. "Some people think if what you say is true—and I have no reason to think otherwise—it may be the first stage in a test."

"A test?" Carl repeated.

"A test to see if these *squid*, as you call them, can be used to control people and to infect a population," Tim said.

"I don't know," Jackson said, rubbing his hand over his eyes. He could feel the fatigue setting in from not sleeping for a couple of nights. "Right now it doesn't make any sense."

"That's because you're tired and probably not thinking straight," Tim said. He glanced at the clock. "Your parents should be arriving any time now to pick you up."

"Oh," Carl said.

"The other thing is the government is sending up a research team to meet with you. They want to go over some of the photos you snapped on your cell phones," Tim said.

"Okay," Jackson said.

"Who knows—they may want to send in a team to take a look at what you've found out there," Tim said. "One thing, though. I want you to keep quiet about what you've seen out there. I don't want a wave of panic to spread through town. Okay?"

Carl nodded. "Got it."

Tim picked up his pencil and began to tap again. "What I can't figure out is why your aunt was burying stuff in the backyard. If you wanted to warn someone, you would either go to the police or tell someone."

"Maybe she was suspicious about who she could trust," Carl suggested.

"Maybe," Tim said. "Or maybe she was just starting to get a bit paranoid."

Jackson just shrugged.

"Did you find more than just the one box?" Tim asked.

"No, why?" Carl said.

Tim coughed into his hand. "Well, it seems that some of your neighbours—Miss Peabody in particular—"

"The neighbourhood snoop," Carl interjected.

"—had seen your aunt burying things on the property on many occasions," Tim said.

"On many occasions?" Carl said.

Tim nodded.

Carl looked at Jackson. "That means there may be more things buried on your property."

"Yeah, I was thinking that, too," Jackson said.

Tim motioned in the direction of the door. "Carl, it looks like your sister would like to speak to you."

"Cheryl's here?" Carl said.

"That's right," Tim said. "And I think your parents are on the way."

Carl's eyes widened. "Oh great." He thought for a moment. "Couldn't you just lock me up as an important material witness?"

Tim grinned and shook his head. "I'm afraid not."

As they walked out of Tim's office, Cheryl came over to them.

"Hey," Carl said.

Cheryl nodded at Jackson and then turned to Carl. "Mom and Dad are on the way, and they're ticked."

"Yeah, Tim told me."

Cheryl shook her head. "If I was you, I'd tell them you were temporarily insane."

"Oh, thanks a lot. You're a big help," Carl said. He looked at Jackson, thinking. "Hey, you probably need a ride home, don't you?"

"Ah, it's okay. I think I'll walk," Jackson said.

Carl gawked at him. "That's over 20 kilometers!"

Jackson shrugged. "The exercise will do me good."

"You coward," Carl said.

"You've got it," Jackson grinned.

Cheryl nudged Carl. "Looks like Mom and Dad just got in."

Carl's father nodded at Tim and then motioned to Carl, "In the car. Now!"

"Yes sir," Carl said, hurrying out.

Jackson slipped back into Tim's office and slumped down into the chair. He hoped Carl's parents would ignore him for now.

After they left, Jackson straightened and looked back through the office window. He could hear Carl's parents yelling at him.

"Do you need a ride home?" Tim asked.

Jackson looked in the direction of the heated discussion outside. "Ah, maybe I'll phone my mom and see if she got the car going."

Tim chuckled. "Come on, I'll give you a ride. I'm heading up that way anyway."

"Really?"

"Yeah. One of the families near you reported a prowler. Apparently he's been seen digging on their property," Tim said. "I thought I'd better check it out."

"Digging? Digging where?" Jackson said, sitting up straight.

"Not sure," Tim said. "We'll find out when we get there."

"Let's go then," Jackson said, hurrying to the door.

"And when we stop by your place, maybe I'll talk to your mom and see if I can smooth things out a bit."

"Thanks. Thanks a lot, Tim," Jackson said. From outside, he could hear someone yelling. He figured he wouldn't be seeing Carl for a long, long time.

Grounded for life, came to mind.

BOOK II
Where Silent Shadows Fall

by R. Scott Campbell

CHAPTER 1

Ethan Liddell bolted upright out of bed and looked around fearfully.

What the heck was that?

He glanced around his bedroom, quickly checking the balcony doors and all the windows.

Nothing.

Just a nightmare? Or had he actually heard something.

Ethan looked over to Brian, who was on the floor in his sleeping bag. "Brian?"

He waited for a moment, swallowed, and whispered, "Brian, are you awake?"

There was a groan. "I am now." He rolled over and looked up at him. "I was just dreaming about Lisa Montgomery and she was just about to ask me out."

"Oh. Sorry," Ethan said.

Brian sat up and yawned. "What's the matter?"

"Some weird noises woke me up," Ethan said.

Brian shook his head and collapsed back to the floor. "You were probably just dreaming. And to think you woke me from a dream about Lisa."

"No, it was some weird rumbling sound," Ethan said.

"Just a dream," Brian said, pulling the sleeping bag over his head. Then, in a muffled voice, he said, "Go back to sleep."

Ethan lied back on his bed, arms folded behind his head, staring up at the ceiling. He closed his eyes and tried to go back to sleep.

He wasn't sure if he had been asleep or not, but he woke up to a loud, rhythmic *whump, whump, whump,* like a thin board was being flexed.

Brian sat up abruptly. "That better not be you!"

"It's not," Ethan said. He sat up and looked around.

The rumbling grew in intensity until the windows began to rattle in their frames. On the shelf where he kept his plastic models, the dust-covered ships rattled and started to vibrate noisily.

"It must be an earthquake!" Brian said, squirming out of his sleeping bag and getting to his feet. "We'd better get outside!"

"I don't know, it sounds like it's coming from outside," Ethan said. He ran to the balcony doors, unlocked them, and heaved them open.

Outside he could hear Bruno, the family dog, start to howl.

"There's something going on out there!" Brian said.

Ethan ran outside, bare feet slapping on the balcony deck.

"Anything?" Brian asked.

Ethan rested his hands on the balcony railing and looked down. "Security lights are on."

"Do you think there's a prowler?" Brian asked.

"I don't know." Ethan searched the backyard, watching for anything moving.

Brian joined him and looked around. "It's gotta be an earthquake."

Ethan shook his head. "Still don't see anything."

"Hey," Brian said, "it's starting up again."

Ethan cocked his head. Brian was right—he could hear the rumble start up again. It was behind them and in the distance.

"Hey, check it out," Brian said, nudging Ethan with an elbow and then pointing behind them. "There's something coming over top of your roof."

Ethan spun around and saw it immediately.

It looked like a dazzlingly bright light clearing the peak of their roof. It trailed a long plume of smoke as it moved.

"It's got to be a meteor or a comet," Brian said excitedly. "It's got to be huge!"

"Or it's a satellite dropping out of orbit," Ethan said. He stared up at the shimmering object, amazed at how fast it was travelling across the sky. As it swung directly overhead, he could hear a powerful *thump, thump, thump,* echoing across the landscape like powerful diesel engine was at work.

"You mean it's burning up in our atmosphere?"

"Yeah, something like that," Ethan said.

Brian frowned. "I think we talked about that in one of our science classes."

As Ethan watched, the object was now almost overhead. The heavy *thrum, thrum, thrum,* like the throbbing of a massive engine, echoed across the sprawling landscape.

"Man, listen to that thing!" Brian said. "That's noisy."

Ethan nodded, watching as the dazzling object started to slow down and begin a curving trajectory towards the wastelands. "Hey, am I seeing things or is that thing changing course?"

"It is! It looks like it's starting to descend!"

Ethan's jaw dropped as the object started a fiery course to the ground, trailing a thick plume of billowing smoke.

"It's heading towards the Tor," Brian said, "and I think it's going to crash!"

The object began to slow once again, changed course a second time, and continued its plummet to the ground.

There was a muffled *whump* and a flash of intense light blossoming in the darkness. It created a rising cloud of dust, debris, and smoke that quickly swallowed up the stars.

Ethan couldn't believe it. It was as if a huge bomb had detonated there. A pillar of smoke plumed into the sky.

"Jeez!" Brian said. "Look at that cloud of smoke!"

Ethan heard a loud droning from behind him. As he spun about, he watched in awe as another two more dazzlingly bright lights swam into view.

The *thrum* coming from them was deafening, like the roar of jets roaring above them.

"Look out!" Brian shielded his face with a raised arm, "they're coming down."

CPSIA information can be obtained at www.ICGtesting.com
Printed in the USA
LVOW122156050713

341441LV00001B/2/P